D1624313

242225
9-11-98

WITHDRAWN

GO BY GO

Also by Jon A. Jackson

The Diehard (1977)
The Blind Pig (1978)
Grootka (1990)
Hit on the House (1993)
Deadman (1994)
Ridin' With Ray (1995)
Dead Folks (1996)
Man With an Axe (1998)

Go By Go

Others Take Notice!

Notice!

First and Last Warning!

A Novel

3-7-77

Jon A. Jackson

D · C · S · S · W

19 98

Rare
PS
3560
.A216
G63
1998

Go By Go copyright © 1998 by Jon A. Jackson.
All rights reserved.

FIRST EDITION
Published August 1998

Dustjacket photo (front)—Frank Little's funeral, Butte,
Montana 1917, corner of Front and Utah.
Dustjacket photo (back)—Meaderville district,
showing the Berkeley, Rarus, Mt. View, Hi Ore,
West Stewart, and Diamond mines.
Endsheet photo—Frank Little's funeral cortege,
coming down Utah and turning onto Front St.
All photos courtesy of The World
Museum of Mining, Butte, Montana.

ISBN 0-939767-31-7

Dennis McMillan Publications
11431 E. Gunsmith Drive
Tucson, Arizona 85749
http://www.booksellers.com/dmp

To the Workers of the World

from *The Waking,* by Theodore Roethke

I wake to sleep, and take my waking slow.
I feel my fate in what I cannot fear.
I learn by going where I have to go.

.

"Take a ride on the Reading. If you pass go, collect $200."
"Go directly to Jail. Do not pass Go, do not collect $200."

("Chance" cards in *Monopoly,* Parker Bros.)

Billings, Montana
1951

The old man looked up. Someone was in his light, a shadow at the open door of the garage. A faint spike of fear stabbed at the old man, but in another second it dissipated into mere irritation. His greatest fear these days was the idle nosiness of his neighbors, in itself an almost welcome nuisance compared to the occasional tenseness he used to endure at an innocent shadow preceding a pedestrian at the corner of a building. He had retired to this mundane suburb for just that reason, to spare himself those foolish reactions, that needle—or rather, the many innocent encounters that evoked it. He no longer reacted to the mailman's shadow at the door; the scratching thump of a crow, landing on the chimney. By now the needle's prick was so rare and fleeting that it surprised him.

In this case, the old man was sanding a wooden kitchen chair, getting it ready to revarnish. This kind of careful but not very challenging occupation was oddly gratifying to him these days. He had backed his 1947 Packard sedan halfway out the opened garage doors, as much to avoid any chance of marring its gleaming black finish as for the light and air of this sunny day in spring. It was still quite cool, but after the brutal Montana winter the folks in Billings, as usual, were in shirtsleeves.

Not this fellow, though. He stood there by the Packard, wearing a suit, a hat, and carrying a satchel. A burly man. The old man's first thought: Salesman. Insurance salesman.

He had no terror of insurance salesmen, however: nobody would try to sell insurance to a man in his eighties, no matter if he looked and felt like sixty. But then the fellow took another step, inside, and the old man almost smiled, managed a faint grimace which could have been tolerance, at least.

"So, it's you," he said. "What brings you to town?"

"Oh, same old stuff, sir. Information–this and that. Been working on the archives."

"Archives!" The old man snorted derisively. "You ought to burn them."

"Oh, no sir! We couldn't do that! What would the Old Man say? He always insisted we keep up the archives."

"Foolishness," the old man said, "and dangerous too."

"Yes," the younger man readily agreed, "they are dangerous. There's stuff in them–," for some reason he hoisted his satchel and shook it for emphasis, "–that could send powerful men to prison. But that's why we have to maintain them, of course: if *we* stay on top of it, we control it. Less danger."

The old man wasn't captivated by the topic. He shrugged and said, "Well, let's go in the house. I'll make some coffee . . . unless you'd prefer a beer."

"Coffee's fine, sir. Here, I'll pull the car in for you." The visitor moved toward the Packard, but the old man headed him off.

"I'll get it," he said. He drove the car inside. Then, while the other man waited, he pulled the two large garage doors closed and made sure the spring-loaded bolts were securely in place. With the doors shut it was rather dark inside; the lone lightbulb was weak and there was only one little dusty window, and the yard door, which was all but closed.

The younger man stood by the yard door and now he said, "Come to think of it, I won't have time for coffee. I've got to be getting on down the road."

"Well, what's your business then?" the old man said.

"Well sir, it's about Goodwin Ryder."

This was puzzling to the old man. He barely remembered Ryder, a former employee. But it seemed Ryder was in trouble now and his visitor seemed to think that he could be of some assistance. He resisted the suggestion: it was not wise to open this can of worms. They argued. The old man was adamant. But he saw, now, that the younger man was just as stubborn, in fact menacing in his insistence. It occurred to him, belatedly, that his visitor might become violent. In fact, he began to feel the prickle of not just a blunted needle, but of many sharp needles.

They were alone. A quiet afternoon in the deserted suburb. The banality of the situation was appalling. The feeling of menace increased when the younger man took a pair of leather gloves out of his satchel and tugged them on as he talked. That was unsettling, but what would be an appropriate response? It might be perfectly innocent. Nonetheless, the old man leaned on the workbench behind and laid his liver-spotted hand as casually as he could on the handle of a claw hammer. The younger man, his voice quite loud now, ranting even, suddenly drew a shocking thing from his capacious satchel. The old man stared. It was nothing less than a coil of new hemp rope, one end of it fashioned into a noose. A hangman's noose.

The old man thought he would scream. But somehow . . . he could not make a sound.

The visitor made sounds. He was talking rapidly, even wildly. The old man scarcely heard what he said, so fixed was his attention on the noose. But he did catch an extraordinary phrase: "Did you think you'd lie down in clover?"

What a ridiculous question.

The F. Mullen House, a.k.a. "The Big Ship,"
Centerville, Montana; side view, Mullen & Main

CHAPTER ONE
Butte, Montana
1917

"Bee-yoot!"

That was how the conductor had shouted the name of the next station, last night as we came over the pass and started our descent into Butte. I was demonstrating it for the benefit of the lone breakfaster in the dining room of the Big Ship.

The Big Ship was a three-storey square brick apartment building, but in those days Butte called it a boarding house. It stood a few blocks from downtown, in Finntown, and I'd rolled in there late in the night, off the Milwaukee Road's "Hiawatha." I guess it was normally chock full of men, mostly miners, but the strike had thinned the guest list. There was only one man in the dining room when I came down and he looked up from his bowl of porridge and sized me up with a low whistle.

"Lemme guess," he said, "yer wid da troupe. You must be da leadin' man."

I laughed and slouched into the nearest chair and lit a cigarette. "What do they call that?" I asked, meaning the goop he was shoveling in his yap.

"Stirabout. It's good fuh ya. It'll stick widja aw day."

"It looks like wet cement," I said. "No offense, but I think I'll pass. Say, what is this 'Bee-yoot' gag?" I explained to the guy where I'd heard it. He laughed.

"Da conducta must be from Billin's, er Hel'na," he said. "It's a old gag. It's like buglin' in da' basin—throwin' up, see? Butte ain't like da rest a dis cowboy state, so dey make jokes."

A serving girl, a bouncy, sturdy teenager with pigtails and a shiny face, came in to ask if I wanted the stirabout. When I made a face she showed me where to get coffee from the urn. I got some and sat down across from the guy. He said his name was Dewey. I said mine was Goodwin.

"Foist er last?" he said.

"Is it my first name? Yeah," I said. "Goodwin Ryder. Some call me Geed."

"Geed. Dat's good." He laughed. "So whaddaya doin' in Butte, Geed? Lemme guess. Yer a dick."

I don't know how I did it, but I laughed it off. Can you beat it? My first time out and some dumb hick mucker calls me dead to rights! "You have a powerful sense of humor," I said. "Do I look like a detective?"

Dewey grinned and stuffed his huge maw with the thick stirabout. He bolted it down and said, "Nah. I was jus' kiddin' ya. Yer too obvious ta rilly be a dick. But den, if you ain't a acta and you ain't a dick, what could ya be? Ya sure ain't no minah. Mosta da dicks try ta look like minahs, natcherly, but dey don't hire no beanpole kids in da mine."

Perversely, now I was a little disappointed that he didn't find me a credible dick. Spitefully, I said, "Well, you must be a dick, for sure."

Dewey laughed. "You goddit, kid! I got da poifick disguise! I *yamma* minah! But not f'long."

"What's up?"

"Butte is perzin," Dewey declared. "D' ayeh is perzin, d' wattah's perzin, d' fergin' doit is persin!"

"Doit?" I mocked. "You mean 'da oith'?"

"Yanh, d' oit, too. It's perzin."

"Persian?" I pushed the gag. "You mean there's a lot of Persians here? Butte is overrun with Persians, maybe?"

"Perzin!" Dewey roared. He was stuffing his mouth with the oatmeal glop while he barked at me. The oatmeal was flying!

"Like perzin gas?" I said, "Like in the war?" I had regained my composure, sitting there at the table smoking a cigarette, my legs crossed, drinking coffee . . . I wondered if I looked like Wallace Reid, the movie actor.

"Dat's it," Dewey says, "perzin gas."

"I'm sorry to hear it," I said, in my best sophisticated tone. "I liked it better when it was Persian. Arabian Nights, flying carpets, harems, Scheherazade. . . . "

"Ya godda 'magination kid, I godda hand it t'yiz."

I got up to stand by the window and look out. I hadn't seen much the night before. To tell the truth, Butte didn't look all that bad to me, no matter what Dewey said. It wasn't some fairy tale city, but it was pretty colorful. The Wild West! It was a jumble of shacks and gallows frames—huge elevator rigs that hauled up the men and the ore—smelters, warehouses, trains, big fancy houses, hotels, banks, streetcars, horse-drawn wagons, cars . . . all jumbled together on the side of a great mountain.

All around were more big, craggy mountains—the Continental Divide, a great jagged ridge, reared up about five miles east of town—and here's this goofy town, well, a city, really— maybe a hundred thousand people, in the middle of nowhere —five hundred miles to the next bigger town and nothing but cows and antelope in between. I thought it looked damned great.

Of course, I was excited because it was my first totally new place, my first job. My first real job for the Agency. I'd been working for the Agency back in Baltimore, doing odd jobs around the office . . . once in awhile they'd let me watch a house, make a note of who went in or out. An older guy,

Jimmy, used to show me a few things. He showed me how to shadow a guy. Don't worry about being seen, he told me, and don't avoid looking at the guy. Just don't make eye contact. Jimmy was a legend. Very businesslike, Jimmy was. Workmanlike, I should say.

Then one day the Old Man calls me in and asks me how'd I like to go out to Montana, do a job for them. I'm all for it. "What do I have to do?" I say.

In so many words he let on that it was strike-breaking. That didn't sound very appealing, but what the hell did I know? It was detective work. It would be fun. The Old Man gives me this pep talk about the miners getting their heads turned around by Reds. This is 1917, the war is stalled and the Russians are having a revolution. The big business people are going nuts, not just in Europe but here. The Reds hadn't won Russia, not yet. It wasn't October, yet. There was no Communist International, yet, but there were plenty of Reds around.

According to the Old Man, a copper mine had exploded in Butte, or burnt up. I think he said a hundred-sixty guys were killed. People said it was because the mines weren't properly ventilated, or something. The Anaconda Copper Company was making big bucks off the War, but they weren't putting any of it back in the mines. After the disaster the miners walked out. They were organizing a union.

Somehow, I had an idea that miners were already union. But no, the Old Man said, they'd had a union earlier, but about three years before this there'd been a squabble—the more radical guys wanted the I.W.W. in, instead of this sweetheart union they had—and it ended up with the radicals, or somebody, blowing up the union hall. The National Guard came in and the men went back to work and there was no union at all, for three years. Then this fire . . . anyway, the

I.W.W. is back, agitating. Some wanted the old union. There was going to be an election.

While the Old Man was laying out the scenario, I tried to figure my role. I couldn't see it. A strike-breaker? What was that, actually? I figured I was a pretty tough kid, I'd grown up on the streets of Baltimore, but I didn't have much taste for duking it out with angry miners. Especially if they looked like Dewey. He was not tall, but he was thick, and hard. He must have outweighed me by a hundred pounds. Of course, at the moment I hadn't seen Dewey yet, but he fit my casting call.

No, the Old Man assured me, what I was supposed to do was infiltrate the strikers, get a line on the trouble makers, find out what they were thinking, which group was likely to win.

I liked that word, infiltrate. It had a sort of military, espionage sound to it. I wasn't exactly sure what he meant, but I didn't want to seem ignorant. I didn't know anything about mining, or unions, but I figured I could fake it until I got the drift. I'd play the greenhorn act, looking for work. That would mean just hanging around, keeping my ears open, meeting other guys. I guessed you could call that infiltrating.

But now, sitting here in the Big Ship, it sounded foolish. Dewey had easily dismissed any suggestion that I was looking for work. I had to be imaginative. For a gag I told him I was looking for gold.

Dewey laughed, choking on the stirabout. "What gold?" he says.

"You mean there's no gold? What happened to it?"

"Dey awreddy goddit. Coppah, dat's what we mine. On'y nobody's minin' right now. D'ey ain't no woik, kid. You bettah go on down d' road. Butte ain't healthy."

"Because of the Persians, you mean? Nasty brutes are they?"

"Perzins! No, I mean d' strike. Between d' Wobblies and d' Comp'ny t'ugs, a minah can get his fergin' head broke, or woise." He cocked a thumb and shot me silently with his finger.

He was a comical guy, I thought, tough, not a lot older than me but much more experienced. He'd been in Butte for several months, he told me. There were thousands of young, single men who lived in the boarding houses and drifted from one mining camp to another. He'd had it with Butte. He was thinking of heading for Colorado, or maybe Idaho. Some of the men were haying in the Big Hole and the Beaverhead, two nearby valleys, he said, to get them out of town and out of trouble and stretch their wallets. I said that didn't appeal.

Dewey thought my clothes were hilarious, especially my shoes. "Great fa dancin', I bet. Woddayiz, Voinon Castle'r sumpin?" He took me uptown to get properly outfitted. I bought some work shoes and a floppy cap, but I drew the line at overalls. I settled for an old black worsted suit like many of the guys wore and packed my prickly tweed away. It was kind of fun, like a disguise. I wore a shirt with no collar and elastic braces. The pants were very baggy.

Dewey was pleased with the effect. "Ya look like a woikin' man, awmost. C'mon in heah. Y' kin buy me a beah and tell me d' troot." When we were standing at the bar, he asked, "Yer a teacha, right? Try'na pick up a few extry bucks fa da summah?"

"Something like that," I admitted. He nodded his head. He seemed satisfied. He introduced me to several young fellows about our age. I was happy to spring for beer. It seemed easy enough. I was infiltrating!

For the next few days I hung around, talking to miners, picking up a little information here and there, but I soon began to get a little anxious. For one thing, I didn't know what I

10

should be listening for. I figure the Agency isn't going to keep me on the payroll forever if I don't start producing. But what am I supposed to produce? Who do I report to? And I'm running out of cash. I'd been in Butte for a week and no contact. I couldn't just go and report in to an office. Butte was crawling with detectives, from Pinkerton, Burns, a couple other agencies, plus the Company's own undercover men. You never knew who the hell you were talking to. The joke around town was that only the spies' wages were keeping the economy afloat. Anyway, the Old Man had said that someone would contact me.

One day I bumped into Sam Hammett, a kid about my age, who I'd met in Baltimore, once. He was working for a rival agency. We almost died laughing when we saw each other. He was dressed like I was before Dewey set me straight, and I guess he was having the same kind of troubles, but neither of us would let on. I hoped I didn't look as out of place as he did. But Sam was always a fast talker, one step ahead of you. He pitched his patter about how he was a reporter, gathering material for a big newspaper back east. He'd quit his agency, he claimed. Now he was a stringer, a leg man. It sounded like a great gag to me and I wished I'd thought of it. Guys were calling me "perfesser." Hammett bought me a beer and in so many words he let me know that he wouldn't queer my act if I didn't queer his. We didn't have to shake on it. I said I'd quit the business, too. I was just passing through. I was on my way to the Coast I said. I was going to join the Army.

"You could have done that back east," he said.

"Yeah, but I wasn't sure I wanted to till I started for Frisco. Thought I'd see the country. But now, I think I'd like to fight."

It was funny, but that seemed to catch his imagination. We forgot about being dicks for awhile and spent the rest of the evening talking about war. He was eager to go, passionate you might say, like a lot of young guys I'd seen. They were joining up all over the place. I'd just thrown the idea out, but now I kind of got caught up. I made up my mind that if nothing happened here soon, I'd join.

So naturally, that very night I'm walking back to the Big Ship . . . and gee, you should have seen the stars. I've never seen stars like that. Billions of them!

"Hello, Ryder," this guy says. I was standing at the corner of Park and Wyoming, I think it was, waiting for a trolley to pass. I've never seen this guy before, but he knows me. He's just an ordinary Joe, kind of a nice suit, good quality hat. And his name is Joe! Joe Davis, he says. "The Old Man says hello," he says.

"What old man?"

"The Old Man who is wondering how your allowance is holding out," he says.

"Oh. That Old Man."

"Right." And he sets off up the Hill. I let him get twenty or thirty paces ahead and I follow, just like Jimmy taught me— hands in pockets, no hurry, looking into store windows. The idea is I'm supposed to be checking his tail. He was clean. He lets me catch up at Broadway. He's looking around like he isn't sure which way to go.

"Davis, is it?" I say.

"I been here for a week," he says, "up there." He nods toward the sixth floor of Hennessey's Department Store. That was the Company offices. We walk on together. "They're expecting trouble," he says.

"You're telling me." The town was very jumpy. Pickets, guys just standing around arguing, fights on every corner. But it was quiet at the moment. Everybody who wasn't in a bar drunk had gone home, I guess. We went to a Chinese joint I hadn't been in before, up a long flight of stairs. A skinny Chinese in a long apron comes up to us and he seems to know Davis. He puts us in a booth with strings of beads over the entry and brings a bottle of rye, chop-chop, without being asked.

I figure, this is it. The pink slip. Next stop, the Army. But, I tell him what I've learned, which is nothing you can't get from the Butte *Miner,* which is mostly where I got it. Davis just sips the booze quietly and listens.

"Is that it?" he says, finally.

I just sat and looked at him. This Davis is a real hardcase, I can tell. But a very ordinary looking guy. The most ordinary guy I ever saw. Forty, maybe less. I was only twenty-two— everybody over thirty looked old to me. But Davis is absolutely colorless. And as deadly serious as you can imagine. He could be chummy, have a drink with you, but you always heard his meter running.

"What do you know about Frank Little?" he says, out of nowhere.

"I'm pretty good pals with a couple guys who know him," I say. "Haven't met him myself, though. He's only been in town a few days."

"Think you can get close to him?"

"Sure," I say, thinking fast. "In fact, I was planning to. I didn't want to try it until I had instructions, though. Maybe you got someone in there already and I'd just muddy the water."

"No, we haven't been able to get anybody close." Davis is eyeing me, calculating. Finally, he nods and says, "Okay, you get close. If you can." He says it kind of sneering, as if he's sure I can't.

"I'm sure I can."

"Only don't get too close. Understand?"

13

I didn't, but I said I did. "What do you want to know?"

"Anything, everything," Davis says. "When he gets up, who does his laundry, what time he goes out, what he eats for breakfast, who he talks to, what he's got to say, whether his stool is hard or soft."

That's Joe's idea of a joke, I guess. When he laughed it was like moths whispering. Kind of dry and dusty. He gave me the willies.

The next thing I know, he hauls out his wallet and counts out two hundred dollars, like he's dealing a hand of gin rummy, and says there is more where that comes from. This makes me nervous. One minute I'm looking for a pink slip in my pay envelope, the next Davis is handing me two big ones. I figure it's expense money and the way the Agency is, every cent has to be accounted for in triplicate, worse than the Army. But when I ask for the chit, to sign it, Davis says, "Forget it."

"Forget it?"

"This is not Agency funds," Davis says. "The Old Man knows about it, but he doesn't want to know about it. Understand?"

I don't understand, but I don't think I want to, either. The one thing the Old Man, and Jimmy, always told me is to keep your hands clean when you're working in the field. Don't get involved in anything illegal.

Now I have to ask myself: What did they mean, exactly, and what does this bird mean? I figure they meant don't break the law and don't get caught in anything that can come back on the Agency. But I'd seen Jimmy going into people's rooms and searching their bags without a warrant or a cop within twelve furlongs. And sometimes he even told people he was a cop, to get information. It was all illegal, but not really serious, somehow. The theory seemed to be—anything's copacetic, if it's done to stop a crime being committed, or to nab a crook. You don't ever want to get caught in some guy's office or house, going through his desk or his files or his safe, but a hotel room . . . or train compartment . . . that's different. And if you actually find some evidence, then bingo!, everything's justified, warrant or no search warrant. But it better be good.

So I'm thinking: Taking this money under the table is not illegal—as far as I know. It's just the amount that's got me edgy. All this goes through my mind in a flash. And all I can think to say is, "Okey-doke." And I take the money.

"There's a lot more in this, if things work out right," Davis says. "You keep this under your hat, kid. I don't want you talking to any of the other guys about it. This is strictly between you and me."

"What about the Old Man?"

"The Old Man is across the wide Missouri," Davis says. "He might as well be on the moon. I'm here. He's got his methods, if that's what you're thinking, and I've got mine. I'm the only one you talk to. Understand?"

I said I guess I understood.

"Let me tell you a little secret, kid. These folks got their hands full here, but it ain't what they think. These miners ain't radicals. They're just yokels. Strong backs and weak minds. They got a gripe—which is, they don't like working conditions. Hell, if it was you or me we wouldn'a gone down in the Hole in the first place, not if they was holding the World's Fair down there. Right? So you gotta wonder what they expected. But the I.W.W. shows up and the Company sees revolution. It ain't no revolution."

"What is it?" I asked, trying to be a bright, alert dick.

"The men are spooked, because of Little. They think something big is gonna happen. They're excited. Next thing you know, some of them'll be talking dynamite, if they ain't

15

already. But, they got families, too. They don't really want to blow up any mines. You blow up a mine, you got no work."

"They hate the company, though," I said. "I don't think they'd mind blowing up one mine."

Davis laughed, the moth laugh. "Blow up one mine! That's rich. You're sharp, kid. Okay, they'd like to give the Company a hotfoot. But just between you and me and the lamppost, don't think that the Company would mind."

I didn't get that.

"Up to now," Davis explained, "the Company has stood back and let the fellers blow off steam. But if any dynamite goes off it'll be Company dynamite and it don't matter who blows it—the Company'll say it was the miners and they'll have the National Guard in here quicker than Frank Little can wink his good eye, just like in '14. And there won't be any more talk about unions and the fellers'll be back in the mines as peaceful as lambs. You'll see."

I hadn't seen it that way, but I thought he might be right. Still, if it was that simple, "Why hasn't the Company tossed some dynamite before now?" I asked.

"Good," Davis says. "Very good. Two reasons. They don't want to destroy their own property if they don't have to, naturally. And they let it go too long before calling me in. Plus you got your revolution scaredy cats. And then, they also got a bunch of pansies up there who sit on their hands and say things like, 'Oh, the men will go back to work soon, because they can't afford to hold out.'" Davis attempted a falsetto, but it didn't come off.

"Crap!" he says. "The men aren't on strike. Little's the one's on strike. Little ain't worried and the men ain't going back to work until he says so."

I wasn't so sure of that. The men had gone out on strike before Little showed up, hadn't they? A lot of the men were excited about Little coming to town, it seemed to me, but

16

he'd only been here a few days and I hadn't noticed any big difference. I mean, the guy wasn't a labor czar, or something, he was just an organizer.

But, no, Davis was convinced. "I've seen Little in action before," he says, "down in Arizona and before that in Idaho. He's one tough cookie. Why, he had every lumber camp in the Idaho panhandle locked up tighter'n a Scotchman with lock-bowel." Moth laughter.

"What happened?" I ask.

"I got him out. It wasn't easy. He's a tough little tick, I'll give him that. But let me put it this way: he's only got one eye left. If he can't see the light with that one, well, maybe I can get him a white cane."

This gave me a chill. I took a shot of the rye and didn't say anything.

Davis knew what I was thinking, though. "Listen, kid, don't take these guys lightly. And don't go high-rolling with that wad. Buy a round of beer when it's your turn, but you don't want them asking, 'Where's Ryder get all his loot?' That could be curtains." He drew a finger across this throat. "These guys may be yokels, but Frank has been downtown. He knows the score. Believe me, he's put plenty of careless Pinks where the sun don't shine. Which reminds me. . . . "

Davis patted his breast. There was a bulge there I hadn't noticed. "You got a gun?"

"A gun? Of course not." I was shocked. Jimmy never carried a gun. He'd always said it just got you into trouble.

"Here, take this one."

I couldn't believe it. Davis hauls out a huge Colt automatic, one of the new Army models, and passes it across the table. "I can get another one," he says.

I wouldn't take it. "If I think I need one, I'll let you know," I say.

17

"Okay. Probably just as well. It might arouse suspicion, though I notice half the town is heeled." And he goes off on a tangent, giving me some more lowdown on Little, how your communist attacks the fabric of society, that sort of thing.

Well, I didn't think anything of it. I more or less believed it, to tell you the truth. What did I know? The way I looked at it, everybody knew that strikes were bad. They made everybody unhappy and the men never got what they wanted anyway and the kids went hungry and what did it amount to? The Company could hold out longer than the men. Everybody knew they had copper stockpiled.

But Davis tells me that the Company is eager to settle the strike because the Allies need all the copper they can mine. They need it for brass, for artillery shells. Well, this appeals to me, of course. My patriotism had just got stoked up by Sam Hammett. I was more than ever thinking of joining up. The draft had started and I was registered. I wanted to enlist before I got drafted. I wanted to kick some Kraut ass before it got over.

Oh sure, I was a bloodthirsty kid, once. We all are. We aren't as complicated as we like to let on. It's a natural thing. Adventure! War! Kick ass! Hell, I was having the time of my life, playing detective! I thought I was invisible in my baggy suit. The Invisible Man! Just loafing around Butte—a hell of a place!—with plenty of moola in my britches, playing detective. Adventure, danger! Nothing like it.

The glory of war was calling, but first I had a job to do.

And the first guy I look up is Dewey.

CHAPTER TWO

"Woddayiz wanna meet Little faw?" Dewey wanted to know.

I reminded him that he'd said it wasn't healthy to try to scab in Butte. I thought I'd better join the union, but which union? I wanted to hear what Little had to say. Dewey said the guy I ought to meet was Sean Paton.

We were in a huge saloon called the M&M. It was crowded with cowboys and miners. The miners had no work and when they weren't arguing and brawling they were talking and drinking in the saloons. I never saw so many saloons in my life. Sometimes I think it was all the saloon life in Butte that started me drinking like I do, but I don't blame it on that. I liked it. I took to it like a duck. The M&M had a lot of gambling, too, but I never took that up, so there you are. . . .

The real center of attraction was the ticker tape. An old grizzled party in a bowler hat would take the baseball scores off the tape, inning by inning, and post them on a blackboard that had lines painted on it to resemble a scoreboard. He wrote the scores with chalk that he kept soaked in a glass. You couldn't hardly read the writing, at first, but it quickly dried into a thick, satisfying script that looked very professional, almost like printing. The bettors were always yelling at him to read the scores, but the old guy ignored them. They bet everything from pennies to real dollars on the games.

Dewey didn't gamble, but he was a Brooklyn Dodger bug. You could almost always find him in the M&M, following the Dodger game inning by inning as it came in on the tape. Between postings he would imagine what was happening and he'd describe to me how Zack Wheat was just now hitting a double to score Stengel, or Rube Marquard was striking out the Cubs. This was before radio–Dewey was ahead of his time. We were having a beer and watching the board when this guy Paton hauls up.

Paton was a tall, rope-muscled miner with a shock of pale reddish hair. He was maybe five years older than me, a big easy lad with a bashful grin. He looked like a farm boy but it turned out he was from the copper country in Michigan. They'd had a big strike up there a few years earlier and he'd fallen in with the I.W.W. and it ended up with him being run off by the mining companies.

Dewey introduced me as a "Ballamaw Awyull, fa gawdsake. He come out West t' pick gold, like it was berries, r' sumpin!"

"He's some joker," I said to Paton. "But I'm real glad to meet you. I hear the union is going I.W.W., so I'm thinking I better join up."

Paton might have been a little suspicious of me, but he was friendly. I bought a pitcher of beer and we went off to a booth where we could talk in peace and leave Dewey to his Dodger fantasies. Paton was an odd duck, I thought, kind of sleepy and nervous at the same time. He had pale eyebrows and lashes. One minute he'd look half awake, the next he's rubbing his hands and his eyes and looking around anxiously. He drank beer like it was air, gulping it down. He'd say, "Ma is gonna kill me," and then suck down a pint. By the time I bought the second pitcher Sean-O was telling me about the statue the grateful people of Butte would some day erect to Frank Little.

One of the beefs the union had, Paton told me, was the rustling card system. This was a way the Company had of keeping book on the men. You had to get a card from the employment office and take it up to one of the mines. If the Company had anything on you in its files you didn't get a card and you didn't get a job. If they found out you were I.W.W., or even a sympathizer, you could be black-balled in every mining camp in the West.

"It's a lousy deal," Paton said. "If you're working the other guys think you're a Company man, a stooge, and if you got a union card your brothers gotta wonder."

"How about you?" I asked. "You working?"

"I was, until the strike. And I got a red card!" He laughed and inhaled another pint, saying "This is the last one." But it wasn't.

"How come you didn't get blacklisted?" I asked.

"Who's gonna tell'm? Anyways, soons we win the strike we'll all go back to work and there won't be no more rustling cards." He reached for the pitcher. "Just one more." His eyes were glassy and he swayed in his seat.

"What if you don't win? You didn't win in Michigan."

"That was the United Mine Workers," Paton said. "Moyer and his crowd. They're all right, but they ain't got the real goods. Frank says they were ness-.... -nessary, the first stage, but they're limited ... they got simple objectives, like wages and work rules and that kind of thing, but they don't address the ... ah, well, the whatchamacallit. They're bushwah."

I didn't know what 'bushwah' was, but all I said was, "Bushwah, eh? That's what Frank says?"

"They don't have no loyalty to the working class," Paton explained. "Y'see, thass why we gotta stick together. We gotta reckanize our ess-.... essential brotherhood. We're all brothers. Ain't we?"

21

"Right, brother. Say, I'd sure like to meet Frank."

"Nothin' to it. He's givin' a talk to the boys at the ballpark, thish . . . thiz affernoon . . . afternoon." Paton inhaled another beer, saying, "Thiss m' las' one."

It was. The big galoot toppled over sideways, lodging his head against the corner of the booth. His eyes sagged shut and his mouth fell open. He started to snore.

"C'n yiz believe it?" Dewey said, popping out of the crowd. "D' fergin' Cubs pulled it out on Evers'es single!" Then he caught sight of Paton. "Jeeziss! Don't tell me."

"He just conked out," I said. "He was only drinking beer. He drank a hell of a lot of it, though."

"No kiddin. C'mon, we gotta git 'm home. Ma Paton is gonna blow 'er stack, but it's gotta be done." We got the big lug on his feet and sort of walking between us, an arm over each of our shoulders.

"How far does he live?" I asked, after we'd struggled a block from the M & M.

"D' Cabbage Patch. Down dere." Dewey pointed with his free arm at a bunch of beatup shacks and hovels down the hill. As we turned into the crooked little dusty lanes a flock of snot-nosed kids came flying up, yelling "Sean-Oh! Sean-Oh!"

When Sean heard them it was like magic. He dug in his heels, bringing us to a halt. Without a word he shook us off and brushed back his hair, took two or three deep breaths and widened his eyes like an owl at sundown. He took a couple of steps on rubbery ankles, steadied, and began to stride along, as sober as Carrie Nation and ignoring the street arabs.

Dewey clapped me on the back and crowed, "I knew he c'd do it! Ain't dat somp'n?"

Just then a girl came around the corner of the lane and stopped, her hands on her hips, gaping at Sean. He didn't notice her, but I sure did. She had on a blue cotton skirt with

The Cabbage Patch

a dirty apron over it, and a white blouse with an open neck that gave a fellow a pretty good idea of her artillery, which was heavy caliber. I took her to be twenty or so, at first, but I soon realized she was more like twenty-eight. She had very fine gray eyes and dark red hair. She wore a polka-dot babushka. Maybe some guys wouldn't have given her a second look, but I never was one to be fooled by a woman's duds, fancy or not.

Sean stalked by her and she let out a howl. She hauls off and slugs him as hard as she can. She was swinging for the jaw, but Sean is so tall she caught him on the shoulder. It didn't hurt him, but it got his attention. Sean doubled over and began to scoot for home with the lady in hot pursuit. All the neighbor ladies are out on their tiny wooden stoops and calling out encouragement and the kids howled along in glee. Dewey and I brought up the rear.

Sean ducked between two tumbledown shacks and scurried into a barren backyard hung with laundered sheets. He tore through a sheet, flung it away and dove into a crazily leaning outhouse, slamming the door behind him and holding it shut.

The onlookers crowded into the yard watching excitedly while the woman kicked and pounded at the door of the jakes, calling Sean a drunken, no-good, booze-swilling, layabout—and those were the polite names. There was only a muffled roar from Sean—"Go 'way! Lea' me alone!"

Suddenly, the woman stopped and looked around the yard. The neighbors melted away like an August frost—something they know about in Butte. One of the kids, wearing only a shirt that hung down over his naked legs, comes sidling up and grasps the woman's skirt. She knelt and wiped his nose with her apron. Then she straightened up and began to pick up and fold the laundered sheets, including the one Sean had flung onto a wooden fence.

Finally, she turns toward us. Dewey and I backed off. I was ready to scram, but she only says, as sweet and calm as if she's talking to a priest, "I suppose it's you I have to thank for bringing the beast home, Dewey Thacker. Well, I dare say you got him drunk. You know he can't drink. I didn't think he had any money." For a second she looked about the crappy, bare-grass yard with those wild gray eyes, inviting us to notice the obvious . . . that there couldn't possibly be any money.

Dewey and I pulled off our caps and stood there like a couple of dopes. "It was my fault, m'am," I said. "I had no idea he could get so drunk so fast."

"And who might you be?" she asked, piling the folded sheets and clothes into Dewey's arms.

Dewey introduced us. When he said this was "Ma Paton," I was taken aback. This was "Ma" Paton? I'd assumed Sean had been talking about his mother, not his wife. The three kids lurking around the scrubby yard were hers, as well.

"You don't look like a miner, Mr. Ryder," Ma Paton said. She had a characteristic way of standing with her hands on her hips, bold and fearless, her feet apart and firmly planted like a solid statue of Venus. She wasn't really beautiful, but she acted like she was and the effect was the same. She was all hair and hips and breasts and very imposing.

She smiled ruefully. "Well, he's done it and it's a done thing. I'll thank you gentlemen to get him into the house." And she skipped past us into the house herself.

I gawked after her, then turned a look on Dewey.

All Dewey says is, "She's somp'n, ain't she?" grinning over the pile of laundry. Later he explained that Ma Paton was a widow who had latched onto Sean after her first husband had drunkenly fallen down a disused shaft in the Mather B, in Michigan. Which explained a violent attitude toward booze.

Dewey set the laundry on the back stoop and led me to the jakes. We tapped on the door.

"Is she gone?" Sean asked nervously. He cracked the door and peeked out. It took us a couple minutes to convince him that she had calmed down and gone in the house. Finally he crept out. But the exertions of the past ten minutes had taken all the starch out of him and we had to nearly carry him into the house.

Mrs. Paton stood by the stove, where a kettle was warming, and directed us to heave Sean onto the bed in the adjoining room. It was a large bed with a brass-work frame and Sean flopped face down on it, his boots dangling off. Mrs. Paton ordered us into the parlor and began to tug off her husband's boots.

It was a tiny house, just the kitchen, bedroom and parlor, but the floors were swept clean and scrubbed smooth. The children's pallets were rolled up and stacked in a corner. There was a heavy, solid oak table and some matching chairs, a good lace cloth on the table. A cut glass Waterford vase with a few wildflowers in it stood on a chipped Dutch tile with a blue windmill on it. A brown palm leaf was stuck behind a crucifix which hung on the faded wallpaper, next to an oleograph of Our Lady of Lourdes.

I got the idea that Mrs. Paton had salvaged a few souvenirs from more prosperous times. It wasn't a completely dismal place, in spite of the barrenness and poverty, but Dewey and I stood around nervously, looking for an excuse to bolt.

Mrs. Paton came into the room, carrying a teapot covered with a quilted cozy and set it on the table. "Sit down," she commanded, then went out to get cups. We sat and she promptly returned with three fine china cups and saucers. I think they were Royal Doulton . . . my mother's folks had some like them.

Ma Paton had shed the apron and the babushka. Her hair was amazing. I'd heard her giving it a quick brushing. It billowed out around her face like a cloud of spun copper. She was very handsome, very impressive. She sat and poured out tea like a great lady—if she'd had a taffeta gown instead of the flimsy cotton skirt and blouse you'd have thought she was a duchess, for sure.

She was smiling pleasantly and saying, "I'm so sorry you find us in such a state, Mr Ryder. It isn't always so, I assure you." But then she looks darkly at Dewey and adds, "Though too frequent." She smiles the duchess smile at me and asks, "Does everyone call you Goodwin?"

There was more than a lilt of Ireland in that voice. I told her she could call me Goody, or Geed, and just for the hell of it, said I was Irish on my mother's side, from Donegal. This wasn't strictly true, but I had an Irish aunt who used to say that the men of Donegal were a mystery to her, and I kind of liked the notion of myself as a man of mystery.

"Donegal, is it? I'm from Wicklow, m'self."

I nodded politely and sipped the tea. I hated tea, but I didn't notice it, for once. I couldn't tear my eyes away. She looked back at me just as boldly. It wasn't something that women did in those days. Women were supposed to be demure.

"You don't seem like most of these miners, Goody," she said, casting a scornful glance at Dewey.

I assured her I was just a working man, looking for work, but she didn't seem convinced.

"It would be nice if Sean had some more refined friends," she said. She smoothed the shirtwaist down over that robust bosom and I glanced nervously at Dewey. He was watching the two of us with a combination of amusement and disgust.

"Goody's a Ballamaw Awyull," Dewey said.

"Just a joke, m'am," I assured her. "He means I'm from Baltimore, is all. But that doesn't mean I'm a roughneck like some of these guys."

Ma Paton beamed and leaned across the table to pour my cup full again. Her bosom loomed like a storm front.

I guess it made Dewey nervous. He stood up. "T'anks f'r d' tea, Missus, but me'n Goody, we gotta go."

"Where are you going?" she asked calmly.

Dewey looked puzzled for a moment, then said, "T' see Frank Little. He's talkin' to d' men dis aftanoon, at d' ballpark."

"You'll not be taking this nice young man to see that heathen Injin!"

"Aw Missus, Frank ain't as bad as all dat."

She turned to me and said, "Frank Little has completely flummoxed my poor husband. Though," she added, with a glance toward the bedroom, from which powerful snoring resonated, "it may not have been a full day's work. Not that Frank Little ever did a day's work in his worthless life. But, I'll not be keeping you. Go on and listen to Mr. Little encourage grown men not to work. I'd like to know if he is going to buy the groceries or pay the rent, or . . . " Her eyes gleamed dangerously, but she controlled herself.

We took off and didn't dare speak until we'd shaken the dust of The Cabbage Patch from our heels. But then Dewey stops and doubles up laughing. I had to join in.

"Did yiz see ol' Sean! Like a rabbit f'r d' briah patch!" He dried his eyes and added, "'Course, y' can't blame 'm."

"Mrs. Paton, or 'Ma', as you so quaintly put it," I said, "is one hell of a woman."

"Y'r telling me!" Dewey held out his palms before him, as if weighing heavy rocks and gave his baggy britches a lewd shake. "Woof! Dat's a woman!"

I was offended. "She's Sean's wife!"

"Unh-hunh," Dewey said, nonchalantly, "but she's a woman, ain't she? She can be a wife to Sean and a woman to d' rest a da woild. Anyways, what's da diff? She ain't yaw wife."

For some reason this annoyed me, though I had no argument with the attitude, normally. "Well, why in hell did you insist on bringing him home, if you knew she'd be so burned up?"

"'R yiz kiddin'? It's bettah'na pitcha show! C'mon, y' wannida see Little," and he set off across town.

CHAPTER THREE

"Boys, it's too nice a day to talk strikes and politics. We oughta be talking strikes and balls."

Frank Little stood on a wooden platform that had been dragged out between homeplate and the pitcher's mound, shouting into the covered grandstand crowded with more than two thousand men, many of them drunk and passing whiskey bottles back and forth.

He was a slender man in his late thirties and he didn't look sinister to me. He was no taller than average and swarthy. He wore a baggy suit with a loose red necktie and his lank, black hair was covered by a dented fedora. It was hot that afternoon and I kept waiting for him to take off his coat, but he never did. He had a thin, rasping voice with a western twang. It was very penetrating and carried well, but it wasn't a real orator's voice, more like a preacher's. A part-time preacher, maybe, a guy who worked in the factory during the week and got to preach the evening sermon one Sunday a month.

I was standing against the wooden backstop of the grandstand with Dewey, about fifty feet from Little, down toward the third base line. Half a dozen of the strike leaders, including Mucky McDonald and Al Wuuri, were sitting on chairs on the platform, smoking cigars and wearing derby hats and suit coats. At least two hundred miners stood between the grandstand and the platform, but I could see over them all right.

Little pointed to his left eye, which was shut and kind of limp and puckered. Apparently there was no eyeball there and I suddenly realized what Joe Davis had meant with his crack about white canes.

Little's voice arced out, in a joking tone, "I never could hit a good fastball or a fadeaway, so nowadays when I see a dozen fellers in a ballpark I figure it's an opportunity for a speech. But, what the hell, let's talk baseball, for a bit."

The men chuckled appreciatively and there were a few shouts of encouragement: "Let's hear it, Frank!", or "Give 'em hell, Frank!"

Dewey dug me in the side with his elbow and said, "Dis guy'll git 'em goin', you watch."

"Wal, we all heard a lot about this new league, this Federal League. A lotta people are kinda disappointed that it didn't work out. Guess who?"

There was no answer from the men. They sat in interested anticipation.

"The players, that's who," Little said. "I guess it's kinda hard for a working stiff, 'specially if he's on strike and not seeing any paydays, to sympathize with a buncha overgrown men who're playing a boy's game and getting good money for it. Hell, we're all a buncha baseball bugs," he gestured at the stands, the wooden outfield fence with its signs advertising Hennessy's department store, Gamer's restaurant, the M & M saloon, and other local businesses, "but it seems a little funny to think of ballplayers as working men. But, it ain't so odd when you come right down to it."

I wondered what the heck Little was driving at. Was this the so-called firebrand? The rabble-rouser who had Joe Davis and the Company so worried? To read the *Standard* you'd think Little was a cross between Billy Sunday and V.I. Lenin, but this squinty bird in baggy pants only needed a moustache to make you think of Charlie Chaplin. I suddenly remembered Sean-O's notion of the town putting up statues of Little and I practically burst out laughing.

"I read the other day," Little went on, his hands jiggling in his pockets, "where Ty Cobb makes twenty-thousand dollars a year! Can you beat that? For playing ball!" Little shook his head ruefully. " 'Course, you gotta admit, Cobb is hittin' three-eighty-five."

Somebody called out, "Three-seventy-five!" The crowd laughed and Little did too.

"Okay, three-seventy-five. But he's still leading the American League! Wal, you know, they say there's only one Ty Cobb . . . and it's a damn good thing for the pitchers! And the Tigers' owners!"

That got another laugh and a few boos for Cobb the bad boy. Little grinned and did a funny little dance step on the platform. Then he stopped and planted his feet.

"There's only one Cobb," he repeated, his voice ringing out, "but what about the other boys on the Tigers? Did ya ever think what they make? Did ya? Wal, I'll tell ya. Before the Federal League got all the bosses in Dee-troit and Pittsburgh and Chicago and New York and Saint Louie all in a tizzy—" he wiggled his widespread fingers, "—an ordinary ballplayer was lucky to get about twenty-five hunderd dollars. Maybe that sounds purty good to some a you, but you gotta stop and think that these boys only play for a few years and then it is back to the farm . . . or the smelter, or the Never-sweat."

A number of miners who worked in the Neversweat stood up and cheered.

"That's right, that's right," Little shouted, grinning, "nothing wrong with the Neversweat. Except that some of these boys don't know nothing but how to play shortstop. They never ran a buzzy down in the hole, or pushed pots in the smelter. Some of them end up with broken legs and torn-up knees and arms they can't lift higher'n their shoulders. Some of them been plunked in the ribs and the head so much they're a little goosey. Now, all of a sudden, they got to start learning how to work at the age of twenny-five or thirty, 'stead of bein' a hero. Okay, okay . . . that don't sound so horrible to some a you fellers, but you got to admit it is a big change from running around a ball diamond for a couple thousand bucks, and going to spring training in Floridy, getting your picture taken by the press and kids asking for your autygraph, and travelling first class on the Pullman . . . I ain't saying nothing about the fancy dames."

Little had to pause for the guffaws and I have to admit I laughed and applauded with the rest.

"It's a change for a feller to be a kind of overgrown kid one day, and the next it's back to pulling on Bossy's tits instead of some other . . . well, you get the drift."

This time the laughter was universal. When it had died down, the men still repeating the joke and explaining it to one another, Little looked more serious.

"These boys found their salaries went up two, even three or four times as much, in '14 and '15, even if they didn't jump to the Federal League—just to keep 'em from jumping. A good outfielder, say a guy like, oh, Bobby Veach, was getting ten thousand. That's right, ten thousand dollars. But wait, you ain't heard the rest of the deal. Today-ay," he said, emphasizing it like a preacher, "now that the Federal League is gone, that same player has been cut back to three or four thousand.

Now why is that? What's that? What'd you say?" Little cupped his ear in response to a yell from the crowd.

"'Cause he's hittin' two-fifty? Ha, ha, ha," Little laughed with the crowd. "Now listen here, fellers, I see where Veach is leading the league in homers. He hit his seventh just yesterday. That don't sound like he's all washed up, does it? Hell no. But we know why his pay envelope is quite a bit lighter these days, don't we?"

Little didn't wait for a response. "The big bosses in the American League and the National League have got rid of the Federal League and they have their own little agreement, the reserve clause—which is in every ballplayer's contract—which says they won't try to hire each other's employees. The Federal League did not honor the reserve clause, of course, which was a headache for the leagues, and a pain in the old pocketbook, too."

There were a few chuckles, but Little went on, "So now the leagues don't have to pay Veach ten thousand, even if he hits twenty homers, 'cause if they don't he can't play for nobody else. And let's face it, fellers, even with twenty homers Veach ain't no Cobb: if Cobb don't play the Tigers don't win, but if Veach won't sign for whatever the Tigers wanta give him, wal, there ain't no Federal League to give him more and there's another Veach down in Toledo, or someplace."

Dewey dug me in the ribs and nodded with a wise look, agreeing with Little's neat explication of baseball economics. "I oise wonnered how dat woiked," he said. I had to admire Little's style. He had a fairly sharp guy like Dewey, thinking he was some kind of brain, and Dewey wasn't any kind of Red.

Little paced around momentarily, head down, as if thinking, and the men waited patiently. He looked up finally, and called out, "Do any of you remember the Player's Fraternity? You don't? None of you?" Little looked dismayed. "Good union men and you don't remember the player's union? Wal, the sportswriters didn't write about it much. They wrote a lot about the Federal League, though, how it was ruining baseball, and they wrote a lot about how much Cobb was making. They didn't write about how much the owners was making off the players. I guess they figured that was the owners' business. And I guess they figured nobody'd be innarested in a player's union. Prob'ly figured the players shouldn't even have a union, same as some people think about miners. Maybe they figured it was just the players ganging up on the poor old owners. A lotta folks who don't know what brotherhood means, folks who don't have a union theirselves, seem to get awful angry when other folks, working men, form a common bond to get justice and a fair pay for their labor."

Little's voice had taken on a new seriousness and I could see that the men were leaning forward to catch each word.

"The ballplayers started a union in 1912. They wanted an end to this deal where a player was bound to play with the same team, forever and ever—unless, of course, he was traded, which is a whole 'nother can of beans. I'm talking about even after the player's owner didn't want him no more. The team can keep him from playing for anybody. Didn't you know that? Why, it's the same as if the Company had exclusive rights to your labor and if you wanted to go work for another outfit, over in Idaho, maybe, they could say 'No dice.' Even if you weren't working for them no more! Sound familiar to ya?"

Little nodded at the chorus of catcalls, smiling wryly. "Oh, so you heard of wage slavery? I thought so. Unh-hunh. But you ain't heard it all, yet." He walked about on the platform while they settled down, his head down and his hands in his pockets, occasionally making that funny little Chaplin dance step. Finally, he went on.

"Wal, naturally, the leagues wouldn't reckanize the union. That's the same old story. Nothing new there. But then, when the leagues got scared by this Federal League business, with an outfit that would sign the ballplayers despite the old reserve clause, then they decided to reckanize the player's union. Now why was that? You damn betcha—they thought the union would help them hang onto their players. And they made a few paltry concessions to the union.

"Now what do you suppose happened to the union once the Federal League went under—actually, I should say, after the leagues bought 'em out? That's right, that's right. They no longer reckanize the Players Fraternity. The union has been broken."

Little stood silently looking at the men, his hands jammed deep into his pockets. That was the moment, I think, that despite his clothes and his goofy little gestures and small-time preacher's voice, I began to see that Frank Little might be who Joe Davis and the Company thought he was. Somehow he looked kind of grand standing there before two thousand hard men. And the hard men were quiet, listening intently.

"Here's a lesson, men. The Player's Fraternity couldn't hold out against the leagues once the Federal League was gone, 'cause they had no real power. They were out at home and the umpire was hired by the bosses. Part of it was that most of their membership was just kids in the minor leagues, kids who didn't know nothing and didn't want nothing but a chance to play ball in the big leagues. These kids wasn't gonna hold firm against the owners.

"The major leaguers—the working stiffs—could see that they didn't have no choice, anymore. Except for Cobb and Tris Speaker, and a few like that, the journeyman ballplayer could

35

see there was a thousand kids out in Terry Haute, and Birmingham, and Butte–" he paused for the hoots to die down "–that was eager to play for anything. For nothing! Free scabs! The journeyman ballplayer had to play for the teams that owned them–owned them like slaves, that sold them to other teams for fifty-thousand dollars, when they was making only twenny-five-hundred. See, that's what the owners figgered some regular players might be worth–not Cobb, but just everyday players. And if the player didn't like his twenny-five hunderd, he could go back to pulling Bossy's tits."

This final line was delivered with withering contempt and while a few men laughed, it was a guilty laugh that quickly died. "The owners said a ordinary ballplayer was worth fifty-thousand, but they paid him a twentieth of that! Oh, if they had to, they'd pay Cobb twenny-thousand, and complain to the papers about how Cobb was greedy. Get that! It's the workers who are greedy! The men who hit four-hundred and steal seventy bases. They're the greedy ones. The ones who git hit on the head and git spiked. The ones who go out and pitch their hearts and their arms out. They're the greedy ones!"

Little's voice had taken on a preacher's soaring tone, but now he stopped and stared at his audience with his single eye. When he spoke again it was in a quiet voice that seemed little more than a rasping whisper, yet could be heard in every part of the ballpark, over the afternoon breeze and the rustling of paper waste under the stands.

"Now I'm gonna talk about men who go down in the Hole. I ain't talking about men who play a boy's game. I'm talking about men. Real men. Men who drill into a rock face and have it cave on them. Men who wear their fingers to the bone trying to claw a way out of a rock fall. Men who don't come up the hoist at quitting time. Men who never come up. Men who are down there still—your buddies, your neighbors, your brothers, who lie under a mile of rock, forever.

"And I'm talking about families, boys. Kids who don't have no food. Wives who cry themselves to sleep at night, 'cause her man didn't come up the hoist. It's your labor, your sweat and your blood, that makes these great mines." He gestured grandly at the hill behind them, with its smokeless smelter stacks and silent hoist frames. Some of the men actually craned around to look at that which they'd seen every day of their working lives. "The Capitalist belittles your sweat and your blood," the organizer cried out. "He thinks you oughta be grateful to have a job, for any kind of pay. But give him a muckstick and see how he likes it a mile down in the Hole, stoopin' over for eight hours in a hunnerd degrees! See how he likes eatin' a cold pasty in the dust and the muck! And see if he still thinks puttin' excape hatches in the bulkheads is a unnecessary expense!"

Waving down the cheers impatiently, Little spoke with fervent intensity. "Some of you probly heard me the other day talkin' about down in Bisbee, in Arizona, how the sheriff and his hired thugs rounded up all the union men, especially the Eye-dubbya-dubbyas, and held us in cattle pens with the help of the sojers. This they did without any warrant or legal authority. And the good people of Bisbee stood by and let 'em do it, even though they knew these boys, had worked side by side with them and went to church with them and their kids went to school together . . . but they let 'em do it. Now why was that?"

Little stood with his hands out at his sides and looked all around the grandstand. The men stared back, waiting for him to tell them.

"They let their union brothers get arrested and some of them was knocked down in the street with rifle butts by sojers.

The papers here made a big deal because I called the sojers no more than uniformed thugs. As a matter of fact, you heard me call 'em worse than that, but they couldn't print it."

There was uneasy laughter and Little went on. "The papers had it that the citizens of Bisbee run off the union men. That was a black damn lie. The good citizens of Bisbee ain't that bad, yet. But they did stand and watch." Little stood silently, mournfully. He lifted his chin and said, "I don't think that could happen in Butte."

"No sir!", "Not in a million years!", and "Never!", ran the chorus of cries from the stands.

"Becau-ause," Little drew out the word, preacher fashion, "becau-ause Butte is a city that knows what brotherhood is!"

"Yes!", "Yer damn right!", and, "You said it, brother!", rang down from the stands. Even Dewey was yelling and shaking his fist.

"And when you come right down to it," Little said, "that's what the union is all about. Ain't it? Ain't it? Ain't it! Yer goddam right it is!" he thundered.

The roars cascaded down, the men on their feet and Little was standing there basking in it. I was yelling myself by now.

When things quieted down, Little took up in a calmer voice, but stronger, as if he'd been nourished by the roars of the men. "But it was fear that kept the good folks of Bisbee from coming to the aid of their brothers," he said. "It was fear of the Big Boss, fear of losing money, fear of something new. And they didn't have the spirit of brotherhood that Butte has always had. . . . " he held up his hand to forestall another outbreak of cheers.

"It's a different kind of folks down there in Arizona, I reckon, or maybe that hot desert sun has baked their brains. I don't know. It damn near cooked my noodle, I'll say that. They ain't like Butte folks. They got a lot of racialism and prejudice down there. They haven't had a lot of Finns and Micks and Dagoes and Hunkies and Cousin Jacks all jumbled together and helping each other out like you have."

That got a pretty good reception, although at first I thought I could sense a little bristling, until the men caught on to the joshing tone.

"It was fear, boys. Fear of the Boss and fear of the union. They ain't used to unions yet, not real unions. And a real union is what we're talkin' about now." He began to talk in a more general way, it seemed to me. It sounded like a speech that he'd given many times before and it was filled with conventional phrases. He spoke of the evils inherent in the capitalist system, the crimes of the bosses, and the so-called nobility of the working man. The men seemed to hang on Little's words, but I thought they were getting a little bored, maybe a little let down. I was. Maybe it was just me.

But then he shifted gears and began to talk about the War, which he said was nothing more than a vicious, greed-inspired capitalist plot to enslave the workers, cooked up by the Big Interests—among whom he definitely included the Company as well as the munitions makers—in order to profit from their labor.

I was stunned. This bordered on treason. I'd never heard anything like it. What the heck, the Kaiser started it, didn't he?

My disgust steadily grew, and my distrust, even when Little pointed out that the price of copper had risen by nearly fifty per cent with the advent of the War—copper being a crucial ingredient of brass for artillery shells—while the worker's wages had not risen at all. If anything, conditions were worse, because the Company was striving to increase production without improving working conditions. That, Little declared, was what had led to the Speculator disaster, a month earlier, when a hundred sixty-five men had died.

If anybody was getting bored, this brought them back to attention. I found myself curiously hoping that Little would continue in this vein. But instead, the agitator suddenly went off on a rhapsody about the great struggle that our brothers were waging in Russia, which they were going to win. And how all the workers of Europe, even in the Kaiser's Germany, would soon rise up to join the courageous Communists.

This was too foreign for my blood. I suppose the miners, many of whom were from the Old Country, felt differently about it, but I just couldn't see Germans and Russians as brothers. I could only think of them as foreigners, alien races opposed to and envious of what I knew was the greatest, purest and most noble nation in the world—America! If Little would only stick to America, he'd do a lot better, I thought.

And apparently, Little sensed he was losing his audience, for he abruptly returned to the War and the Company.

"They feed you all this malarkey about the Huns and they wave the flag and tell you to be true to your country. But do they care about the country? They're selling copper to the Huns right now! Sure they are. They sell it to people who they know turn right around and resell it to the Huns! And the Huns make it into artillery shells that they fire at our boys!"

I was shocked. Could this be true? Would Little dare to make up such an audacious story?

"You don't believe me?" Little shouted. He was looking right at me. I thought he was talking to me alone. I looked around kind of embarassed, but I saw that the rest of them, even Dewey, seemed to have the same feeling.

"Hell, the Bosses are the same people as the Huns! They own stock in each other's companies, they trade together, they belong to the same club," Little declared. "But you're the ones who have to fight their war. You're the ones who have to die on the battlefield, in the trenches, or," he paused, "in the mines that they won't properly ventilate. And if you protest, then you're a coward and a traitor! You're holding up the war effort! But they're the real traitors. They don't care about this country and they don't care about you or your families. They use the trumped up War as an excuse for breaking unions and grinding more work for less pay out of the workers."

Abruptly, he took a new tack.

"What can we do? Is there any way out of this nightmare? Are the Bosses too tough for us? Well hell, boys, are you dumb? Are you weaklings?"

The men screamed as one, "Hell, no!"

"You're damn right! We ain't no damn sissies. But we gotta stick together. That's first. And we gotta organize. Not some damn sissy bullshit union that plays patty-cake with the Company and is nice and polite . . . " Little pranced around, miming an effeminate type while the men hooted, and then he suddenly whirled and snarled, ". . . I mean a real union, for real men! A union with balls!"

Little held a partly open fist out before his groin, as if clutching his own testicles and brandishing them. "We ain't afraid of no goddam Huns. Give us guns and we'd kick the Huns' asses in an afternoon, as soon as we got through kicking the asses of the Capitalists!"

The men howled. Little paced, head down, hands jammed deep in his baggy pockets. Thinking while they settled down. When he spoke again, his voice was calm.

"I got nothing against the Germans—I mean the German people, not the Kaiser." He laughed. "No, Germans are working men, too. Hell, I don't even hate the English." He had to pause while the many Irish roared. Little laughed. "Sure some of them are bastards, but they got the same problems we do. They got bosses like we do. The same bosses, in fact—the ruling class that sends troops into Ireland is the same ruling class that grinds the worker down and lives in ease off the sweat of your brow. The bosses who turn brother against brother for their own selfish purposes."

I didn't think too much of this familiar stuff, but then he brought up a theme that was a little too close to my situation.

"It's the old game," Little warned the men. "I'll be damned if I know why it works so well, but the bosses seem to be able to feed on our own suspicions. We gotta trust one another, we gotta be brothers, or else there ain't no union, but there's always the Judases that will take the bosses' coin while pretending to be one of us. The stooges destroyed your last union, in '14. They sold you down the river."

This line of talk naturally made me uneasy but it appeared to have been a tactless error. The old union still had plenty of loyal supporters, evidently. There were angry shouts and scuffling in the stands, along with exclamations about dynamite being good medicine.

"Stop this!" Little screamed, waving his hands over his head. The men paused in mid-punch, looking at the slender orator on the platform.

"You stupid men! You wanta see why you don't have a union? Look at you! I'm talking solidarity and you're swingin' from the heels!" He laughed, then. "You look like a buncha monkeys."

The men looked sheepish. Little grinned and waved his hand forbearingly, saying, "Ah, what the hell . . . you're all wound tighter'n a whore's. . . . " He didn't finish.

"Whore's what?" somebody yelled.

"Alarm clock," Little popped back.

I burst out laughing and pounded Dewey on the back, I guess out of relief.

"No man is an island," Little intoned, finally. *"No* man stands alone. Brothers, those ain't jokers up there." He pointed up the hill. "They want your blood. They won't settle for nothing less. It's their ball and their bat. That's the simple truth. The only problem is, it don't do 'em no good if you won't play. They can take their goddam ball and bat and go home, but they can't play by theirselves. Without you, all they got is a bat and a ball."

The men roared.

"They can't play ball without you," Little shouted. "They despise you, they crap all over you, they pretend you don't exist. To them you are the lowest of the low. They don't want their kids to go to school with yours, their wives don't go to tea with your wives, they want your wives and daughters for maids and mistresses. You're just part of the machinery. But the fact is, they can't do without you. Without you there ain't no damn ballgame."

Now Little's voice began to mount, it sounded raw, embittered, and he shrieked, "Are you men? Are you men? If you are men, don't let them make the rules, anymore. It's time for you to make the rules. This time . . . " he paused to let their roars build, then wane, ". . . this time we bring the umpire! This time we win!"

The roars cascaded, the men on their feet and stamping. They screamed "We win! We win!".

Little thrust his arms upright, fists clenched and his jaw thrust out belligerently, his single eye glaring up into the cheering stands. But at last, he slowly dropped his arms to his side as the noise subsided, and he broke out a sunny grin and muttered, "That's all I got to say." But then he suddenly grabbed his throat and made a burlesque of choking, with his

43

tongue extended and exclaimed, "Whoo-ee! This is dusty work! Let's go get a beer!"

And he jumped down and disappeared into the crowd.

I immediately pushed forward, trying to get to Little, but it was impossible. He was lost in a mass of enthusiastic supporters. Finally I gave up and turned away. Dewey was waiting for me. While we walked back uptown, I said, "Little is some orator, don't you think?"

But Dewey the worldly cynic wouldn't admit to being excited by Little. "I heard better," he said. "Dat crazy Sean, d'ough, he t'inks da guy's anudda Jeeziss." Dewey shook his head.

I could understand that, though I didn't say as much to Dewey. Little reminded me of a country preacher I'd seen in Alabama, where I used to go on visits to my father's family. I reckoned he was another Billy Sunday, what with all the baseball talk. I asked Dewey if he thought Paton could introduce me to Little.

"Ast him. He used to know him up in Michigan."

Uptown, everybody was talking about Little's speech, but even though we rambled around to various saloons, the orator didn't seem to be out and about. I spent some of Davis' money, buying beers and drinking a few shots of whiskey, myself. Finally, I left Dewey in the M&M, checking the scores, and walked back to the Big Ship. I felt grand. Butte was a hell of a place. Night had fallen and I saw a bunch of shooting stars, more than I'd ever thought possible.

CHAPTER FOUR

In the morning the mountain that Butte was trying to dismantle stuck its scarred head into the bottoms of thick black clouds and those clouds rained on the town until the mine tailings were washed down onto the streets and the vacant lots became greasy lakes and the gullies were scoured raw. My room in the Big Ship was on the top floor. I wrenched my thin blanket tighter and listened to the rain thunder on the flat, tarred roof and gurgle through the rainspouts and finally seep into the ceiling, making a wet patch that slowly spread out from the southwest corner, gradually overtaking the tide marks of a previous rain.

I had to piss but I didn't want to get up yet. It was damn cold for August. I nursed the blanket for comfort and listened to the voices of the other men through the thin walls. Down the hall there was a man telling the story of his travels. It sounded like there were several men who had gathered in the room to wait out the downpour rather than walk uptown. The story-teller's voice was Deep South, Mississippi perhaps. It rose and fell softly, almost singing, with a quality of wonder and awe as the story-teller talked about his travels to The Great Salt Lake, where a man couldn't drown if he wanted to . . . then about the "geezers" and hot pools in Yellowstone Park, where the moose and the buffalo came right up to you and the grizzly bears just waved as you walked by and went on with their berry picking. It was better than a radio play, but there wasn't any radio in those days, of course. It had another, ancient quality, too, of something tribal and comforting, a way of showing a good face against the elements. I dozed to the melody of the voice.

As usual, I started out day-dreaming about a couple of girls back home, but their faces kept being replaced by Ma Paton's. I fought it for a minute, maybe, and then I began to dwell on the shape of her hips in the thin cotton skirt, and the surprising pinching-in of the waist, and inevitably, the swelling of the bosom. I imagined with startling clarity just how her slim belly would look, white and firm with a slight mounding of the abdomen and a sense of the underlying muscles . . . it was too unsettling, what with having to piss, anyway. I forced myself to think instead about Frank Little.

The memory of Little's speech kept merging with the melody of the story-singer down the hall. After awhile the substance of it, the baseball stuff and the Russians and the Kaiser, melted into the weave of the singer's song and I could not really remember what Little had talked about . . . I could see him dancing on the top of the dugout and singing in the rain. I finally drifted off, for a few minutes anyway.

When I awoke again, the singer was still telling his stories and I lay there with my hands clasped behind my head and carefully recalled everything Little had said. His attitude puzzled me. It was so different from anything I'd ever heard. He wasn't for any of the things most people were for, and yet he seemed so self-assured. For the first time in my life I wished I'd paid more attention in history class. I wished I knew more about geography and philosophy. I'd quit high school before my last year, but I'd always enjoyed reading; in fact everybody in my family said I read too much. For some reason I started late; I didn't learn to read until I was in the third grade and I guess I had an idea that I had to catch up to everyone else. Anyway, I read constantly . . . illustrated magazines, newspapers, cowboy novels and stories, and even good stuff—Dickens, Thackeray, and Mark Twain. I attempted Dostoevsky, but it was too dense and I gave it up, one of the few books I ever began that I never finished. Tolstoy's books were too huge to even begin.

Ma Paton's image popped back into my day-dreams.

"It's like a feen in your blood," the singer crooned.

For a moment, I thought he was singing directly to me, the voice sounded so clearly. But the singer was referring to the lust for travel, which he claimed was a fiend, in his case a youthful addiction to "swingin' freights."

"I was standing in the rain, in Birmingham, Alabama," the singer sang, "coming home from Miss Grace Obera's house, where I'd filled up on chicken and biscuits—we were fixin' to get married—and here come a freight train just a-trun'lin through, and I heard that lonesome whistle blow—'whooo-woooo'—it was that ol' feen, calling me, and I seen a boxcar with an open door. Well boys, I just stepped forward and. . . " And they were off again, this time to someplace called Shinbone Valley, where folks had never heard that the War Between the States was over.

I wanted nothing more than to snuggle up and listen to the singer, but my bladder wouldn't let me. I got up and dressed. As I went down the hall I passed the story-singer's room and paused at the open door. The men, sitting around smoking cigarettes, looked up at me, expectantly. Their faces, framed in cloth caps, were pale and passive and seemed like so many worn, soiled flowers. Their expression was in no way hostile, merely curious, but I felt like an intruder. The story-singer, sitting on the bed with his back to me, turned around and smiled, exposing a few, brown, snaggled teeth. His eyes were as blue as a summer sky. I was embarassed and fled down the hall, followed by a low flutter of laughter.

Dewey was not in his room and I was too late for breakfast. The serving girl, a cheerful, bouncy one, said Dewey had most likely gone uptown. When I went outside the rain had stopped and the clouds were blowing away rapidly. By the time I reached Sean Paton's house the sun was shining brightly and the ragamuffins had come out to splash in the gleaming puddles, streaked with iridescent chemicals.

For a minute I couldn't think why I was there. I wasn't aware of having chosen to walk that way rather than uptown to find Dewey. Then I remembered that Sean could introduce me to Little and I knocked on the door.

"Hullo?" Paton said. He didn't seem to recognize me at first, but then his puzzled look gave way to a sheepish smile. "Oh, hullo. C'mon in." He was wearing overalls but his feet were bare and his hair was tousled. Obviously, he'd just gotten up.

He led me into the parlor. Mrs. Paton appeared, standing in the entrance to the kitchen, wiping her hands on her apron. The light wasn't good, but she seemed to be wearing the same skirt and blouse. The light came from behind her and I couldn't quite make out her facial features, but her figure was outlined. I felt a little surge in my stomach. The feen, I thought, and almost laughed out loud.

"Ma, this here is . . . " Paton turned to me, ". . . uh, it's Gordon, ain't. . . . "

"It's Goodwin," Ma Paton said, firmly, "Goody Ryder."

"Oh. I guess you met. Yesterday," Paton said, shamefaced.

"Yes, we met," she said. She disappeared.

"Siddown, siddown," Sean said. I sat on the same wooden chair I'd used the day before and Sean pulled up another across the table from me. It seemed damp and chilly in the house.

"So, what's new?" Paton ran his fingers through his unruly red hair and said, apologetically, "You wouldn't have a butt, would ya?"

"Sure." I pulled out a pack of Caporals and handed them over after I'd taken one out for myself. We lit up and I said, "I just wanted to see if you were all right. You weren't feeling too good when I left."

"He wasn't feeling anything," Mrs. Paton corrected, entering with a pot of tea under a quilted cozy. She set it down on the table and went back to fetch cups and saucers.

As soon as she'd left the room, Sean made some mysterious grimaces in her direction and a silent appeal to discretion with his finger to his lips. I nodded.

"We gotta get outa here," Sean whispered.

"Okay, I'll think of something."

Mrs. Paton returned with the cups and a bowl of sugar. "What are you two whispering about?" she asked, in a mood of superior amusement.

"Oh, I was just asking if Sean felt better, m'am."

"I'm not your mam," she replied, in a good-natured way. She sat down and poured tea.

"Actually, I was wondering if Sean would take me over to the Company offices, so I could see about getting a card."

"There's a strike on, in case you haven't heard," she observed. "Of course, a few men are working." She glanced pointedly at her husband. "The ones who aren't trailing Frank Little around like sheep."

"Company stooges," Paton said, bitterly.

"Well, I ain't a stooge," I said, sipping the weak tea, "but I need work." I set the tea down. I hate tea.

49

Sean shrugged. "I could take ya over there, but there's pickets. It won't be no picnic."

"I'd like to take a look-see," I said. "If it doesn't seem like a good idea, well. . . . "

"Okay. It's yer funeral," Paton said. "But I don't wanta be seen with ya, if yer plannin' ta scab. But I reckon we could walk uptown together."

"That's fine," I said. Paton nodded and went into the other room to get his shoes.

Tension immediately began to build in the room. I tried to avoid looking at the woman across the table, but it wasn't possible. Her thick red hair billowed out framing her strong, handsome face. She gazed back at me boldly, as before. I looked away.

"I didn't think I'd see you again," she said, quietly. "After yesterday." She smiled. "I reckoned I didn't make too good an impression. You probably think I'm some kind of Irish fishwife."

"Oh no. Certainly not."

She smoothed the front of her blouse down, causing the material to stretch over her bosom provocatively. "I'm glad," she said. "Glad you didn't think so poorly of . . . of us. I'm glad to see friends of Sean's, really I am, but so many of them seem so tough. And you don't seem tough."

I had to smile. "No, m'am. I'm not tough."

"Now there you go again," she said. Her smile softened. "Calling me m'am."

"I'm sorry."

"You're from back East," she said, refilling our cups.

"Yes, m'am, Baltimore. Oh, sorry. Missus Paton."

"My goodness, you will make me feel like an old married woman, Goodwin. But you say your family is from Galway, originally?"

"That's right." I sipped at the insipid tea.

"Or was it Donegal?"

"I meant Donegal," I remembered.

"I knew it was somewhere in the west. I'm a Dublin lass, myself."

"You're a long way from home," I said. "Do you miss it?"

"Oh yes, Ireland is very beautiful, you know. Not in the way America is, of course. It's quite different. But there isn't much opportunity there. Not that I've done so well here," she gestured at her surroundings. "Mind you, I'm not complaining. I know Americans hate it when foreigners complain."

"You don't seem like a foreigner to me. You seem to fit in quite well."

"Oh, I'm a full citizen now, but thank you. And I don't consider that my opportunities are used up."

She had a splendid smile. She had one of those faces that the movies would have loved . . . Johnny Huston would love it . . . a frank, pretty face that was attractive without being beautiful. The chin was strong but not jutting, the cheek bones not too pronounced, the brow wide but not overly intellectual. Her eyes were large and smoky gray. It was an apple-pie, Irish-American face. The figure and the hair were extra special, though.

"What kind of opportunities are you looking for?" I asked, flippantly.

"I embrace," she crossed her arms over her bosom, "all opportunities." She gazed directly into my eyes and I was momentarily incapable of speech.

But then she glanced over her shoulder, toward the bedroom where her husband was grunting with the effort of pulling on his boots. She seemed to consider something for a moment, then took a deep breath and turned back to me.

"Goodwin, I must talk to you . . . privately." She spoke in a low and urgent voice. "It's about Sean-O." She looked down. "I'm very worried for him."

I, of course, had nothing to say.

"Where are you staying?" I told her and she said, "I'll send a boy. Soon." Her eyes seemed misty and she reached out a hand toward mine. I watched, as transfixed as a nestling at the approach of a snake. Her hand fell on mine. It was cool. She squeezed my hand gently and said, "Will that be all right?"

"Uh, yeah, sure."

She patted my hand, almost as if comforting me. "That's good . . . Goody. My name, by the way, is Sheila."

Sheila! I almost laughed. Her name seemed too apt. But it was a fine name. I broke off my rapt gaze as Sean returned, and jerked my hand away from hers. I stood up hastily.

"Now, Sean, you'll not be getting into mischief again?"

Sean managed a shaky laugh and threw an arm around his wife's slender waist. "A course not, Ma. Say, we better get a move on."

Mrs. Paton followed us to the front door, saying, "I'm going to hold you responsible, Goodwin Ryder!"

"Aw, Ma," Sean said. I didn't say anything.

At the Company offices, there were at least two dozen men lounging against the buildings, some of them carrying placards that said such things as, "No Scabs!", or "Support Your Union!" Sean and I held back, a full block away.

"I don't like the looks of this," I said. "Maybe I oughta think this over."

Sean grinned. "Well, where to?" he asked, hopefully.

I brightened his day by gesturing to a nearby saloon, The Board of Trade. Over a couple of beers, which seemed to calm Sean's morning nerves marvelously, I suggested that maybe I ought to join the union, instead of trying for a rustling card.

"If I have to cross a picket line to work, the heck with it," I said. "I got a few bucks saved and I reckon I can hold out for a couple of weeks, anyway. The way I figure it, the union's bound to win this strike, like you say. I'd be a sap to go in now, against the men instead of with them."

Sean fully agreed with this. "There ain't gonna be no work for scabs, soon."

"How long do you think it will be? Before the strike brings the Company around, I mean."

"Could be any day," Sean said. "Frank says the price a copper is up and going higher, what with the War and all. The Company won't want to miss out on the boom times. They'll settle before long."

"That's exactly the way I see it," I said. "It stands to reason, don't it?"

"That's what I been tryin' to tell Ma," Sean said, "but she won't see it."

"Say, Dewey and I heard Frank yesterday at the ballpark. It was something!"

"Ya did? He's a humdinger, ain't he?" Sean enthused. "Boy, when the strike is settled you're gonna see some changes in this old town, and I'd say it'll all be due to Frank."

"I thought he was one of the most stirring speakers I ever heard," I said. "Say, do you think I could meet him? He's a pal of yours, isn't he?"

"Well, sure," Sean said. "I mean, I know him as well as any of the guys. Frank isn't one a your stuckup guys. He don't act like a bigshot at all. Well, you seen him."

"Could you introduce us?" I asked, pushing gently. "I just wanted to tell him how much I liked his speech, and all."

Sean stalled for awhile, out of caution, but after a couple more beers he agreed to take me around town, looking for Frank. "There's no telling where he'll be now," he explained. "He has breakfast in Harrington's and pow-wows with Campbell and Wuuri and some of the other local fellers, but they'll of left by now. After that he usually just kinda walks around town, talking to the fellers, trying to keep our spirits up."

We set off on a tour of Butte's taverns, in each of which we had to have a beer, which I cheerfully bought. We finally ran Little down in Cassidy's, talking to a group of ten men in the card room. Sean and I stood on the fringes listening while Little exhorted the men to stand by their brothers and assured them that the whole world was looking on at their struggle for justice and fair play. When the informal gathering broke up and Little prepared to go on to his next inspirational station, I pushed Sean forward, whispering, "Ask him."

"Why, hello, Sean," Little squinted up at the big fellow. "How are you doing, lad?"

"None too good, Frank," Sean said, but then he grinned and said, "but we'll stick 'er out."

"That's the stuff. Good for you."

"Say, Frank, this is my pal Goody Ryder. He's just come to town and he'd like to meet ya."

Little shook my hand warmly and welcomed me to Butte. "Things are kind of tough right now, young feller," he said, "but you stick around. It'll improve."

Up close, Little looked even less impressive than he'd seemed at first on the dugout, the day before. But he had a friendly, reassuring manner. He was one of these birds who hang onto your mitt a trifle long, however, and I practically had to pry it loose.

"I enjoyed your speech yesterday, Mr. Little," I said, trying to act a lot calmer than I felt. All of Joe Davis's warnings came back to me. I wasn't scared, but I was nervous. I was a bit taller than the labor organizer, which helped, somehow.

"Call me Frank. So you're a miner, Goody?" Little looked at me shrewdly.

"Well, not yet, sir," I said. I hoped to hell he couldn't see how jumpy he was making me. "I'd like to give it a try, but I can't see crossing a picket line when guys like Sean, here, aren't working."

"Good for you. Wal, don't get discouraged, Goody. Things'll change, they'll change. Things'll be booming before long. Maybe sooner than we think. Tomorrow, even. You keep your pecker up, young feller. And you, too, Sean-Oh."

Little made as if to go, but I blurted out, "I was kind of hoping to talk to you, Frank."

"What about?" Little stopped and put his hands in his pockets. He looked a shade suspicious.

"About your speech," I said, off the top of my head.

"What about it? You said you liked it."

"Oh, I did. But, you know . . . I noticed that it kind of had it's ups and downs." I gestured with my hands, moving them up and down.

"Ups and downs? Now what does that mean?" Little smiled condescendingly, glancing to the other fellows listening. "You know something about speeches that I don't?"

"Oh, no sir. It's just . . . well, when you got to talking about Russia, and all . . . I noticed that the men got kind of restless."

Little looked me over, assessing me. Then he said, "Wal, that's interesting. What else?"

"The baseball stuff was real good," I rushed on. "I could see the men liked that. But you left it and started talking about Russians and Communists and international brotherhood.

55

That's all good stuff, too, of course, but I got the feeling that they don't really care about that, so much. You see, it seems to me that it's kinda hard for an American working man to be worried much about foreign stuff. I know we got a lot of foreigners here—but they're Americans now! They left Europe, left it behind. I don't mean to criticize, but. . . . "

"Oh, you mean to criticize all right, Goody," Little said agreeably, "and you're doing a good job of it. But you don't have to be afraid to criticize. That's the trouble around here." He began to speak louder, including a few men who had lingered and now pressed in to hear more of Little's talk.

"There's nothing wrong with criticism. A man can take criticism. It's the Comp'ny can't take it. They don't want to hear it. They won't hear it." He went on in this vein for a few more minutes then concluded and, taking me by the elbow, steered me toward a nearby booth, saying, "I want to talk to this young feller, men." He nodded toward Sean, shooing him off.

I couldn't believe my luck. I'd just started shooting off my mouth, because I couldn't think of anything to say, and it had turned out to interest Little. Little ordered beers but I insisted on paying.

"So you're new in town," Little said. "Where exactly are you from?" It seemed Little knew Baltimore. He mentioned a few streets and hotels, which I recognized, and a few names of men I didn't know. He asked me if I was for the Orioles or the Terrapins. I said I'd always been for the Orioles, but I wasn't really a baseball bug, like some.

"Wal, I like it," Little said. "It don't amount to a fart in a whirlwind, but that's the point, ain't it? It takes a feller's mind off his troubles, worrying about how his team is going. But you liked what I said, at the ballpark?"

"Oh, sure. That was good. I never thought about it before, but you made us see how baseball was sort of like life."

"Wal, it's bigger than life, you might say. Not the game itself, exactly, but the rest of it, the glammer of the players and the way the owners deal with 'em, all of it. A lot of life's little drammers are played out for us on the ball diamond. Like this labor struggle, for instance. But you didn't like the other stuff, the Russians? It upset you, made you nervous?"

"Yes sir. I guess that was it. I kind of wanted you to stop talking about that."

"Wal, that's the point, Goody. It's in the papers ever'day, but folks don't really want to talk about it, even though it's real important to their lives, more important than they know. It makes them nervous, because they don't know what to think about it. It's mostly because they're not used to it. It's the same with a lot of things. Like the folks in Bisbee I was talking about. They didn't know what to think and so they let somebody else do the thinking for them. It's the same with something as common as sex, even. People don't like to talk about sex, except in certain, accepted ways."

Little was certainly correct there, I thought. In those days I didn't even like to hear the word "sex." It made me uneasy. It wasn't a word that I or anyone I knew ever used. I'd have been just as happy, in fact, if Little would drop it. But he wouldn't.

"People don't talk openly about sex and so it stays mysterious," Little said. "Fellers tell dirty jokes—hell, I slipped in a couple in my speech, just to loosen the boys up—and we kind of leave it at that. So we don't have to really talk about what it really is." He sipped his beer thoughtfully. "But we all do it, that's for sure. Ain't that so?" He grinned.

I laughed uneasily. "Oh, well, yes sir. But. . . . "

"Go on." Little sat there very calmly, listening. He was making me nervous and I couldn't tell if it was intentional.

"It seems like there's something else to it, this talk about revolution, I mean."

"Wal, there is. There's more to it than just getting folks used to the idea. You're right. But the first job is to get folks talking and thinking about what causes a revolution. The Russians are having a hard time of it, right now, but they've had hundreds of years of hard times. This isn't their first revolution, you know. But we've had it kind of easy. We had our revolution more'n a hundred years ago and things have gone along, mostly improving, but the American revolution wasn't what you'd call a real revolution."

I was taken aback. "It wasn't?"

"Not like the French revolution, or some of the rebellions in Europe and England. That was the common people objecting to an oppressive system. Ours was more like a bunch of businessmen pulling out of an unprofitable cartel. But that's not how we were taught in school, was it? But our revolution had plenty to offer to the common man, that's for sure, only now it looks like our revolution is getting stabbed in the back. Things are getting out of hand. The Big Interests control every-thing, anymore. We don't notice because it was done so gradual. But if Jefferson and the boys were around today, I bet they'd be plenty gravelled to see what's happened to their revolution in just a handful of generations. Nowadays, you can't even mention revolution without getting beaten and throwed in jail . . . or having young fellers like you get annoyed."

Little grinned, to show me he was joking.

"Heh! I guess you're thinking, 'There he goes again,'" Little said. "Wal, I'll take that up some other time, if you're really innarested. You strike me as a feller with an education. Did you go to college?"

I was flattered, but I said I hadn't. "I read a lot, though."

"You ever read Marx? Karl Marx? Or Engels? No? You oughta, you know. A man isn't educated if he hasn't read Marx. I got a few pamphlets. You could come by my room, sometime, if you're innarested. It's Mrs. Byrne's place, over on North Wyoming, three-sixteen, room thirty-two. I'm not always there, but you could drop by sometime, maybe you'd catch me."

I said I'd like that, but for some reason I didn't suggest a time. I just let it go, for now.

Little seemed to relax, but then, out of nowhere, he said, quietly, "You wouldn't be a Pinkerton, would you, son?"

I was stunned. I guess my mouth fell open and I couldn't speak. Little was looking at me calmly, a thin smile on his lips.

Finally, I stammered, "No, Jeeziss, hell no, Mister Little. Why, you can ask Sean, or Dewey Thacker. . . . "

"They don't know anything about you, Goody, and I don't really know them any more than you do. You just got into town, didn't you say? Know anybody else in Butte? Somebody who can vouch for you?"

I gulped and shook my head. The people who could vouch for me in Butte weren't exactly Frank Little's pals.

"Wal, maybe you are and maybe you aren't. It don't make a lotta difference." Little hitched forward and offered a friendly smile. "Gotta fag?" He took one of my Caporals and lit it with a kitchen match that he lit one-handed on his thumbnail, blowing the smoke out slowly.

"What I mean is, it don't make a difference to me, Goody. But it makes a hell of a lot of difference to you." Little squinted at me through the smoke. "It makes a difference to a young

59

feller who and what he follows—the scum or the decent folks. These men here," he gestured at the bar, "drink a little beer and maybe a few of them cheat on their wives with the gals in Venus Alley, and they swear and chew tobacco and bet on the ballgames, and most of 'em don't go to church as much as they oughta . . . but they ain't the scum, Goody. They are the salt of the earth."

He gestured again, this time upward, up the Hill, and said, "The scum is up there, Goody. They say the cream rises to the top, but so does the scum." Little smiled. "A lot of 'em are real good pillars of the community, upstanding men, deacons . . . but they'll screw their fellow man quicker'n a frog'll eat a fly. And they probably'll believe they're doing it out of principle. Maybe they are, but them have gotta be some awful rubbery principles."

His single eye glowed. "It don't make no difference to me, Goody, but you oughta know what's in it for you—if you're one of them. I'm not saying you are. But these men here don't like Pinks. Pinks have a way of disappearing, no questions asked. I'm not a violent man, myself. But Mirabeau said, 'You can't make a revolution with rosewater.' I'm a shot-and-a-beer man, myself."

I had no idea who Mirabeau was, but I didn't like to say so. I contented myself with a show of offended dignity, saying, "Well, I'm no Pink."

"Wal, you sure as hell ain't no miner, Goody. What's your game?"

"My game? Well. . . . " I thought fast. I hitched myself closer across the little table and dropped my voice. "To tell you the truth, Mister Little, I'm a reporter."

"A reporter?" Little frowned skeptically.

"I'm writing an article for the *Smart Set.*"

"Mencken's rag?"

"That's right. I didn't want to say anything to Sean, or the others. They wouldn't understand and anyway, the idea is to get the real picture, the working man's angle."

"Unh-hunh. Which is why you told me," Little said.

"Well, you kind of caught me out. I guess I never figured that someone would take me for a Pink."

Little considered me for a long second or two, then shrugged. "It don't matter."

"Well, I reckon it does! You couldn't get too far with your revolution, surrounded by Pinks."

"Think so? I wonder. Once upon a time I'd of agreed with you, Goody, but now I don't know. What's the use of a revolution if you can't convert the unbelievers, eh? You can't make all the Pinks 'disappear.' You got to convince 'em. They got to be part of the revolution, too. Anyway, it's no use hiding. After awhile the revolution has got to come up out of the underground. The revolutionist has got to stand up and holler."

"Even if he gets knocked down?"

"Even if he gets knocked cattywampus, Goody. You get knocked down, but you get back up and fight."

"Is that what you're doing?"

"That's what I'm doing." He hoisted himself to his feet. "If you really are a reporter, stop by, if you got the time. I've got a lot to say, if the *Smart Set*'s really innarested. Maybe you can give me some advice on my speeches."

"Mister Little," I said, "Frank . . . could you kind of keep it quiet, about me being a reporter?"

Little winked with his good eye. "It'll be our secret."

I breathed a sigh of relief. And I swear, that's the only thing I ever stole from Sam Hammett.

The seven stacks of the Never Sweat

CHAPTER FIVE

I don't really recall the details of the first time . . . I just know how it came about. I'm pretty sure it was at Columbia Gardens. That was a big amusement park just outside of Butte. You had to take a special trolley. One of the Copper Kings built the park. It had an artificial lake, a pavilion, a roller coaster, a midway with other rides and carnival attractions.

We didn't meet on the midway. It was up on the mountainside. There was a little trail, beyond the lake. Obviously, many lovers had been that way, seeking privacy. She'd told me in the note she sent to The Big Ship, handed to me by the bouncy serving girl, just where to go and to wait for her.

"Who brought this?" I asked the girl.

"Just a kid," she said. "I think it was one of them Patonses. Devvy, it was."

Patonses? Ah, I realized then. It was from Sheila. Ma Paton.

I was not a virgin. I was a man of twenty years, having grown up in Baltimore, on tough city streets. I had my first experience in an alley, behind a wooden fence between two sheds—we would have used one of the sheds, but we were afraid to trespass. So why was I trembling as I got off the trolley and made my way through the sparse weekday crowd on the midway, looking for the lake and the trail? Well, I'd never had an invitation like this before, a bold summons from a grown woman, with a map.

I wasn't sure how far up the trail I should climb. I was already well above the amusement park and there was a fine view of the city in the distance and the blue mountains beyond. I stopped by a big rock next to the trail and lit a Caporal. I gazed out at the splendid scenery, wondering what I was doing there.

And then a voice floated down from above. It sounded impatient. "Well come on!"

I looked up. She was standing by the edge of some scrubby pines. I remember the pine aroma, now, when we entered the copse, the needles underfoot. It was not so shady, really, but warmed by the sun. She drew me on, holding my hand.

When we found a little, sunny clearing we stopped and I just stood there, looking about, not knowing how to proceed. The clearing was like a fine, open terrace, beyond which was all the world ... the mountains, the distant city, just a portion of the park below, and a vast blue sky on which a few distant clouds were poised. The air was very still, silent except for an occasional rattling cry from a magpie or a jay. It was a moment of great expectancy ... but somehow, I couldn't start.

And she just stood there, smiling. Waiting.

Finally, out of desperation I started talking about the clouds. I remember she said something about building cloud castles when she was a little girl, walking along the beach near Dublin, I guess. 'Along the strand,' she said. She used to imagine all sorts of things. . . .

"What sorts of things?" I asked her.

"Oh, the usual—knights and ladies, pavilions with pennants snapping in the breeze ... castles in the air. What do you see?"

I thought for a while. These were not castle-building clouds. These clouds were like discs. They have them in the mountains but nowhere else. They had an edge to them. They were a little too real and I said so.

"Real?" Sheila laughed gently. "Here, sit down."

We sat down on a large, flat boulder that was warmed by the sun but kept bearably cool by the shade of a few aspens on one side. At this time of the day, the aspens cast a mottled, greenish shadow. It was remarkably like a huge divan under a thin canopy and strangely soft to the touch.

"Yeah, real. I don't mind that. They don't mislead you into believing things that can't be. I just meant they weren't the kind of clouds to construct castles out of."

"You're a strange boy."

"Don't say that. I hate it when people say that. I'm sorry," I apologized, seeing her face stiffen. "I don't mean . . . I don't know what I mean. I'm just tired of things not being true."

Sheila frowned. "What do you mean?"

"It's harder to explain than the clouds," I said. "Look. See those trolley cars down there? They're real. And this hill is real and we're really sitting here. But when we walk back down this hill and get on the trolley and ride back to town, why, with every foot we get closer to town, things will get less real. Problems will start to pop up—everything is a problem, in a way. Look, I know I'm not making sense. . . ."

"Go on," she said. She leaned back, supporting herself on one extended arm and rotating her hips slightly toward me. It made her breasts slide sideways and the shift, the movement and the awkward, not quite arrested poise of them under the shirtwaist created a tension that transfixed me. I had a sudden mad flight of imagination in which I saw her breasts as pendulums, swinging back and forth . . . were they really at rest? Or would the cloth yield and allow them to shift further down in their gravity-bound arc? I tore my eyes away and tried to think of what it was I'd been trying to say. It was something about the reality of things and how it shifted . . . was she wearing a shift?

"Do you miss the sea?" I improvised, mindlessly.

"The sea? You mean the Irish Sea? Oh yes. The sea is lovely. But the mountains have some of the same beauty, of course."

I didn't understand that, but I was glad to hear her talk of something that didn't arouse me. But then she went on, throwing me back into confusion.

"They are both large," she said, "vast you might say, and natural. Yes, that's it. They both have a natural power and beauty, a kind of enchanted splendor."

Vast, I thought. And natural. And an enchanted splendor. But then I realized that she was talking about the sea and the mountains.

"Ah, yes," I said. "Ah, that's a little bit like what I was trying to say, before. Natural things, like mountains or clouds—or even trolley cars—they have a certain realness. But people—" I waved a hand, frustrated at my inability to find the words. "Business . . . and the things we have to do and what we say to each other, when we're all together in the city—that doesn't have the same kind of realness. Yeah, that's sort of it. Only not quite. It's getting to it, but not close enough, yet."

We sat there for what seemed a long time without saying much. All that confused talk about clouds and what was 'real' . . . until finally I said, "I guess we shouldn't be here."

"No, of course we shouldn't," Sheila said, in a matter of fact way, adding hopefully, "but as we are here. . . ."

"You're probably worrying about the kids," I said.

"The kids are fine, for now. I don't see them for hours when I'm there. They go out in the morning and come back when they're hungry. Sometimes I . . . well, I certainly didn't come up here to talk about the children."

That was my cue. I should have said, "What did you come up here for?" But I flubbed it. I just stared out over the valley, at the town of Butte, looking so clean and orderly from this distance. Even the mines looked all right—bare spots on the hillside set about with clever little buildings and toy structures.

She knocked my cap off.

"What the. . . ." I turned to her in surprise.

She grabbed my hair, sank her fingers into it and shook my head. She was laughing but it hurt. I had to pry her fingers away. We tussled. And then, somehow, we were kissing and rolling together under the pale green-and-silver shade of the aspens. I could feel her belly, just as I'd imagined it, warm and womanly against my own. Her breasts were as firm as sponges against my chest.

She kissed wonderfully. Her mouth was cool and hot at once, sucking and sinewy, soft and biting. She filled my arms in a marvelously satisfying way.

I suppose to her I was as spooky as a yearling buck, but she didn't complain. She kept running her hands down my side and my thighs, slipping them under my coat, caressing me. I was doing the same, loving the feel of that soft, firm flesh under her thin skirt and blouse.

We went on like that for some time, kissing and caressing, and then . . . somehow it went on too long, without progressing to the next step, to the "real" event. A kind of deadly caution began to creep into our caresses. It was fatal. We finally drew apart, although reluctantly.

"Well," Sheila puffed the word out as she sat up. She straightened her blouse and skirt, patting and brushing at her tousled hair. Primping.

I was embarassed. I knew I'd blundered. Why hadn't I touched her breasts, her sex? It was too late. I cleared my throat and whisked imaginary dust off my clothes and hair. I sat apart from her. Naturally, I got out a cigarette and lit it.

A cigarette is a great thing, especially in moments like that, when there isn't anything really useful to say. You smoke your cigarette and then it's a little later and the difficult moment is past.

I suddenly felt awfully exposed. It was as if the whole town of Butte—not to say the people at the Gardens—could look up and see the two of us, sitting alone on the hillside. I no longer felt so protected by the thin curtain of the scrawny pines. We weren't doing anything, but we weren't innocent, either. It was an unbearable situation. There was nothing to do but go, which made you ask yourself, Why did we come?

We stood up and made a show of politeness and I tried to think of something amusing to say but nothing came. We pretended to brush the leaves and pine needles off one another, careful not to touch in some suggestive way—which is a different kind of horribleness than if we had touched. And finally we set off down the steep path. It came out on a walk that led by the flower gardens and down along the edge of the lake where the swan boats were. We didn't venture onto the midway . . . the Electric Theater and Katzenjammer Kastle . . . the people . . . too many people, even though it was a weekday. Butte wasn't such a huge city that we could expect to be anonymous in a crowd. I was sure that someone would see us and tell Sean. I didn't feel like the invisible detective at that moment. In fact I was more scared than I ever was trailing some robbery suspect.

But Sheila seemed as calm as an ewe grazing through a meadow. She had a shawl and she wrapped it about her, cupping her elbows in her palms. We strolled back to the trolley, side by side, more or less, but pretending not to be together.

Sheila asked me for a nickel. I was surprised. She had come up there without a return fare! The motorman had stepped outside the car to smoke his pipe. We paid separately and clambered aboard. The car was empty and Sheila cleverly chose one of the lateral seats at the front, so that I could sit in the first of the row seats, close by but not necessarily "with" her. We waited nervously as several others boarded, but none of them were acquaintances, nor even so much as glanced at us.

At last the motorman looked at his pocket watch, knocked the smoking ashes out of his pipe, and boarded. He looked the passengers over briefly, as if counting us, and sat down. He gave the handle a jerk and the trolley slid off toward town, making a convenient racket as we rocked along.

"We shall have to find a place," Sheila said, smiling as if chatting to a casual acquaintance. Just a neighbor, perhaps, whom she'd met on the trolley.

"Where?" was all I could think to say. I was kicking myself, now, for letting this chance get away without "doing it." Her place was out of the question and so was the Big Ship. Other than the amusement park, where was there? I didn't want to suggest a hotel, though I suppose there were hotels for that purpose, there always are. Butte didn't seem big enough for that kind of place. And anyway, a hotel seemed degrading.

"I'll think of something," Sheila said. She added, in a louder voice, for the benefit of eavesdroppers, "It's so refreshing to get away for an hour or two."

When the car approached Clark Park she stood up and waited by the door. She pulled her shawl tighter around her and stepped down, clomping in her heavy shoes. They were rough shoes, I noticed, men's shoes. She wore black stockings and the same blue skirt as before.

I thought: She's not really dressed for an afternoon at Columbia Gardens. Perhaps she has no other clothes. But then, how could she dress for a tryst? Every housewife in the Cabbage Patch would have noticed. I was ashamed of myself for not noticing before and I hoped she hadn't been embarrassed. Then I realized that she was the kind of woman who is never embarrassed. She knew who she was.

The car slid away and I saw her face, strong and brave, so lovely, framed in coppery hair. She stood looking after the car. A strong, brave adulteress. I turned away and didn't look back.

CHAPTER SIX

That same evening Sean Paton came up to me in the M&M and said, "You perfessers can talk the pants off the devil, I guess. Whadja do to my old lady?"

I was caught completely off guard. I searched Sean-O's face but he seemed to be joking.

Paton laughed. "Don't git so jumpy, kid. You ain't exactly Wallace Reid, you know. But you must have somp'n. Ma said you was by earlier, looking for me. And, she told me to tell you to drop your laundry off t'marra."

"My laundry!" I was dumbfounded.

"Yanh. She sez you young guys don't take care a your laundry. She can do it with the kids'es."

"Say, that's real sweet of her," I said with a snort and a wink, "but I take my stuff to the Chink, over on Mercury. They do a good job for next to nothing."

Paton winked back. "And besides it gives you a good excuse to walk by the hoo-ers' cribs in Venus Alley, eh? Oh for the single life! But lissen, you better not cross Ma. If she says bring it by, you bring it. I'll catch hell if you don't."

"Well, for chrissake, I'm not going to have your wife looking at my drawers," I said, huffily. "Anyway, I can't pay her any more than I pay the Chink, and that isn't right."

"Aw, what the hell, kid. You can buy me a coupla beers and we'll call it square," Sean suggested cheerfully.

71

I bought a pitcher of beer. "Where were you today, any-way?" I asked. "I was looking for somebody to jaw with. I don't know what happened to Dewey."

"I was over to that little ballpark in Dublin Gulch, listening to Frank. Say, you struck it off real good with Frank the other day," Sean said, wiping the foam off his chin. "He asked me about you. Said to tell you to stop by the room if you get a chance." He looked impressed. "What did you guys jaw about for so long, anyway?"

"Revolution," I said.

"I didn't know you knew anything about that stuff," Sean said. "Say, you're a college man, ain't you?"

"Well, I can't say I got a degree. You ever hear of Johns Hopkins?"

"What's that, a new kind of union suit?" Sean laughed.

"It's a college, dope! In Baltimore. Pretty well thought of, too. Mostly a medical school, but they teach the whole curriculum, besides."

Paton was impressed by "curriculum," I could tell. "You know what?" he said. "I'm gonna call you Doc. It just fits you, in a way. You got that touch—class."

"'Doc' sounds like a gambler," I said. "Did Frank say what time I should come by?"

"Frank? No. He's over at Walker's, right this minute. I just bumped into Tommie Dowd, who seen him there. You going? Me, I'll stay and finish this pitcher then I'm hitting the trail. Ma's in a good mood and I mean to keep her that way."

The thought of Sheila waiting at home in that mean hovel for Sean to come to her bed was more than I could bear. I left him to the pitcher and went around the block to Walker's tavern.

The saloon was nearly empty. An old geezer in a pinned-together coat was spryly hopping along the bar, sucking down the dregs of one beer after another from schooners left standing.

"Where the hell is everybody?" I demanded, loudly. There wasn't even a bartender to watch the till.

The old coot jumped in terror, then pointed with a bony finger toward the back of the long, hall-like room. I could see overturned chairs and spilled beer schooners. A broad back filled the rear doorway. Shouts came from beyond the door and I saw some movement. I hurried back there and craned over the bartender's burly shoulders.

The alley behind the bar was crowded with men, most of them miners with a few cowboys and townsmen, all of them shouting furiously. In their midst was a whirl of dust and confusion, difficult to make out at first, but soon revealing a tall cowboy with windmilling arms. The cowboy was wearing a huge white ten-gallon hat and whooping crazily.

The cowboy reeled back, fetching up against the brick wall of the narrow alleyway. Onlookers scurried to get out of his way and in the sudden opening he dashed up onto a rubbish pile and whipped off his giant hat, waving it over his head and roaring like a madman: "Wahoo! Lemme at 'im!"

He clapped the hat back onto his head and charged into the mob, his knotted fists the size of baby's heads looping at the end of his long ropy arms.

The crowd fell away and I could see a skinny, crouching figure with a bloodied face, staggering but gamely holding up his clenched fists, as if he actually meant to oppose the maniacal windmill. And, in fact, as the cowboy closed on him the pint-sized opponent hauled off and socked him right in the crotch.

The cowboy buckled with a strangled scream, closely followed by a deep groan of exquisite agony. The crowd groaned in sympathy and many shouted, "Shame!" and "Low

73

blow!" and "Oh, coward!" But the skinny fighter didn't hesitate. He waded right in and punched furiously at the cowboy's shoulders and head, now brought to his level, knocking off the cowboy's hat.

This did not have the effect the skinny fighter had intended. The cowboy somehow forgot his agony and scrabbled wildly on the dusty bricks for his hat, found it, jammed it on his head and sprang back into the tumult in earnest. In short order the smaller fellow doubled low and covered his head with his arms while blow after bombarding blow rained down on him.

"Good lord, it's Frank!" I shouted, suddenly recognizing the cowboy's victim. I somehow squeezed past the bartender and started into the packed arena. Almost immediately a powerful hand grabbed my collar, nearly choking me, and slammed me up against the brick wall. The bartender pinned me there with a brutal forearm across my neck.

"Oh no y'don't. 'Sa fair fight! One t' one!" the bartender barked.

"Fair?" I gagged.

"One t' one," the bartender insisted.

But he was too late. The miners abruptly came to their senses, realizing that it was anything but a fair fight and that their eagerness to see a fight, any fight, had blinded them to the fact that one of their own was being badly mauled.

"It's Frank!" they shouted. "He's hurting Frank!" And a massive wave swept over the cowboy, who went down in a cascade of flailing arms and fists. Boots thumped on flesh.

Freed from his attacker, Frank Little looked up, then looked around to see what had happened. It was almost comic. When he saw the mob on the cowboy he waded into their midst, pulling them roughly aside.

"Hey! Hey! Stop it boys! Stop it!" he shouted, at first to no avail. Finally, he resorted to the old dodge of yelling, "The coppers! The coppers are coming!"

Immediately the men ceased to pummel the cowboy and began to mill away from him. They pushed past me and the bartender, almost strangling me in the crush, eager to get back into the saloon before they could be caught by the phantom police. Within seconds only a few remained, looking over Frank's shoulder at the curled up cowboy, who was now cowering under the shield of his arms as Frank had been.

Once he was satisfied that the cowboy wasn't seriously hurt, Frank stepped over to the trampled sombrero and stooped as if to pick it up. But he stopped and, instead, gave the hat a mighty kick that sent it sailing off into the darkness. Then he turned and walked back into the bar, glaring challengingly with his one eye at the bartender, who still had me pinned against the wall.

The bartender released me. I slid down the wall, almost unconscious, but he hoisted me up and slapped my back violently, nearly dislocating my head, then shoved me through the door into the saloon. He slammed the door on the supine cowboy, lying on the refuse heap.

Frank stood at the bar, gulping down one of several beers that the miners were pushing at him, and wiping the blood off his face with a bar rag. He turned and saw me then and declared with a grand gesture, "Wal, here's the feller saved my tail. If it wasn't for young Ryder, you bums woulda let that crazy galoot knock my last eye out."

It was delivered in a joking way, as if to show that Frank didn't mean the men any ill will, just a little annoyance. Relieved, several of them rushed to offer me a beer. But Frank shoved them all aside and snatching up a couple of full

75

schooners off the bar he herded me into a booth. He waved the men away, snarling, "Giddouda here, y' shiftless traitors!"

The miners hung back, leaving us to ourselves. They soon fell to recounting the battle royal to one another.

Little grinned as best he could and leaned across to me. "I wasn't kidding, Goody. If it hadn't a been for you, there's no telling how far that crazy cowboy woulda gone. He was hoppin'!" He fingered a loose tooth and winced.

I gulped beer and gasped, "What the hell happened?"

"Aw, it was my own fault. The galoot was all likkered up and he found out who I was and started in to rag me about being a Red, and why didn't I get a decent job. Hell, I been used to that. But I guess I just got a little fed up with it, for once, and said something to the effect that if I couldn't get a better job than punching cows I'd go back to beating off."

I groaned and shook my head.

Little smiled ruefully and prodded his battered face. It was lumpy and already starting to bruise and swell. "It wasn't a good notion," he admitted. "I think I got a couple loose teeth, which I don't have so many I can afford to lose 'em. But you!" Little clapped his hand on mine. "You saved my hide back there."

He beamed at me, forgetting his own aches and pains. "That was a real act of brotherhood," he said. "That was mighty fine of you."

I was embarrassed. "Aw, no, Frank. I just happened in and there wasn't anyone around and when I went out back and I saw you were having a rough go, why. . . . " The fact was, I hadn't been able to do a damn thing. I drank my beer to hide my confusion. Little still clasped my hand, now with both of his, holding it firmly.

"I would have done the same for any man," I said, and I meant it. I never could stand to see a fellow getting a beating,

76

fair or not. I gently and slowly withdrew my hand from Frank's. "Of course, seeing it was you . . . but really, Frank, I'd have done the same for most anybody."

"I know, I know," Frank said. "You're a good feller, Goody. I know you'd a done it for another, but all the more so for a brother. Am I right?" His face was red and bruised and already beginning to puff up. He'd have a couple of black eyes for sure.

I shrugged. "I guess so."

"I knew it!" Little leaned his face across the booth to look me in the eyes with his single, black one. "You have a sense of brotherhood, Goodwin. Now don't you?" He sat back, then, adding in an easier manner, "I think I'm right in this."

Frank hoisted his beer in a toast. "To you, Goody—where'n hell'd you get a name like that anyway?"

"Goodwin's a family name, on my mother's side. Back home they call me Geed."

"Wal, Geed, the other day we were talking about standing up for it, weren't we? I didn't expect to have to take on a ten-foot cowpuncher, though."

We both laughed, almost hysterically, the excitement of the fight wearing off, and toasted one another again. When he'd calmed down, Frank said, "Thanks again, Geed. You were a brother," and he patted my hand gently, just a couple of times.

This was another fine occasion for a cigarette. I had decided to switch to Fatimas and I got them out and offered them to Frank, who took one. Frank bellowed for and got two more free beers from the miners. We sat and smoked and grinned at each other.

Frank said, "Wal, now I can't afford to let you outta my corner, Geed. You got to come by and get a little reading matter off of me, and maybe a two-dollar college course in

Karl Marx. I'm gonna turn you into a regular, full-time revolutionary."

I laughed. "Me? A revolutionary? That'll be the day. I'll write about it, but I'm not getting sucked into it."

"Hell, you're already in it. You know, the Chinese say if a man saves your life he's responsible for you from then on, and you saved my life, Geed. No bull crap about it. That galoot was out to stomp the living bejeezus outta me."

I wouldn't hear it. "Anyway," I said, "I don't know that I buy all this revolution talk."

"Wal, hell, of course if a feller can't buy it, he won't buy it. There ain't nothing you can do about that but point the way. But I got a feeling about you, Geed. You got the makings. It takes a man, you know, a real man. No sissies need apply. A man that'll stick by his brothers, that's a real man. And you're no dummy, neither. No, Geed, don't shake your head. I got a feeling, and I'm never wrong about that."

We talked our way through several more beers and it ended with me agreeing to come by, soon, in the next couple of days. By then Frank's supporters had to have him and he drifted off into the crowd.

I wandered out into the night and headed back toward the Big Ship, feeling pretty good. All the excitement had pretty much pushed Sheila out of my mind, which was all to the good, I was sure, and it had provided me with a great occasion for making up to Frank. I felt like a detective again.

CHAPTER SEVEN

She wouldn't let me in. I was dumbfounded.

"Sean told me to bring the laundry," I insisted. "I waited until he left."

She kept me standing on the tiny front stoop. She took my laundry with a false smile, saying, "You great ninny, loit'ring 'round the corner all morning—do you think the neighbors have no eyes?"

"Oh. Well, how 'bout if I come back later, after dark?"

She ground her teeth in exasperation.

"Well, what the hell?"

"Go to 825 Quartz Street, about two o'clock, this afternoon. Go to the back door. If someone else answers the door, say you're looking for Jim Tracy and go away."

"Hunh?"

"Your laundry will be ready tomorrow, Mister Ryder," she said loudly. "Thank you," and closed the door.

I stood there baffled for a minute, then stalked away. I guess I'd been so blinded by desire that I hadn't given proper thought to the consequences of a married woman allowing a single man into her house while her husband was gone. In a place like the Cabbage Patch there was no privacy. The houses were little more than shacks. Just walking down the street you could hear the people talking inside and walking around.

I went uptown to the Carnegie library and whiled away a few hours reading a Frank Norris novel about wheat growers in California. I got so involved in the story that I nearly missed the time. I hoofed it up the hill to Quartz Street and found a solid new brick house at 825. To my relief, Sheila answered my knock on the back door.

"Come in here," she said, her arm snaking out the door and drawing me inside. In the darkened vestibule she threw her arms around me and kissed me passionately. What a change! No strained moments of embarassment now! And in a strange house! But I kissed her back, all right, figuring she must know it was safe.

"You needn't worry," she said, "the old hag is out. But we haven't much time. What kept you?"

She didn't wait for an answer. She led me by the hand through the kitchen, the dining room with its massive oak table and the chairs hanging from hooks on the wall; through a parlor with fancy, tasselled furniture and heavy drapes, a gaudy glittering crystal chandelier and tiled fireplace; and up the stairs to the main bedroom. Here she began to hastily unpin and unfasten her clothing, urging me to hurry.

I needed no urging, though all the while I was shucking off my clothes I was demanding to know whose house this was and what she thought we were doing.

"Oh, do get a move on," Sheila said. She wore only a flimsy linen shift that made her seem more naked than total nudity could have. She began to tug at my belt and trousers until I was down to stockings and underdrawers. At this point she dashed out of the room and returned almost immediately with a large bath towel which she spread upon the crocheted bedspread. Kneeling upon the bed she quickly shucked off her shift and waited, hands on her thighs, saying, "Come on, for the love of the saints!"

I was struck by the amount of tawny, reddish hair between her thighs. She was not as slim as I had supposed and her belly did not precisely resemble the slightly mounded, girlish one I'd pictured while lying abed. She was a full-bodied woman, even more lush and sensual than I had imagined. It aroused me tremendously. My erection actually made it difficult to pull my drawers off. Sheila laughed.

A few moments later we were wildly entangled on the high four-poster bed. Sheila was highly experienced, I discovered. The act lasted barely three or four minutes.

Sheila cried out with alarm. "Surely you haven't come off already?" She set to work immediately to arm me again and quickly succeeded. This time we went at it with less frenzy, more rythmically, and ultimately with greater satisfaction.

"Oh, that was lovely," she breathed, when we had both reached the desired end. "No, no, don't move. I want to feel your weight upon me," she insisted. "You weigh hardly anything, for a man. Ah yes, that's nice. Don't draw away. You're a sweet, sweet man." And she clenched me to her with her powerful legs, hooked over my own skinny shanks.

Before very long, however, she rolled me off her, got me up, straightened the bedspread and put the soiled towel in the laundry. We were both dressed and back down in the kitchen, the two of us neat as pins and innocent as Hansel and Gretel. She began to polish silver and chat with me in a relaxed way. She explained that she had taken on some housework to feed the kids, now that Sean wasn't working.

She had an ear cocked and when the front door was heard opening she instantly whisked me out the back door, saying, "Come for your laundry in the morning, before nine."

I strolled back to the library, hands in pockets and whistling. The air was clear and the summer weather fine, warm but not too warm. I felt about as fine as a young man can feel. A little drained perhaps, but there are times when a certain hollowness in the loins is extremely gratifying.

I had just settled down with the Norris book again and found my place when a hand fell on my shoulder. A voice said, "How come you're not off haying, or fishing?"

I looked up in surprise, then shock. It was Frank and his face was grotesquely swollen and discolored. He didn't have just a black eye, he looked like the disemboweled guts of a sheep that had been left lying in the sun. I almost expected to see flies on his face.

Little acknowledged my shock with a shrug. "I got a loose tooth, too." He stuck his fingers into his mouth and wiggled a canine. "Probably drop out by itself. Jeez, I can't afford to lose too much more a myself, can I?" His laugh was cut short by a painful grimace.

I could hardly bear to look at him. "Damn, that cowboy did a worse job than I thought. I hope it looks worse than it feels. Whew!"

"No, it feels about like it looks." He winced through another attempt at laughter.

I glanced around. "Where's your cohort?" I asked. I wasn't used to seeing Little without the company of pickets or at least some miners that needed haranguing, but he was alone. "What are you doing in here?"

"Can't a feller—even a socialist—take advantage of Mr. Carnegie's charity? Why, this is my favorite place. A feller like me can't carry his lie-berry around with him, you know, and there's one a these outfits just about anywhere the train stops. It's amazing. Makes me wonder if Mr. Carnegie knows what he's doing, making it possible for the public to read the truth for theirselves. I bet he'd have conniptions if he knew what went on here—the womb of revolution." He gestured grandiosely and managed another painful grin.

"Ennaway, it's a good place to hide out from your supporters, when you don't much feel like getting out and about." He made a vague gesture toward his battered face. It really was too awful to look at.

"What's this?" Little said, picking up my book. "Novels? Wal, Norris's not so bad as some—at least he's from the West, 'stead of some jackass like that Henry James, traipsing around Yurrip and drinking tea in drawing rooms. Gimme a real writer, like Jack London. A socialist, on top of it!"

He tossed the book down and said, "Wal, c'mon, let's get out in this nice sunshine and get a little exercise."

We walked up the hill, toward some of the bigger mines. When passersby glanced at Little, their mouths would fall open and they would hurriedly look away. But soon, as we approached the fenced zones of the mine heads, there were few pedestrians. There were picketing strikers here, who waved and called out to Little, some of them derisively asking if I was his bodyguard. They didn't take his battered face too seriously; they were too used to injury and disfigurement.

Little paused to chat briefly with these men, encouraging them and addressing them briefly on the usual subjects—patience, brotherhood, solidarity. Then we walked on to the next mine, where the act was repeated, and so on up the hill to Walkerville, a rough-looking neighborhood crammed amongst the gallows frames. On the way, Little waved gaily to a priest who was talking to a miner outside a church.

"I thought of being a priest, once," he said as we huffed on up the hill.

"I thought you kind of sounded like a preacher, the other day, at the ballpark," I said.

Little laughed. "Wal, it comes natural. My ma got religion at one point and took to going to tent meetings. She allus drug me along. But then she took up with a feller I didn't get along with, or maybe he just didn't like me—this was in Spokane—and they sent me to live with my Grammaw, on the rez."

"The 'rez'?"

"You know, the reservation. My Grammaw was a near full-blooded Shoshone. She lived on the rez, over by St. Ignatius, in the Flathead. They're Salish—very fine people—and she'd married a Salish, but he was dead and gone by then. Ennaway, they were all Catholic. There was a good priest there, Father Michel. I learned a lot from him."

We had walked beyond Walkerville as Little talked about life on the reservation. It sounded like a pleasant life for a boy, though they'd been horribly poor. We came into the back country suddenly, a rough region that looked out to the north upon even more mountains. Below us to the south lay the deep, broad valley of the Silver Bow, with its hillsides scarred by mines but its floor a greenish brown that was bordered to the south by forested mountains, one of which had a bare reddish face. Along the east stood the great wall of the Continental Divide. I could make out the lake and the pavilions of Columbia Gardens over there, on the mountain-side. Beyond, one could see the smoke of a pair of locomotives drawing a long train down out of Homestake Pass. The enormous engines looked like fairy toys from this distant vantage.

"Whew! That's something, isn't it?" Little said, accepting a cigarette. " 'All the kingdoms of the world, and the great glory of them . . . '—and man's wee piles of crap." He chuckled and shook his head ruefully.

"Wee piles of crap," I echoed. "Quite a mess, really."

"We sure are an enterprising bunch of devils, though, ain't we?" Little said. He made a sweeping gesture, including all the massive mountain ranges on either side and the immense valley below. "It's a hell of a lot of country out there, but everywhere you look there's smoke."

It was true, I saw, even if the smoke was only from the chimney of some distant sheepherder's wagon. Beyond the city at our feet it was seemingly a vast panorama of emptiness, yet there was an isolated house and barn over here, an abandoned smelter or a mine over there . . . some sign of man in every quadrant, dwarfed by the grandeur of the landscape, to be sure, but steadfastly present and advertising an intention to spread.

"It's something to see," I said.

"Man busy, using it," Little observed, sadly. "Not just the land, but each other. It looks like there is plenty of room for all of us, don't it? So how come we're killing each other?"

"I guess we're just ornery, by nature," I said.

"You think so? The Indins didn't think so. Not the ones I knew."

"I thought they were always on the warpath with each other, or with the settlers."

"I reckon the settlers was a different sort of thing," Little said, "but they didn't seem that wrathy toward each other when I was with them. 'Course, things had changed. They kind of had gotten the white man's idea that all Indins was the same. Before that they just figgered the Salish were the real people and then there were all these others, Blackfoot and Shoshone, and even white people. It took them a long time to figure out that all the white people weren't the same, that some of 'em were enemies of other ones."

"Well, I guess it's like I say, people are just naturally ornery."

"But the Indins don't treat their own people so bad as the white man does. They don't make 'em go down in the mines and then don't pay 'em a good wage and kill 'em if they complain. They didn't go in for that."

I suggested that he was overstating the case. The miners didn't object to mines, as far as I could see, only the pay and the conditions. Little allowed that he was, but only a bit.

"Sometimes the Indin in me gets in the way of the Marxist," Little said. "Sometimes, Marx seems like just another white man to me, more like Mr. Carnegie, or the men who run the Company—Mr. Kelley and Mr. Ryan, and them—than like Chief Joseph or Victor Charlo."

I was not familiar with those names. Little said he wasn't surprised.

"There's two kinds of men in this world," he opined. "Those who are happy to ride on the backs of their fellow man and those who wouldn't think of it. Old Charlo is in the second bunch. Most men are, I believe. But the first bunch, they cause enough trouble for all the rest of us that it's a full-time job just trying to get 'em off our backs.

"The hell of it is," he went on, "a young feller like you has a tough time trying to sort 'em out. You don't have no 'sperience with life and a rich man looks kind of grand to you. He dresses nice, prob'ly has a autymobile and a fancy home and his wimmen folk look prettier'n angels."

I said it sounded like a complicated deal. I supposed there were plenty of people who would argue the other way. Frank agreed that it was so, but that you could usually tell who was on the right side, easy enough.

"If a man's rich and his kids got plenty to eat and his wife has time for tea parties and the like, and still he's complaining about poor men, whose children are starving, and 'specially if he says the poor man is greedy. . . . Well, I can see you're bored. We'll go at it some more, another time, and I will tell you about Marx. Let me ask you one thing though, now that I got you up here. Which would you prefer? Riches or fame?" He waved his hand over the grand scenery below.

"Are you offering?" I laughed. "Oh, I haven't thought much about all that, Frank."

"Sure you have," he said. "Ever' man thinks about such things. And now you're looking down on it all. There's riches down there and fame. Which do you want?"

I didn't take much time to think about it. I said, "I like to spend money, but I never chased after it."

Frank smiled. "Fame is yours," he said, grandly.

"Fame," I said. "I don't rightly know what it would be." I thought then of looking down on Butte from the other side, from over Columbia Gardens, with Sheila. "None of this is very real to me. The place I come from is a long way from here. What is real, out there?"

Frank looked at me strangely, then he said, "There ain't no difference, Goody. The Indins don't trouble themselves with real. Ever'thin's real . . . the dreams and the stories and the ever'day grubbing. It's all real."

"You think so?" I said.

Frank laughed, a little ruefully. "I ain't sure I know anymore, myself. I been away from the Indins too long, been bothering my head with Marx. I'll leave you with one thought, though: What is the value of a pound of copper? You just think about it and tell me, next time. Now let's get down off this stinkin' hill, before it caves in under us."

Little paused, however, and looked out over the panorama. The air had grown cool and a breeze riffled his black hair. I could almost see him as an Indian chief, despite his one eye and his lumpy, discolored face. On further thought, he resembled a pirate more.

Little chuckled to himself and muttered, "Man is a enterprising devil, all right. Which reminds me. One a the fellers saw that cowboy leaving town this morning on the Northern Pacific."

87

"What cowboy? Oh, you mean the one that . . . "

"Yeah." Little touched his chin gingerly. "The feller that saw him said he was talking to a Pink."

"No kidding? How did he know the guy was a Pinkerton?" I asked, casually.

"He reckanized him from before. According to the feller, it was McParland, the guy who tried to frame Big Bill Haywood, in Boise, a few years back."

I was not familiar with the case. Little told the story as we walked back through Walkerville and then down Excelsior Street. In 1906, the ex-governor of Idaho, Frank Steunenberg, had been killed by a bomb attached to the front gate of his house. A man named Harry Orchard was arrested. A Pinkerton detective, James McParland, had been allowed to interrogate the prisoner for several days, during which time Orchard confessed to Steunenberg's murder as well as a couple dozen others, and additionally implicated five leaders and members of the Western Federation of Miners, who he claimed had hired him to do the evil deed. Bill Haywood, the secretary-treasurer, and Charles Moyer, then president of the union, were the key targets of Orchard's accusation.

"Bill, a course, is in the I.W.W., now," Frank pointed out. "They all got off. They had the good sense to get Clarence Darrow for a lawyer. It was a hell of a big case. I'm surprised you never heard about it, being a reporter interested in the I.W.W."

"In 1906, I think I'd have been in the third or fourth grade," I said. "What does this McParland look like, anyway?"

"Oh, he's just a ordinary feller. Kind of hard to describe, but the feller who saw him reckanized him sure enough."

"And McParland was working with the police?"

"Sure. The Pinks get along fine with the coppers. This McParland is a hard one, though. A man like that, he's about

88

the lowest of the low. He calls hisself a detective and I guess he thinks he's a kind of hero, or something. Well, come to think of it, the Pinkertons don't call themselves detectives—that's what the newspapers call them. Among themselves, they're operatives. Ops. Detecting isn't their real business. Their real business is betrayal. They just carry out operations, for their clients, the bosses. Operative sounds more business-like. Doesn't actually conjure up Judas, does it?

"This McParland, he made a name for hisself back East, in the coal strikes. Well, he started out back in your part of the country, in Pennsylvania. He joined the union, there. He took their oath of brotherhood. He met with the brothers every day, ate at their tables, drank in the saloon with them, played with their kids, for Godssake! And then he turned around and testified against 'em, and nineteen of 'em went to the hangman. Oh, he's a piece of work, that one!"

I had nothing to say to this. I walked on, feeling chilled. But Little hadn't done with McParland.

"Imagine a man whose whole life is scheming and spying and treachery! Why, what kind of life can it be? He'd have to spend his whole life looking over his shoulder. Darrow said it right. He said a detective wasn't a liar, he was a living lie."

"Well, they killed the governor, didn't they?"

"Who? Haywood and Moyer? No, a course not. They were in Colorado at the time. Harry Orchard killed him. He also claimed to have killed some twenty or thirty others. It was a hell of a confession. Some of the people he claimed he killed turned out to be still alive! No, Orchard was a lunatic. I don't know how a man could take his confession seriously, and lucky for Big Bill, the jury didn't. The thing that gets me is why anyone would think that the union would want to kill Steunenberg in the first place. The man used to be a union man hisself, 'though he called in the militia to break up a

89

strike in Coeur d'Alene once he got in office. But that was water under the bridge. He wasn't governor anymore. The union don't waste time on guys like that."

"Why was he killed, then?"

"Who knows? Maybe he knew something about the mine owners and they were afraid that he'd blow the whistle on them, now he was out of office. Or maybe Orchard just had it in for him, and when the deed was done, the bosses saw an opportunity to pin it on the union. Orchard was as crazy as a shithouse rat. What gets me is, he's still alive, living in a special house on the grounds at the Idaho pen. It's something, ain't it?"

I had to admit it was something, all right.

We had cut back toward the district and now paused by a fanciful house with turrets and parapets. Little said it was an authentic French chateau which one of the sons of W.A. Clark, the Copper King who had built Columbia Gardens, had imported brick by brick and had rebuilt on the site.

"It's a pretty thing, ain't it? Not many of them in the Cabbage Patch, is there?"

CHAPTER EIGHT

You can get away with sin for a while, and that's long enough. Sometimes, if you're careful, by the time you're found out it doesn't really matter. But not always. And of course, sometimes it just isn't possible. The most agonizing part of being found out, sometimes, is that it wasn't your fault. You didn't make any serious mistake—somebody else did.

Sheila had taken a bunch of menial jobs since Sean was out of work: scrubbing floors, doing the laundry, polishing silver, waxing the furniture in the big shots' houses. They didn't pay worth a damn, naturally, but it was enough for the milk and bread her kids needed. But from my point of view, the great thing was the jobs gave us a place to . . . well, let's say meet. And did we meet! On Monday, we used the widow's canopied bed, on Quartz Street; on Tuesday, it was some department store owner's place, right on Park Street. Then, on Wednesday . . . let's see . . . it was a linen closet, in a doctor's house. We did it every which way, just about every day of the week. I remember I bent her over a brocade upholstered easy chair, once, watching the street for the lady of the house. Another time, we did it on a fine Persian carpet. . . . It seemed just a matter of time before we got caught, or Sean got wise. And naturally we longed for a more extended, relaxing occasion, an overnight. So we cooked up the idea of going to a resort, Hot Springs, about fifteen miles out of town.

She told Sean that one of her employers, a lawyer I think it was, wanted her to accompany him and his family to Hot Springs and look after the kids, so he and his wife could have some free time. It worked out pretty well, at first. I even rode the daily excursion train out there ahead of time to spy out the lay of the land, eyeball the staff in case there were some familiar faces. Some of the room maids were from Butte, but Sheila said that she didn't know the girls and was pretty sure they wouldn't know her. It was a fine outing. I had taken a list of her sizes uptown and purchased some decent clothes for her, which she put on in the women's room on the train. I have an idea that dressing up may have been the most lasting pleasure of the affair, for Sheila, though we both definitely enjoyed the weekend. We locked ourselves in the hotel room and had a hell of a time. She came up with some variations that we hadn't already tried. The great thing was the relief from tension, the feeling that you could relax and enjoy yourself, which we did.

Sex always seems like a big thing, but there's only so many hours you can spend at it, finally. We became restless and daring. We were eager to flaunt our romance in public. I guess we missed the tension. Crazy, but we were kids. We had to show off our romance, or maybe it was just Sheila wanting to show off her new duds. We tried the dining room first. We had an entire roast chicken, with stuffing and mashed potatoes and gravy. Very fancy. I enjoyed spending the money. After that we took a stroll out along a horse trail. The horses were beautiful and the people riding them looked very fine. Sheila said that she would like to ride horses someday and I said that I would not. There was a dance band in the pavilion. I was a pretty good dancer, in those days.

Anyway, the next couple of days we tried the hot plunges and the rowboat on the artificial lake. But the chief entertainment was sex—repeated, frenzied sex, with all the variations we could imagine.

It was great to wake up in bed together. It just about broke Sheila's heart to leave. I had to abandon our plan to travel separately. We couldn't pry ourselves apart. I joked that someone might have to throw a pail of water on us. Sheila didn't think that was funny.

"I can't bear to put on these old rags," Sheila said, in the train. But she did it.

We couldn't even part at the Butte station. I convinced myself that there was no great danger in me walking along the street with her. We were legitimate acquaintances, weren't we? No one could imagine that we had just returned from a weekend in bed at the Hot Springs—though all you'd have to do is glance at our faces and you could see we'd just climbed hot from gluey sheets. But no one seemed to notice.

I left Sheila at the approach to the Cabbage Patch. She was blinking back tears. I guess a glimpse of luxury had made the Cabbage Patch unbearable.

I wandered uptown and drank a beer at the M & M. Some of the fellows asked me where I'd been. I said that I had gone to Hot Springs for the weekend, but that it had turned out to be a bore. I was operating on my mentor Jimmy's maxim that it was better to lie as little as possible. I couldn't imagine how it could make a difference.

What we didn't know was that Sean had bumped into the lawyer—the one Sheila was supposed to be babysitting for—uptown, on the Saturday. Sheer accident. They didn't really know each other to talk to, of course, but the guy was supposed to be at Hot Springs. So Sean beats it over to the guy's neighborhood and, sure as hell, there are the kids playing in the backyard. He didn't know what to think. He went right uptown to the M & M, looking for me, for advice, I guess, but nobody had seen me around for a day or two. So he runs over to the Big Ship and hears that I'd gone out of town. This must have struck him as odd, but he didn't make too much of it.

When Sheila returned on Sunday, she found Sean sitting in the house, all too sober and with the children crying. The first thing he says is, "Did you have a hard weekend with Mrs. Jones and all those kids?"

From the look on his face and the tone of his voice, she knew right away that something was up. It could only be one thing, she figured. So she says, "No. I had a very pleasant weekend with my friend, Cora Monger. The Joneses never showed up, and I aim to find out why, first thing tomorrow."

"Cora? Why Cora lives way to hell over in Deer Lodge!"

Sheila explained, as if annoyed, that when the Joneses didn't arrive as planned, that she had taken the round-trip ticket they'd given her and cashed it in for one to Deer Lodge and then had borrowed money from Cora to get back.

"But I'll sure get the money back from Mrs. Jones," she said, angrily. "They can't expect me to go on down there and wait around for them all weekend. I was that fed up," she said, in a still-annoyed, self-justifying tone, "what with you lying about drunk all these weeks and after breaking my back day after day to provide for the kids, and then they don't turn up! I said to myself, 'Well, Missus, you shan't be treated so! You shall have your bit of a holiday, and Mister Paton can just tend to the kiddies and bide at home for a change.' So there!"

Sean was instantly contrite. He hadn't had the nerve, nor perhaps just the presence of mind to enquire of the Joneses about the outing, and now he fell in quite readily with Sheila's prompt explanation. He apologized for everything, especially for letting little Alex get sunburnt. Sheila went to look at the kid and was enraged at the sight of the kid's poor peeling butt. Apparently, Sean had let him run around stark naked for most of Sunday, which had been a very hot day.

Sheila went out to fetch some salve from a neighbor and contrived to send a message to the Big Ship, warning me that Sean suspected something and that she had claimed to have gone to visit a friend in Deer Lodge.

Uptown, I had already run into Dewey in the M&M. He said he'd been out of town, too, on a fishing trip down in the Big Hole valley with some other miners. He had come back early, dying to catch up on the fate of his "Bums."

"Yiz wutn't b'lieve it, kid. Dey don't git no papers, no scores, nuttin'! Dey go to bed at dark, or even before, cuz dey gotta be up by dawn ta fish! D' owls hoot all night 'n' d' rooster crows in d' middle a d' night, 'n' d' frogs'r croakin' 'n' d' cows'r mooin'–I coutn't sleep wid all d' racket!"

"What about the fishing?" I asked. "That's supposed to be great out here."

"Fishin'? Are yiz kiddin'? Dese guys don't know nuttin' from fishin'. Dere's no lakes, no ocean, not even a dock – jist d' rivah, and d' rivah is so fast 'n' cold 'n' dere's great big rattlesnakes all ovah d' jernt . . . I wooden go near it!"

He informed me that Sean had been in asking about me and that he seemed upset about his "old lady." I didn't know what to think about that. When I got back to the Big Ship I read Sheila's message, but it didn't tell me much.

The next day Sean sought me out in the M&M and as soon as I'd bought him a beer, he asked, "Did you see Ma at the Hot Springs?"

"What the hell? What's that supposed to mean?"

Sean hastened to reassure me that he wasn't suggesting anything. It was just that he'd heard that I had gone to the Hot Springs and Sheila had been supposed to go there too. He just wondered if we had bumped into one another.

Well, what could I say? I didn't know anything about the friend in Deer Lodge and I had to assume that someone had seen us out at the Hot Springs. "Sure, I saw her," I said. "I just didn't want you to get any funny ideas."

"I don't know what to think," Sean said. "First she tells me she's goin' to the Hot Springs to help the Joneses with the kids. Then I bump into Jones. Turns out they ain't gone to the Hot Springs at all. Now the lying whore tells me she was visitin' a friend. I'm thinkin' maybe she spent the weekend with some slickster."

"Ah! I guess the lady I saw her with must have been the friend."

"Oh, she was with some lady? What did this lady look like?" Sean put on a shrewd look. When I said I couldn't remember what the lady looked like, Sean asked, "Well, was she young or old?"

I thought for a few seconds and said, "Young."

"Young, eh? Hmmm, that must of been Cora Munger. Kind of small, but a nice figger?"

"Yeah, that's it," I said.

Sean shook his head, smiling sadly at me.

"What?" I said.

"Cora is about forty and ugly as a quart of warts. Doc, I hate to see you get sucked into something like this."

"What do you mean?" I asked, cautiously. I was suddenly conscious of the size of Sean's calloused hands. When he made a fist, they resembled nothing so much as ten pounds of hard sausages. Fortunately, they were not formed into fists, yet.

"She was with a man, wasn't she?" Sean asked with quiet resignation.

"Naw, naw, nothing like that," I protested.

"It's all right," Sean assured me. "You don't hafta cover up for her. I'll find out anyway." His hands curled into knockwurst. "I'll hafta thump her before she admits it, but I hadda thump her before. It's not a new story. She allus denies it, for awhile. Fine'ly she comes clean." He shrugged. "I know it prob'ly looks purty sorry to you, Doc, but I been used to it before now."

"You mean, it's happened before? Often?"

"I don't know what often is. Three or four times? Hell, she was married when she started fooling around with me. I should of known better then. But, let's face it, she's a lotta woman. What the heck, a guy's gotta figger, a woman like that . . . no one man could be enough."

"Jeez, I didn't know," I said, genuinely taken aback. "I mean, how could I know?"

"I know, I know," Sean said, shaking his head sadly. "She looks like an angel. And she's a good mother! She loves those kids and she'd kill for 'em. She loves 'em more than me." This last was spoken ruefully.

We sat there for a long moment, sadly shaking our heads at the perfidy and mystery of Woman. Sean had another beer, on me, and promptly inhaled it. He sighed gloomily and began to gather himself for departure.

"She's a wonderful mother, no doubt about it," he said, with a sigh, "but she's gotta pay."

"Oh no," I said. "You can't do that. Why, she's a woman. She's . . . she's so . . . so attractive! You couldn't hurt her. Why you wouldn't hurt a fly!"

"I don't wanna," Sean said, regretfully, "but she's gotta pay. She knows that."

"Oh no, no, no. She's a sweet little thing. Besides, you're used to this, uh, this situation. You said so. And thumping doesn't seem to have stopped her before."

"No, it don't stop her," Sean agreed. "She don't seem to learn. But me being used to it don't help, neither. It hurts."

He looked me in the eye, almost pleading. "It hurts so. Don'tcha see, Doc? I'm still crazy about her. Even after all the times she's . . . done it. A guy can't help thinking about those other men, 'speshly when yer'n bed." He blushed. "I s'pose it all sounds awful trashy to you."

"No, no, of course not. I mean, well, it's kinda tough, I can see that. But, every couple has problems. And look here, you're crazy about her—" this hurt to say, but I took a deep breath and plunged on, "—and I know she thinks the world of you. You couldn't hurt her. And besides, it's bad for the kids!"

"Bad for the kids? You must be daffy, Doc. It sure ain't good for the kids to see that kind of sorryness going on and the old lady gettin' away with it! How do you think it makes me look? How can they respect the old man—even if I ain't really all of 'em's old man—if I let that go by? I'd look like a sap."

"No, no," I said. "It's not like that. No kid likes to see their Ma getting thumped. It looks bad for both of you. Besides, they don't know anything about all this. It happened at the Hot Springs, for crying out loud. You're wrong if you think the kids understand that their mother has done wrong. To them she's Ma, their loving Ma, and you're the mean ol' Pa who's thumping her."

"Oh no, they'll hear about what she done. They allus do. It gets out. We think kids are innocent, but they know things. This is the first time in Butte, but it got out in Ishpeming and then in Houghton, again in D'loot. And the thing that hurts so bad is, it's allus the same kind of guy. Well, maybe I was the 'ception, I mean when her first old man was alive. But it's us'ly some slick, fancy, uptown kind of guy. Some of them don't even look like men. I bet it was the same this time, eh? What'd the guy look like? Go ahead, you can tell me—I wouldn't know him. Some skinny little shit with pomade on his hair and a fancy suit, prob'ly a moustache—no offense, Doc, a moustache looks good on you. But this guy looked like a sissy, I'll bet. Sometimes I wonder if they actually do it. It wouldn't be a real man, a working man, a miner. What'd he look like?"

"I told you, I didn't see any guy. She was talking to some woman. It was just in passing, at the train station." I didn't want to say any more than that. Jimmy always said it was a mistake to elaborate, thinking to authenticate a lie. Keep the information to a minimum. But I could see that Sean didn't buy it. He evidently assumed that I'd seen her with some guy and I was covering up. I let him think that.

"You didn't know him? Naw, you wouldn't. But you must of been surprised! Shocked, even. You must of noticed. I bet he was about five-eight, skinny, patent-leather shoes, wearing a straw hat, maybe. Smoking a skinny little cigar?"

I refused to say. I insisted that I hadn't seen a man. But I was foolishly glad that I was tall and thus didn't fit the description, barring the moustache.

"It don't make no difference," Sean said. "I'll find out. I know a couple of the girls who work out there. That Sandy Boynton is one. You know her? Cute little piece, about eighteen, and no better than she should be. Fact is, she's prackly a whore herself. I'll ask her. She'll know, or she can find out."

"Jeez, I wouldn't do that. Don't do that," I pleaded. "What the hell difference can it make?"

"Fer cry-eyes sake, why not? What'm I gonna do? You say I shouldn't thump the friggin' whore, I shouldn't try to find out who the bastard is and jump him. Why, I can easy get a buncha guys—Dewey, Carl, Jack—yer welcome to come along, if you wanta, be glad to have you . . . and we'll teach the sneaking sonuvabitch to fool around with other men's wives."

"It doesn't do any good," I insisted. "Don't you see that? She's done it before and if you beat her and beat up the guy that won't stop anything. She'll be angry at you and sorry for him! It might even make her more determined to do it again —you know how contrary a woman be! And if there was a guy, well, he's probably long gone. Probably some guy she met there. She probably went over there with her friend, innocent as hell, and this—"

"This friggin' snake-in-the-grass," Sean interjected.

"Yeah, this snake, he probably saw she was good looking— you gotta admit, you've got one hell of a fine looking woman there—and figured she'd be a sucker for a good time. In all honesty, pal, she hasn't had much in the way of good times lately. And he was able to turn her head for a few hours."

"For a couple-three nights, more likely," Sean said.

"But it isn't all her fault. Hell, I'm not trying to make excuses for her. A wife's place is home, taking care of the kids and keeping the home. She does a hell of a job of that. And besides, she's . . . well, she is a peach."

"Yeah," Sean said, almost wistfully, "she is maybe too good lookin'. She sure turns heads. I even noticed you liked her."

"Well, yeah, of course, she's not my type, but. . . . "

"Nothing funny meant, Doc. It's just that you're a man, like any man, and you can't help noticing. Am I right?"

"Well, sure, Sean."

Sean was pensive, weighing the situation. But then he shook his head and said, "Nah, I gotta thump the whore."

I begged him. At last I said, "Just promise me you'll give it a day or two. You're hot behind the collar right now—who wouldn't be? You're not thinking calmly. Give it a day or two and think about what you're doing. What difference will a day or two make? She doesn't know you know. Just keep a close eye on her. Then, well then. . . . " Suddenly, inspired, I offered, "If you want, I'll talk to her."

"You'll talk to her? What about? Jeez, what kind of sap do you think I am, I can't take care of my own woman?"

"It was just a suggestion. I could maybe explain that she was hurting you, in a way that you maybe can't tell her yourself. Sometimes husbands and wives, they don't talk about things because they're so close to the problem, they figure the other one knows how they feel, but maybe they don't. What the heck, maybe she's got a reason. Maybe she thinks you don't love her, or something."

"Oh fer crying– Well. . . . You mean you'd do that? Jeez, yer a pal. All right, all right, I won't do anything. For now. And I'll talk to you before I do. All right. Say, you couldn't let me have a few bucks? Just till I get back to work? I'll make it all square with you."

I cheerfully loaned him ten dollars, out of which Sean bought two more rounds of beer.

My mother, who was a God-fearing woman, nonetheless had a ribald side to her. I once heard her say, in reference to a friend's husband, caught in bed with the friend's sister: "A stiff prick has no conscience." (I was only a child at the time, about the age of Sean's son, Devin, so perhaps he was not so wrong about the falsely presumed innocence of children.) But I was just trying to save poor Sheila a beating. And myself a thrashing, of course. The bit about becoming her marriage counselor was just sheer inspiration.

It's amusing now, and I wonder that I never thought of writing about it. I guess it just wasn't my kind of thing. I wrote about detectives and killers. I suppose I considered this *Lady's Home Journal* material.

101

But then, I didn't write about Frank Little either. Oh, I used some of the material in an early draft of *Poisonville,* but I had to cut it out. My editor didn't see it as my kind of stuff.

And she was right: it was too political. The kind of audience I was writing for, they didn't go for that stuff. They wanted gangsters, gun molls, hard-boiled private eyes. The editor said it didn't ring true. I was just as glad to cut it out. It was all too true.

CHAPTER NINE

I drifted slowly along Park Street wondering what I would say to Sheila when Sean arranged for me to talk to her. I imagined the circumstances in which this farcical conversation would take place and it struck me that we would probably be alone. Well, we'd have to be alone, wouldn't we? Sean couldn't expect that I'd conduct this business in his presence. Which raised an interesting possibility . . . I envisioned Sheila's warm thighs, her remarkably thick, reddish bush, her surprisingly slender waist.

"Same place," a man said, quietly but distinctly.

"What?" I was startled and didn't comprehend what had been said, at first. Then I recognized Joe Davis walking on. I stood for a moment, collecting myself, then followed.

We sat in the same bead-curtained booth as before and the same Chinese man brought a bottle of whiskey even as he ushered me to Davis.

"Hey, bring some a them egg rolls," Davis told the waiter, "the pork kind, with a dish of them seeds and the hot plum sauce. That's a boy." To me, he said, "I love that stuff. So, how are you and the Reds gittin' along?"

"Oh, fine. Fine. Frank has been real friendly."

"Frank, is it? That's swell. So whadja find out?"

"You mean his plans, and all? Well, I guess they got a vote coming up, about which union will be in—the I.W.W. or the Mine Workers. And then there'll be a—"

"Naw, naw, I can read that in the *Standard,*" Davis said. "I mean about Little, what he does, what his habits . . . ah, here's the grub. Yeah, that's fine, just put it down and we'll order later," he addressed the waiter.

"Here," he turned to me, "try these chopstick things. They're kinda clumsy, at first. You hold 'em like this." Davis demonstrated how to use the chopsticks, picking up an egg roll deftly, dunking it in the plum sauce and the sesame seeds, then taking a bite. "See? Nothin' to it."

I struggled with the utensils and managed to drop an egg roll into the sauce. I fished it out and took a bite. The sauce was powerful and nearly brought tears to my eyes, but I smiled and chewed away. With the next one I was more successful. Like Davis, I washed it down with whiskey, a combination that nearly made me gag, but I persevered.

"What do you want to know all that stuff for?" I asked, between bites.

"Oh, it might come in useful. You never know," Davis said. "So whadja find out?"

"Well, he lives at Mrs. Byrne's boarding house," I said. "He invited me over, to look at some books and stuff."

"I bet." Davis smiled a crooked, queer grin. "So, what happened?"

"I haven't been, yet."

"Well, go. That's good stuff. Take a gander at the layout, find out where he keeps his gun."

"His gun? I don't think Frank carries a gun."

"No? I'd be awful surprised if he don't," Davis said. He gobbled down the last of the egg rolls and swilled more whiskey. "What about these other two ducks he hangs around

104

with? McDonald and Wuuri? He meet with them regular, or what?"

"Well, they're I.W.W., I guess, but I kind of got the impression they aren't regular members, or something. He never talks about them. They're just miners. I guess, if the union gets in, they'll be officers. They're his local contacts, it seems like. He usually meets them for coffee in the morning, at Harrington's, about eight o'clock. And then they go their separate ways and whether they meet again during the day, I don't know."

"How about at night?"

"Not that I can see," I said, sipping my whiskey. The fact was, almost everything I knew about McDonald and Wuuri had come from Sean. I hadn't actually met them or talked to them. I realized that I should have. I made up my mind to meet them as soon as I could, tomorrow.

"You know what they're doing, don't you?" Davis said. "They're fixing to control the vote at the union meeting. McDonald and Wuuri, and probly a buncha others they got lined up and which they paid, will be there and they'll second anything Little suggests and shout down the others. They'll talk it up for Little and talk down the rest. That's called organizing. If there's any ordinary Joes that object, they give 'em the bum's rush—if they ain't already spotted 'em and kept 'em outta the meeting."

I was shocked, but I suspected that there was at least an element of truth to Davis's allegations. It sounded like something that might happen, something a dedicated revolutionist might do and justify in the single-minded pursuit of his cherished goal. I recalled Frank's crack about revolutions not being made with rosewater.

"What about this goof, Paton?" Davis broke into my thoughts. "You shaggin' his old lady?"

105

"What! Oh, no, nothing like that. Sean's been real helpful. He introduced me to Frank."

"So, d'ja have a good time at the Hot Springs?"

"You know about that? Yeah, it was all right." I had no idea how much Davis could know about that. Did he know that Sheila had been there? Or perhaps his spies had only tipped him that we'd arrived together back at Butte. I had a feeling that it was just the latter. I couldn't imagine that Davis was having me closely watched, though it was likely that any Agency men who happened to see me about town, especially around the train station, would pass on the information.

"Good. That's good. I mean it. I'm glad to hear you're enjoying yourself. A little moola helps, don't it? Well, there's more where that come from. A lot more."

"No kidding?"

"Yeah, really. How does a thousand bucks sound?"

It didn't sound real to me. My base salary was $25 per week. I also got expenses, but never as much as the $200 that Davis had given me just last week. I still had a lot of it left, despite the expenses of the weekend. A thousand dollars sounded like too much money. I couldn't help wondering what I'd be asked to do for that kind of loot.

"A feller could buy a car," Davis said, "and not just a Model T, neither."

"The Agency is paying a grand? Is this the bonus you were talking about?"

"Yeah, it's a bonus. And no, the Agency ain't paying it. The Agency never paid nobody a grand for nothing. Somebody else is paying it, for a little extra work."

"What kind of work?" I asked, suspiciously. "I don't know about this extra work. Does the Old Man know about this?"

"Lemme put it this way," Davis said, "the Old Man knows, but he don't know. Get it? Naw, the bonus is strictly on the side." I didn't get it, and said so.

"Okay, how's this? The Old Man knows about it, but it ain't something that he wants to know. If you do something for somebody else, and it don't actually involve the Agency, well that's jake with the Old Man, long as it don't come back on the Agency."

"You mean, if something goes wrong."

"You got it, kid. Only, nothing can go wrong. You got my word on it. It ain't even any extra effort, hardly. And bingo! An extra thousand spondulicks for the kid."

I liked the sound of that word, especially with the magical "thousand." A thousand dollars had a nice, multiple resonance to it, but "spondulicks" set off chimes in my head, like a golden carillon.

"What, uh, what kind of work is worth a thousand of those things? Those spondulicks?" I asked.

"It ain't exactly work. I mean, it ain't as if you was a contract miner, or nothin'," Davis said. "It's more in the way of, oh, 'exercizing your regular function, as a operative'"–Davis parodied an Agency directive. "Though this is more like a non-regular function, you might say. Sort of an extension of your regular work. The logical extension, say. Only this time, instead of turning the bird over to the Law, we handle it our ownselfs."

I wished Davis would come right out and say what it was, but he didn't seem able to and curiously, I couldn't bring myself to insist. It was as if I knew, somehow, what Davis was driving at and was unwilling to hear it actually spoken, as if it were taboo. Still, something had to be said; there had to be some kind of clarifying hint.

"The thing is," Davis finally said, "Little has got to go."

This was almost a relief, although the implications of the statement filled me with dread.

"What do you mean, 'Go'?" I asked, as coolly as I could.

"I was told you was a sharp kid," Davis said. "They said you had plenty of sand." His voice was flat and uninflected, as if he were reading from a text. "To me that says you're either in or you're out. As for the grand, let's just say that's for starters. There could be even more, depending on how it shakes out and how well you do. So, whaddaya say? You in? Or out?"

I didn't know what to say, but I knew I had to say something. The idea of saying "Out" disturbed me. I knew it would not please Davis. "In," on the other hand, still had a nebulous sense to it. "In" to what? It wasn't clear. It left open the possibility for a later negative, if the business didn't appeal to me. Or so it appeared.

"If you're saying that you're going to run Little out of Butte, and you need my help . . . well, I guess I'm in," I said. "At least, if you're . . . I mean, if I don't . . ."

Davis held up a hand to stop my rambling and his face took on a solemn look. "Listen kid, if you're in, you're in. There's no going back on a deal like this. There's other guys involved and I gotta perteck them. I can't have any 'Yes, I'm in—no I'm out,' crap. A man has to make up his mind, so other men know they can count on him. That's the way it works and that's how it's gotta be."

"Well, if you have other guys . . . I mean, why me?"

"They're good men," Davis said. "Men I can count on. But there's some things they can't do. Now, maybe I could get by without you, but it'd put us back and we ain't got a lotta time. The thing is, I gotta feeling about you. I figger you're the man I need, if you're the man I think you are. Just so you know, now. What's the word?"

"Okay," I said, suppressing a sigh.

"Fine, fine," Davis said briskly, "I never thought you'd let me down for a minute. The last time we met we talked about dynamite. Well, you can forget about dynamite. Dynamite's out. The thing is, Little is dynamite, all by hisself. This union vote don't mean nothing. Either way, Little is gonna turn this new union Red. Now, the Comp'ny's got their beef with unions—who don't?—but they can live with them, as long as they ain't too radical. It's the Reds they can't deal with. The Reds screw up everything, see? If the Reds take over the union the whole hill will go up in flames and a lotta innocent folks are gonna get hurt. Little hypnotizes the guys. The guys don't really listen to what he actually says, see, they just figger he knows what he's talkin' 'bout 'cause he sounds good. And they follow him like sheep. And that's how come he's gotta go."

Davis had spoken earnestly, with the conviction of a man of experience. I thought he was right. From all I'd heard, Butte had seen plenty of violence already in its brief history. All the mines had, from coal mines in Pennsylvania to the silver mines of Idaho, and the unions had been involved. Whether they had started it hardly mattered, in a way. When dynamite was involved, the results were indiscriminate destruction. Sometimes I wished they'd simply quit agitating, no matter how just their cause might be. The results were too painful.

"What do I do?" I asked.

"I need somebody I can trust," Davis said. "This town is crawling with guys who'd croak Little for beer money, but I don't need that kinda guy. What I need's a guy who keeps his head, who can take orders and carry 'em out. A guy who'll help control the strong arms and weak heads. Also, a guy who can get me close to Little."

My heart sank at this last. "A finger man," I said glumly. I poured myself another shot of rye and tossed it down. It stayed down with no encouragement.

Davis shrugged. "I wouldn't put it like that. The thing is, Little needs to be taught a lesson. He's gotta know that Butte ain't a healthy place for him. I thought he'd get the point the other night, with the cowboy, but there was too many of his followers around. You must of heard about that."

"I kind of stumbled onto the scene," I said.

Davis's eyes narrowed and his small mouth pursed seriously. I felt he was gauging me, trying to figure out how reliable I was.

"I need somebody to steer him into the right neighborhood," he said. "I'll have a few guys, a car. We take him for a ride, give him some friendly advice, and give him a head start on the road. After," Davis went on, "you gotta leave town your-self. It'll be too hot for you. Little's congregation ain't gonna be too happy with the news of his departure. We'll try to keep your name out of it, but you never know. They'll be looking for someone to blame and you'll be handy. It'd be best if you get on the train to Spokaloo, stick on it clear through to Portland and then go on down to Frisco. The Agency office in Frisco'll be expectin' you and they'll take good care of you. You'll like Frisco, kid. It's a real town, not like this dump."

"So the cowboy was an agent," I said.

"Not so's you would notice," Davis said.

"Frank just shrugged it off, you know, even though he took a beating," I said. "What makes you think he won't shrug this off? Won't that make things even worse? There could be a lot of trouble."

"He won't shrug this off, don't worry. He'll prob'ly be on the same train as you. Maybe you can buy him a beer in the club car. You'll have plenty of moola. Anyways, he won't

110

stick around, but I ain't buying his ticket, neither. And if, by chance, he does stick around, you won't wanta be here. Get me?"

I got it, but my mind was whirling. Why did this have to happen? The job had seemed fairly simple and straight-forward. Infiltration and undercover work was interesting and exciting, but luring a man into a trap. . . . You could call it what you liked, it was still betrayal. At best, Little was going to be hurt. It could be anything from a twisted arm and threats of worse, to actually breaking bones and knocking out teeth. Little could be seriously hurt.

A sickly queasiness invaded my gut. Maybe it was the com-bination of egg rolls, hot plum sauce and rye, but it felt more like this mess. Frank Little, I knew, was a man of conviction and courage. You could break his bones, but threats would never dent his spirit.

"Why is the Company doing this?" I asked. "If Frank is so dangerous, such a threat to public safety, why don't the cops arrest him and lock him up?"

"They'd love to," Davis said. "I was talking to one of the big shots up on the Sixth Floor about it. He says they went to the D.A., this guy Wheeler. He's prackly a Red hisself! Get this: Wheeler says he can't do nothing to Little, 'cause he hasn't broke no law! How do you like them apples? The Law can't touch the commie bastard until he overthrows the government! Then, a course, it's too late. There ain't no more law."

I didn't understand.

"It's like this, kid. Little is a traitor, ain't he? You heard him, running down the country, running down the flag, running down the War. He's against everything: the President, Congress, the sojers—against our own sojers! He's against a great Company that came out here and at great expense and risk started up a industry where there wasn't nothing but bearshit, buffalo and Injuns, a industry that pervides jobs and homes and a living for thousands of miners and their famblies.

"What it comes down to, he's against America. A man is free, here, not like back in the Old Country. A guy keeps his nose clean, works hard, he can make something of hisself. Hell, he can be President if he wantsta. You can't do that in the Old Country. Over there, no matter how hard a guy works, he's allus just a friggin pissant. The Kings and the Dukes, and them, they got it all locked up. Here, nobody bothers a guy and nobody bothers his family. A man's home is his castle. Nobody tells him what to do. If he wants to quit his work and move to another city or state, where he thinks he'll maybe do better, nobody gives a hoot in a whirlwind. He's free, right?

"Now, what happens if the Communists get in? They throw over the government. No more 'lections, no more jobs. What you got is anarchy. That's what they call it and they're proud of it! You know what anarchy is?"

I shook my head uncertainly. I'd heard the word but I wasn't secure in my understanding of it. Frank Little sometimes spoke of anarchy, but I had gotten the impression that Frank was not for anarchy. I supposed I'd gotten confused.

"Anarchy is everybody running around like they was crazy," Davis explained. "No law'n'order, no government. It's a mob, a riot. Lookit it this way: do you know how to run a mine, or a smelter? No, a course not. Do any of these miners, outside a their own job? Hell, no. Do you know how to run a railroad? Do you have the capital, the moola, and know-how to invest it to start up a mine or a railroad? It takes dough and it takes brains. So how is this country going to run if a buncha Commies and anarchists take over? It'd be like caveman times. No railroad, no telegraph or telephone, no 'lectricity, no mines, and no law. Can they run them things? Don't make me laugh. Why, they might as well be a buncha monkeys, like ol' Darwin said.

"And religion! Well, they're dead set against religion. They don't believe in nothing but their ownselfs. Let's face it, I ain't so much for religion myself, but any fool can see it does a world a good, 'specially for the kids and the wimmen folks. It tells you how to act and what's right."

I nodded. My mother had been keen on religion, and some of my relatives were ministers and deacons.

"Lemme give you a f'rinstance," Davis went on, warming to the subject. This wasn't his usual line of talk, I figured, but I guess he felt I needed to be set straight and he rather enjoyed waxing philosophical. I had the impression that he surprised himself with how neatly his ideas sort of dovetailed and explained things. Perhaps he'd occasionally given thought to such things at odd moments, such as the long hours of a stakeout of a suspect's house, and now he was sounding off.

"Say a feller comes down the road some night and for no reason decides to rub you out and take your money and maybe shag your old lady. What's to stop him from it, or even killing your kids? The law and religion. But if there ain't no law or religion, what could you do about it? There ain't no more law, if anarchy's in. Frank Little and his gang have thrown over the law and got rid of the cops. Now, they're the law. Is Little gonna help you out? Maybe . . . if you happen to be a pal a his. But if you ain't . . . well, you see the way it is."

This rambling diatribe addled my mind. I didn't even try to make sense of it. I just said, "So what do we do? Shoot him?"

Davis said, "Be nice if it was that easy, wouldn't it? But it's better not to. We don't want no so-called martyrs. It's better if he can just be run off. Then it's like the people themselves got fed up with his filthy mouth and his rabble-rousing. Now they're talking about a sedition law, which is we could arrest these birds for talking down the country and throw 'em in the pen for a few years 'til ever'body forgot about 'em. But they're just talking about it and who knows how long it'll take, if they ever pass the law. Naw, the thing is to make it look like the Vigilantes run him off."

I had never heard of the Vigilantes. Davis explained that they were a bunch of good citizens in these parts who, some forty years earlier, had gotten fed up with the stagecoach bandits, the claim jumpers and other outlaws and had "cleaned up on them." The Vigilantes rode by night, caught the culprits and hung them, with a note pinned to their bodies, reading "3-7-77." These mysterious numbers were said to refer to a grave, three feet wide, seven feet long and seventy-seven inches deep.

"They just hung them? No trial or nothing?" I asked.

"They had a kind of saddle trial," Davis said, with a smirk. "And some they just tarred and feathered and rode 'em out of town on a rail. Not a railroad. A fence rail. You see, there wasn't no law in them days. It was frontier times. Sort of like anarchy, you might say, only it hadn't got that bad yet. In fact, the way I heard it, one of the worst outlaws was the sheriff hisself. They hung him. See, the people had to act for their ownselfs. And it's gettin the same now. We got guys like this Commie, Wheeler, who's s'posed to be a District Attorney, but won't do nothing. Frank Little, now, he don't care nothing for the law. You heard him. To hear him talk, the cops are the crooks. According to him, you and me are worse than the cops."

Davis sat back and lit a particularly strong cigar. He poured us each another jolt of whiskey and knocked his back quickly, then refilled his glass. He looked pensive for a moment, then said, "I been in this line of work for a long time, kid. The

Law," he said, with a kind of reverence. "A couple of times I had to kind of bend the Law. I didn't want to, but I did it. I did it so I could catch a crook. The Law's hands is tied sometimes, until they can get the goods on a crook. That's where the Agency comes in. We're kind of like the cops, but we can do things they can't. And we can find out stuff they'll never know. Sometimes, we can nab the crook before he kills somebody or robs a bank. I know. I done it. And if it's done in the service of the Law, in the spirit of the Law, then it's all right. The Supreme Court even said so. And that's kind of the deal we got going right here.

"Now you take this Little, he's worse than any crook I ever run acrosst. Most crooks are out to break the law. He wants to destroy it entirely! Before he's done there won't be just one man killed, it'll be dozens, hundreds! And there'll be wimmen and kids, babies, killed too! A guy like Little can wreck a whole country. He's gotta be stopped!"

I was alarmed by Davis's vehemence. I would never have suspected the stolid operative of such passion.

"All right, all right," I said, trying to calm the man. "It's just that I don't care for the idea of a bunch of guys jumping one guy. They got a word for that out here. They call it bushwhacking."

"I wouldn't call it bushwhacking," Davis retorted. "I'd call it snake killing. You see a rattler, you don't wait till he strikes. A rattle's a harmless thing, but it's a warning. Anyway, it won't come to that."

Davis dropped the metaphor. Maybe he feared I wasn't as tough as he'd thought.

Davis turned the conversation in a more general direction. He spoke again of detective work, how it was often seamy and unappealing, but still exciting and adventurous. And essential, in a world that was inherently evil.

Crime, he philosophized, was a constant. He pictured the police, and their ally, the Agency, as soldiers of the Law, knights warring against the tide of evil. He could see that I responded to that metaphor and he expanded on it, using the war in Europe as his theme. The Huns, he said, were a type of arch-criminals. The Democracies were police. Little, with his imported foreign ideas was in league with the Huns, by implication.

He suddenly recognized that he'd gone too far down a murky trail. There was something weird about equating Communism with a reactionary regime like the Kaiser's. The two weren't exactly asshole buddies, though I didn't object. Still, I looked a bit skeptical, so Davis dropped it. He was tired of philosophizing, anyway. It was awfully complicated.

"So, how about it," Davis said, finally, "you're in?"

"I'm in, sure," I said, "it's just, like I said, I don't like the idea of leading a guy into a trap where a bunch of guys are gonna maybe hurt him."

"You keep harping on that," Davis complained, "but it ain't like that. It ain't as if Little was a lamb, or something. Look, we're just gonna talk to him. We'll spell it out so even a half-blind man can read it. After that, it's up to him. It's his own choice, when you get right down to it, which is more than he gives these poor suckers. He can either go quietly, or not. Anyway, you don't even have to be there. Once you get him to come along to the place I pick out, we'll take over from there and you can skedaddle on to Spokaloo."

"What is this Spokaloo you keep talking about?"

"Spokane. And then on to Frisco. And don't forget, you got a thousand spondulicks in your britches. A good-looking kid like you can have a hell of a time in Frisco with a cool thousand." He watched me closely for a moment, then shook his head, saying, "You still got some doubts? Okay, okay.

Think it over. In is in. I'll tell you what. My plans aren't set yet, but we gotta strike while the iron is hot, before things get completely outta hand. Prob'ly before the union vote. You meet me here tomorrow night, about dark. I'll fill you in then and I gotta know, one way or the other."

I agreed and after a couple more drinks from the rye, I rose to leave.

"Hey, doncha wanta eat?" Davis asked.

"I'm full up," I said. The very thought of food was nauseating. I needed fresh air.

"Well, I'm buying. No? Suit yerself. Tell you what: talk to Little," Davis said. "Ast him about a few of the things we talked about. See what he's got to say for hisself. It'll make ya sick."

I nodded and staggered out into the cool night. There were a million stars, but they seemed awful blurry. I'd had too much whiskey and talk. Davis's words buzzed in my ears like bees. I took deep breaths and when I felt better, set off for the Big Ship.

CHAPTER TEN

You don't remember a hangover. It's the kind of thing you want to forget as quickly as you can, which is probably what makes alcoholism possible. Usually you can forget all about it by mid-afternoon, or even earlier when you're young. But I'm pretty sure I had a hangover the next day. I can't be certain, but I think it was one of those where you sincerely and devoutly swear an oath on whatever is most sacred to you, that you will never, never take another drink of whiskey. If I'm not mistaken, that was the occasion when I swore never to drink rye whiskey again. It was Old Overholt whiskey, I'm sure of it now. And I've never touched rye since.

It was a beautiful, sunny morning but I didn't appreciate it. Whiskey was out, but a cold beer seemed like a wonderful idea. I eased out of my lumpy bed at the Big Ship, decided I couldn't face Dewey and the stirabout, and slipped out to walk uptown. The M&M was full of gamblers and cowboys, early (or very late) drunks and anxious looking miners. I was shaky. I had a couple of beers and felt better. I amended my newly minted resolution to permit a shot of bourbon, which cured me.

I strolled around to Harrington's and looked in the window. Sure enough, Frank was in there, talking to McDonald and Wuuri and a couple of other men I didn't know.

Plotting, I told myself. Figuring out how to take over the union meeting. There was no telling how long they'd be. I

119

went back to the M&M, looking for Sean. I was anxious to talk to Sheila. I figured I'd put my offer to counsel Sheila into practice. But Sean hadn't been in yet.

I deliberately refused to think about Davis's proposition. It was too early. I'd talk to Frank first, then think about it. I had another beer and then sat down to a big breakfast of eggs and country sausage, with fried potatoes and toast, gravy on the fries. Stuffed, I set off for the Cabbage Patch. There were the usual gangs of ragamuffin kids hurtling about the streets. I thought I recognized some of Sheila's among them, but couldn't be sure.

Sean answered the door. He seemed glad to see me and invited me in. I said I was there to pick up my laundry. Sheila wasn't around. Sean didn't offer me tea, but immediately borrowed a cigarette.

"By golly, you were right," Sean told me. "Things ain't as bad as I thought. The old lady was frisky as a week-old heifer last night."

This wasn't exactly welcome news. "What about the slicker at the Hot Springs?" I asked acidly.

"Ah, who gives a rap about that? Prob'ly some guy who bumped into her and she just let him go for a walk with her. Sorry I bent yer ear last night. I was just upset, that's all. I bet she prob'ly was just being sociable. Who says she did anything more?"

"You did."

"You didn't see her being more than friendly, didja? There ain't sump'n you didn't tell me?"

"Well, I can't say I did." I was uncertain how to deal with this. I wasn't inclined to feed Sean's suspicions, but I had looked forward to a session with Sheila, especially if Sean would leave us alone. But everything seemed different this morning.

120

"Don't you think I ought to talk to her, anyway?" I asked. "I could maybe find out if anything did happen."

Sean shrugged. "I don't see how you could," he said, "and to tell you the truth, I ain't sure I wanta know if it did."

He blushed. "I got to thinking, and you was right. It never did no good to thump her. Maybe I oughta just let it alone."

I was glad Sean hadn't beat Sheila, but his complacency toward her obvious adultery was annoying. I had counted on seeing her and talking to her. In fact, it seemed urgent, now. "Where is Sheila, anyway?" I asked.

"She's working at the widder's up on Quartz."

The canopied bedstead, I thought. "Well, that's all right. I'm glad you worked it out. I'll check with you later. I've got some stuff to do, uptown."

"Sure. I'd like to come with ya, but I'm watching the kids."

The kids were nowhere to be seen, but I didn't comment. I hoofed it up to Quartz Street and knocked on the kitchen door. Instead of Sheila a fat, middle-aged woman with a bandanna tied around her head appeared.

"Vot you vant?" the woman asked crossly.

"I was looking for Mrs. Paton."

"Vot you vant py her? She pizzy. She is no time for poy-friends, now. You talk her some time else."

"I'm not a boyfriend, m'am," I said, straining to be polite. "I'm a friend of her husband's and he sent me up here. It's about one of the kids."

"Ach, all right," the woman said and went off, muttering some foreign language and pointedly closing the door, leaving me on the steps. A few minutes later Sheila came hurrying out, the fat woman hovering in the background.

"Goody! What are you doing here?" She looked nervously over her shoulder.

"It's Kevin," I said, knitting my brow in a warning grimace. "Kevin? Kevin who?"

"Your kid, Kevin. Sean sent me."

Sheila looked blankly at me, then began to catch the drift. "Oh, little Devin! Has something happened?" She managed to register alarm.

"Not exactly," I said. I gestured surreptitiously and Sheila stepped out into the backyard, letting the door bang shut behind her. The older woman shrugged and withdrew.

"Goody, what the devil is going on?"

I grinned. "I just wanted to see you, and that old battle-axe was being awful nosy."

"For heaven's sake," she hissed, "are you drunk? At this hour?" She sniffed the air and didn't like what she smelled.

"I'm not drunk," I objected. "I just wanted to see you." Now that I had her, I was damned if I could remember what it was I'd wanted to see her about. But she looked fine. Her hair was in a bandanna and there was a smudge on her cheek. I felt like kissing her, right there.

She seemed to sense it and permitted herself a coquettish smile. But for the benefit of listening ears, she assumed an anxious voice and said, "What's the matter?" Under her breath, she added, "The old lady's using our bed this morning. I can't get out, anyway."

"You have to," I said. I remembered what I'd wanted. "I have to talk to you."

"Oh, that. Sean's cooled off. He told me you had 'seen' me at the Hot Springs. But I soon made him forget all that nonsense."

"Don't," I said. "I don't want to hear about it."

"I'm sorry," she said. She looked contrite. "But I can't leave. Mrs. Hekkonen–the housekeeper," she gestured with her head at the kitchen, "will be here all day. Didn't you get my message this morning?"

I hadn't.

"I have to talk to you," I insisted. "I might be going away, soon."

"Oh my saints. When? Where?"

"I can't talk here."

She thought hurriedly, then said, "All right. I'll have to tell Mrs. Hekkonen it's about Devin."

"I thought it was Kevin."

"Kevin is the Mahoney boy, two doors down," she said. "Mine's Devin. It means poet, in Gaelic. He's all right?"

"As far as I know. The last I saw, he was hooking a trolley on Montana Street."

"Oh, that little. . . . You go on ahead," she said. "I'll meet you up at the Gardens, at our old place."

Twenty minutes later I was resting on a rock, panting, and looking back at the city. I saw a streetcar winding out toward the amusement park and hoped she was on it. Up here things seemed better. The air was sweet and cool, though the city had been hot in the July sun. Here the flowers were in bloom and the mountains looked mystical in the distance. A breeze stirred the pines and aspens around me and a large hawk, or eagle, sailed lazily away beyond the park. It made me wish that the strikers would never go back and start up the smelters again.

The city clung to the raw hill like a skin disease, the neighborhoods merging into the rash of chemical stains and tailings, beneath the huge, industrial structures, surmounted by the lift frames. Gallows frames. The word made me shudder.

Clothes flapped on backyard lines, cars and trolleys beetled in and out of the warrens of larger buildings uptown. From this distance it was not simple to say which were the workers' hovels and which were rich folks' mansions.

I was suddenly sick of Butte. I had a mind to take the next trolley back to town and hop on the first train out, no matter the direction. I would join the Army and not say a word to anybody about it. But I knew I wouldn't. For one reason, and I'm afraid Sheila wasn't the reason. It was the Old Man. I'd have to quit the Agency and that would mean a telegram at least. It wasn't just that Joe had told me not to contact the Old Man, although I understood the necessity for that: any telegram I sent would immediately expose me as an agent. Western Union was supposed to be confidential, but an operative couldn't rely on that, not in a tinderbox like Butte. No, the real problem was what such a telegram would have to say.

There was no way I could explain to the Old Man, in a telegram, why I was quitting without finishing the job. The Old Man had taken me in, literally off the streets, and given me a real job, an interesting job, and one that paid good money. I had respect for the Old Man, maybe even some affection. He'd been more like a father to me than my real pa. The Old Man was the Agency. He wasn't the founder, but he represented in the public eye the Great Detective. He was a confidant and protector of American presidents. Thanks to him all other agencies were just other agencies, the rest of the field. It was his leadership, his vision that had called into being the Secret Service. For many years he had campaigned for a national investigative service or bureau, but lesser minds had yet to heed his vision. I felt proud, even thrilled to know him, to say nothing of fancying myself a kind of protégé. I couldn't bear to think what his response would be to the idea of me quitting.

But I was on shaky ground here, I knew. The Old Man knew about the Frank Little business, presumably, but he couldn't be a party to it. I understood that, in a way. I didn't think any less of the Old Man for turning his head away from such a sorry business. The Old Man had told me that it wasn't the Agency's business to judge their clients. We must be objective, do what we'd been employed to do, and avoid . . . well, avoid what? Obviously, an operative should avoid just what I was now involved in up to my neck. But was this really what the Agency had been hired for? How had this happened? It was Joe's doing, I felt. Somehow, Joe had gotten the Agency —well, me and himself, at least—involved in something that the Agency shouldn't be involved in. Joe had implied that the Old Man approved, but I wondered how much the Old Man really knew about it, back in Baltimore.

Maybe I ought to alert the Old Man to the realities of the situation, I thought. But how? For that matter, I wasn't sure that I really understood the situation myself. Maybe it was just as Joe had described it. If I could only talk to the Old Man. But I couldn't.

What made me most uneasy, I realized, was the feeling that I was out on a limb here, two thousand miles from home. It didn't seem fair, but maybe that's what being on your own meant. Maybe accepting the unfair was part of being a man.

I was especially graveled to realize that Joe Davis clearly felt that I was the kind of man he could come to with a proposal to bushwhack a man like Frank Little. I had to ask myself if I really was such a man. Up to this point in my brief career I had never been involved in anything in the least illegal, and definitely nothing violent. I had only been in one tight scrape, when I'd been angrily confronted by the lover of a client's wife. I had shadowed the man in order to find out his home and thus his identity. It hadn't been any problem in the

125

crowded restaurant where the man had dined with the errant wife, but after they had parted the guy had wandered around Baltimore, in and out of shops and bars, until it got later and later. The crowds had melted away, and finally it was just the two of us on an interurban trolley. The man had thought he recognized me, but I had been able to joke the guy out of it. We'd ended up laughing about it, and I had even gotten out at the same lonely stop, walked away in the opposite direction with a wave of my hand and then doubled back. It had been fun and not really dangerous after all, the man being no heavyweight. In the end, it hadn't mattered if the man had believed me or not.

But this situation made me sick to my stomach, assuming that this queasiness wasn't another symptom of last night's rye. My hair-of-the-dog cure had worn off and I wished I had a cool beer. I was tempted to walk back down to get one. Instead, I lit a cigarette and tried to dope out this jam.

The fact was, I had to admit, I was concerned about Frank. What if Frank didn't leave? What if he resisted Davis and his thugs? I had a dread that Frank would put up a fight and Joe might react with his pistol. He might even shoot Frank!

A sudden clarity. It was as if the projectionist had adjusted the focus. As soon as I thought it I knew I'd been trying not to think it. I pushed it to the back of my mind, for now, and tried to concentrate on what Joe had said.

Joe had sketched a vague scenario of me luring Frank off by himself, away from his friends, on the premise of meeting a significant person. I envisioned a lonely street, some empty warehouses. Who could I suggest Frank meet? I considered this problem calmly. Suddenly it flashed on me: Burton Wheeler, the District Attorney. A suggestion of a deal with the mine owners, with Wheeler as the trustworthy go-between. What a gag that would be! I had a feeling that it would work and I congratulated myself for thinking of it. Joe Davis would laugh his moth laugh when I told him. He'd love it.

Then what, I wondered? A lonely street. Warehouses. An alley. Joe and his gang waiting. Frank and I enter the alley. It's dark, maybe a single streetlight halfway down the block, otherwise nothing but deep shadows. How many men would be lurking there? Would Joe step out into the light, or would he direct the action from the shadows? Say he steps out.

Frank is alarmed. "Where's Wheeler?" he says. Davis laughs, dry as dust. He waves a gun. The others appear. They have guns, too, or maybe just clubs.

I shuddered in the warm sun. Somehow, clubs seemed more ominous and cruel than guns, which seemed almost innocently mechanical by contrast. A man with a club would use it more readily. Guns can be merely brandished for effect. They needn't be fired. Nothing calls attention to itself like a gunshot.

I forced myself to go on, to visualize it.

Say Joe threatens Frank. Tells him he's got to go. Frank would laugh, tell Joe to go to hell. A thug takes a swing. Frank fights, just as he had in the alley with the cowboy. I vividly recalled that scene, the blood, the yells, the sound of blows, Frank cowering with his arms protecting his head.

Suddenly, a gunman—Joe?—steps forward and shoots. Frank staggers. He looks back at me, astonished and accusing, his life's blood spurting from his wounds. Frank steps toward me, his arms outstretched, but he never reaches me. He falls in the gutter, his blood flowing into the rain (it would be raining).

I look across the fallen body, horrified, and see . . . the gunman.

At that instant, sitting under the pines on the sunny hillside, I knew real clarity. I understood that the gunman would still have the gun and that I would now be a threat to the gunman's security, to his very life. And even if there were no gunman—

127

I was frozen. Forget the warm sunshine, forget Columbia Gardens, this foolish paradise of fun and pleasure. I stared up at the deep blue sky. It was so clear and so dark blue. I felt lonelier than I ever had in my young life.

Where was this Butte, this Montana? It was so very far from anyplace I had ever even heard of. What in hell was I doing here?

Suppose the gunman let me go. Suppose Joe Davis actually gives me the thousand spondulicks. Even suppose they let me get on the train to Spokaloo. Would a telegram tell the sheriff of some town down the line—Deer Lodge, say, or Missoula—to arrest the murderer of Frank Little? Would there be a witness to say that Goodwin Ryder was the last man to see Frank Little alive? That we had walked off together into the darkness, in the direction in which the body was found? Would Joe Davis be anywhere near Butte? Would the Agency come to my defense? Would the Old Man appear and take responsibility?

I shook myself and burst into nervous laughter. Jeez, I thought, you're sitting up here scaring the daylights out of yourself. What an imagination! Too much imagination. My mother had always said so. She'd said I would grow up to be a novelist, I was so full of tales. She called me her "little Dickens." I almost laughed.

It was so ridiculous. The way I'd imagined it, you'd think they were after me, not Frank. It was Frank they were after, I reminded myself. I lit a cigarette shakily. Joe had said they didn't want any martyrs. What they wanted was Frank Little out of Butte. That's all. Frank wouldn't be hurt at all. Well, not mortally . . . no, that wasn't the word I wanted.

Anyway, I couldn't see any advantage for the Company in hurting, that is, really hurting . . . well, okay, killing Frank. Besides, he was no fool. He'd see they meant business and he'd hit the road, pronto. And then he'd come back, of course, underground and pursuing his cockeyed dream of a new American revolution. Frank had been around. He'd no doubt faced this exact same situation many times before. You get out, you come back, and you try again. And again.

But I remembered what Frank had told me: there didn't seem to be any advantage to killing Governor Steunenberg, in Idaho. And yet, McParland had nearly gotten a noose around Big Bill Haywood's neck.

I stood up and stretched, trying to clear my head. Where was that woman? I needed her badly. I was a young man, I told myself, and I'd have a lot of fun yet. I wasn't going to let this little problem get me down. Of course, a guy couldn't ignore the danger. Evidently, there were some angles to this detective game that I hadn't considered. Well, it was time to consider them. Time to grow up. I wasn't a kid anymore. It was time to be a man. To take hold of my future. A man had to do things sometimes that he didn't really want to, that he didn't approve of. But he had to be tough. The fact that an old pro like Joe Davis had come to me at this time meant that people were beginning to take me seriously. And I had to admit that Joe's proposition interested me, even excited me. And there was the thousand dollars, too. Don't forget that. I wondered if my father had ever had a whole thousand bucks in his pocket at one time.

I began to look at this detective work in a calm, logical fashion. This proposition was the ultimate extension of a detective's role, I saw. Frank had said that the business of the detective was betrayal. I couldn't accept that, but now it seemed to me that there were elements of truth to it, whether it was gathering information against an adultress for the divorce court, or worming your way into the confidence of a thief who would drunkenly boast how he'd swindled his employer, or fingering a traitor—these were all genuine instances that I knew about from my mentors, Jimmy and the Old Man. It was all the same, really. You acted on behalf of the Law, in the spirit of the Law, for the people—as Joe Davis had put it. But there was no denying that you acted against the interests of the person you pursued and ultimately betrayed. Well, that was the way it fell out. Who should you be for? The people, or the ones who broke the law?

At last, she came. I saw her red hair bobbing up the trail. Then the white shirtwaist and the blue skirt. I waited behind a tree. As she passed, glancing about and breathing hard, her face flushed, I leapt out behind her and grabbed her by the waist.

Sheila spun around. I swept her into my arms and kissed her. She kissed me back furiously. Her hair was a cloudy blaze in the sun and her skin was hot. Her tongue probed into my mouth wickedly. I drew her back into the trees and pushed her down on the ground. She protested momentarily, then eagerly gave in to my passion. She helped me undo the buttons of the blouse. It had three odd buttons—a large blue one and two smaller ones. And then those wonderful lush breasts were free, crazy things like nothing else in nature the way they were so cunningly formed, round but sloping and curved in a way that suggested weight and lightness in the same swooping line. They bobbled and swayed, the areolas large and swollen from the heat. I bent to suck at them hungrily, like a baby, laughing. Then she drew up her skirt. She had no stockings on and her thighs were white and soft.

"You madman," she whispered, and hooked her legs over mine. I could feel the hot sun on my bare ass. I buried my face in her hair and her neck, kissing her as she grasped my achingly stiff cock in her warm hand and drew it into her body.

For a short eternity there I had no thought of crimes or anything else.

CHAPTER ELEVEN

When I told her I was leaving she thought it was because of Sean. She told me not to worry about him.

"No," I said, "it has nothing to do with Sean."

"Then why?"

"I've got to. I can't stay."

"Because there's no work? Is it money you're worried about? You'd leave me because you're running out of money? I shouldn't have let you spend like a sailor at the Hot Springs."

"No, no, no," I assured her. "I don't want to leave you. It has nothing to do with that."

"Then it's me," she said.

"Don't be silly."

"Then tell me."

"I can't. It's too dangerous. Dangerous for both of us. For all of us."

"Oh, dear. I was afraid of something like this." She buried her face in my chest. "It's all right, you know. I don't care."

I pushed her away and looked in her face. "What do you mean? What do you know?"

"I knew you were no miner the moment I first laid eyes on you, in the back garden. I'll be very embarassed if I'm wrong. But . . . you're a spy."

"My god! Does Sean know?"

"Of course not. I only knew this minute. It had to be something like that, though. Didn't it? Anyway, it doesn't matter."

"Doesn't matter? Of course it matters. It's why I have to go."

"Oh, dear. You've been found out? Well, I shall go with you!" In intense moments like this her voice became more Irish, lilting and charming in accent, but declamatory, as well.

I nearly laughed. It was ridiculous, of course, and I said as much. "Anyway, I haven't been 'found out,' as you say. No one knows. Well, only one or two, who have to know."

"Then why must you go?"

I sighed. "It's the job. It's over. I'm being sent on."

"You want to leave," she said, accusingly.

"Of course not! Don't be so silly. I have to go."

"I see. You are in trouble. What's gone wrong?"

I sighed. "Oh god, I don't know. Everything seemed to be going so well. Now it's all confused."

"You have to tell someone, you know."

I didn't dignify that with an answer. The need for secrecy was one of the first things Jimmy had taught me. Only he called it security. You didn't go around shooting your mouth off, telling your business. Your business was finding out the other guy's secrets, penetrating their security, which was usually not very secure.

"You should," Sheila said. "It isn't difficult. You simply start by telling the truth and you go on telling the truth."

"Like you told Sean about the Hot Springs, I suppose?"

She shrugged. "That was for his own good. Sean Paton wouldn't know the truth if it stood on its hindlegs and bought him a pint of Guinness. Besides, I had to think of you. I didn't want him to hurt you."

"Well, it's the same way here. Sort of."

132

"You mean someone could get hurt? Hurt badly? Then you must tell me. I'm part of you, now. It concerns me. Unless, you don't want me."

"You know it isn't that. It doesn't concern you, that's all. You couldn't be hurt, regardless of what happens to me."

"Oh, then it is serious. I suppose it has something to do with this wretched strike. Let's see . . . you would be a Pinkerton, then? Or a Burns? A strike-breaker, is that it?"

I was dumbfounded. I said nothing.

"But it must be more than that. It must be something to do with Frank Little."

This was too much. "What makes you say that?"

"It would have to be. Why else would you have befriended my poor, foolish Sean? You're a much superior man, you know."

Her words pleased me, but they worried me, too. "I'm just a guy on the road," I said, "picking up a few bucks. There's no work, so I took the first offer."

"Oh, it's more than that, I should think. You're not just a wandering lad. You're intelligent. You have a future, Goody. You'll not be a miner. There's nothing of the miner in you. Only now, something has gone wrong. They've asked you to do something you don't care for, that you hadn't bargained for."

I could only stare in amazement.

"Women aren't such fools," she said lightly, smiling. "It's the men who are fools. Men long to be important. They want all their business to be important. Except for a harmless fellow like my Sean, and even he idolizes a man like Frank Little and plays at secret brotherhoods like the I.W.W. It makes him feel more important, as if earning a living weren't important enough."

I wished she would quit referring to "my Sean," but instead of objecting I countered, "And women like to be self-satisfied philosophers!"

"Yes, I suppose we are. We sit back and watch our men make bloody great fools of themselves until they endanger everybody, including us and our children. And then we must set to work to straighten it all out."

"How nice for you."

"Not so nice, as a matter of fact. Life is not very easy at the moment, for instance. Thanks to you and your strike and falling in love with you and wanting to leave with you."

I groaned. "I wish that were all. I'd take you away in a second." I'm not sure why I said that. Actually, it was only when she said that she had fallen in love that I realized that I was in love, too. A half-hour earlier I had wanted to leave Butte and hadn't given a thought to her accompanying me.

"It's not easy, I realize," Sheila said, thoughtfully, "but it's not impossible, either. You must believe that. Otherwise, you're simply lost. Your problem concerns Mr. Little. Is he a spy, too?"

"Frank, a spy!" I laughed. "That's the craziest notion! The problem is the Company is out to get him!"

"And they want you to help, now that you've become his friend," Sheila said, matter of factly. When I didn't reply, or even look at her, she went on: "Then why don't you?"

"Are you crazy?" I demanded. "How can you say such a thing?"

"I see. It's a question of loyalty, then," she said. "Men often talk about loyalty, and honor. Wonderful words, those. Frank Little is your friend, I think. Or you think. But he's also your enemy. To me he's a dirty little one-eyed Indian who never did a lick of work in his life but has managed to stop nearly every able-bodied man in Butte from working and supporting his family as he should."

"That's a woman talking," I said sarcastically. "I don't suppose you're interested in higher wages or safer working conditions. Oh, the wages would be nice. You could buy a new hat. But the working conditions . . . you don't have to go down in the Hole, in the stink and the heat, a mile underground . . .."

I remembered that I didn't have to do that either, and wouldn't. I dropped it, embarrassed.

"A hat?" Sheila laughed. "Do you fancy me in a hat? What sort of hat do you think I should buy? What would go well with this gown?" She stood and spread her wrinkled cotton skirt, twirling clumsily in her heavy shoes. "Something with an egret plume, do you suppose?" She sounded like a stage duchess.

I smiled despite myself. "Quit play-acting," I said.

"So they want you to help them get rid of Mr. Little," she prompted, standing above me, looking down with hands on hips.

"Something like that."

"Well, if I were a man, I should do it. Then the strike would be over and you would be a kind of hero, wouldn't you? Though, of course, not the kind of hero the newspapers could write about. A few men would know, however, and applaud. You would be promoted, I dare say. When you become the boss, in New York City, will you send for me?"

"Will you be serious? I'm in trouble here. If I don't go through with this I reckon I'll be out of a job. But that's not the point. They're going to do it, with or without me, and I'm in it up to my chin."

Sheila was serious, then. "Yes, I can see that. You're damned if you do and damned if you don't. Unless," her face lit up, "you stop them."

"Stop them? How? I can't go to the cops."

135

"Why not?"

"For all I know, the cops are part of it. And even if they aren't, what can I say? These guys are after Little? I have no proof. The cops would laugh. And then I'd be out on the street, and the street is something Joe Davis knows something about. I don't know if my life'd be worth a plugged nickel."

"But Mr. Little would be safe. He could go on with his wretched strike," Sheila pointed out. "Perhaps he'd give you a job. No? No, I suppose it isn't likely, is it? Gratitude isn't likely from his kind. Though why I say that I can't imagine. I don't know the man. Perhaps he's the exception. One of Nature's Gentlemen. Sean thinks he's a saint."

Suddenly, her face lit up, again.

"Now what?" I said, sourly.

"You could go to Frank Little," she said. "It's that simple! Tell him you've discovered a plot against him. He could leave town, perhaps just for a short time, or he could make it public. At any rate, your role needn't be made public."

I considered this with interest. It had merit. "But would he trust me?" I asked, more to myself than to Sheila. "I'm sure he likes me, but I'm not really 'in,' you know. Maybe Sean could tell him!"

"Oh no," Sheila said, "not my Sean. I'll not have you mixing him up in your dirty business."

"Oh, is that it?" I said, angrily. "It's 'your dirty business,' and 'my Sean,' is it? This is how you really feel about me?"

"Oh, no, Goody. It's not that, not a'tall." She was very Irish in her anguish. "I do love you. You must know that I do. But Sean . . . he's such a poor, dear man. He's not much good for anything but hard work and drinking beer. He means no harm, Goody, but he's never the man for such business as this. He's not the man you are. You're a man of a different calibre, Goody. I'll not have you roping a poor laddy like Sean into it."

136

"Ah, I suppose you're right," I said, somewhat mollified by her words. "Still, I don't see how he could get involved, really. He could just say he'd heard it from someone reliable."

"A lot of good that would do," Sheila said. "Why should Frank Little listen to that blather? I dare say he hears rumors like that everyday. No, no, it must come from you, Goody. As you say, you're not of the inner circle, but that in itself is a point, is it not? He probably already suspects you are a spy, I shouldn't doubt; he'd be a bigger fool than I think he is, if he didn't."

She was right. I was merely resisting a difficult task. I didn't relish going to Frank and confessing that I was a spy. Maybe it needn't be decided immediately. I could talk to Frank, sort of feel him out about things, drop a few hints. And I still had to see Joe Davis. For all I knew, Davis might have dropped the whole plan, or could be argued out of it. The Old Man could have contacted Davis by now and ordered him to drop it. It was possible. It would be a major mistake to move too fast on something like this. It could clear itself up, without me doing anything, and if I'd already squealed to Little, there I'd stand, with egg on my face. No, it was better to be cautious. This was no time to go off half-cocked.

I didn't mention any of this to Sheila. Instead, we discussed the merits of her suggestion in a general way, she as an enthusiastic advocate, me with judicious caution. I ended by agreeing to consider it further and, in the meantime, to sound out Frank on his reaction to previous, similar situations.

As we walked down the hill, I amused Sheila with an account of how I'd talked Sean into not 'thumping' her.

She raised an eyebrow. "That was good of you," she said, "but you mustn't think it was your doing, you know. I have my own ways of handling Sean-O."

"Oh sure," I said. "The way he talked, he's had to thump you in the past."

"He hit me once," she said, "years ago. I took it without a word. He was drunk, to be sure. Afterwards, he fell into bed, in a stupor. When he awoke, in the morning, he couldn't get up. I had pulled the sheet up over his head and tied it down that tight, you see. I had to crawl under the bed to do it. He didn't know what to do, poor helpless eedjit. He shouted for help. I wasn't in the room."

I had to laugh. It was a marvelous joke, I thought. But her story was not ended.

"I waited in the kitchen, till he'd shouted himself hoarse," she said, laughing. "Then I lugged in a bloody great kettle of boiling water."

My laughter dried to dust in my throat.

"I told him, if he didn't repent and beg my pardon, I should scald him to death. I sprinkled a few drops on his belly, to show him how hot it was. Oh, he begged my pardon, indeed he did! And swore never to strike me again. And he hasn't."

We walked on, but I couldn't find anything to say to this.

"A man has to sleep every night, you know," Sheila observed, cheerfully ignoring my uneasiness.

In response to this confession to bloody-mindedness, I couldn't resist a little cheerful malice, myself. I told her that Sean had asked me to talk to her.

"You talk to me? About what?"

"About marriage. About being a good wife, and all that."

She was furious. "You? That's ridiculous. What do you know about marriage? Why you're only a boy."

It was my turn to laugh. But I assured her it was just a ploy to get to see her. That restored her good humor and she observed that it might come in handy yet.

"Sean's a great silly fool," she said. "He doesn't deserve a fine wife like me."

I fully agreed with her.

CHAPTER TWELVE

The first thing Frank said when he answered the door of his room, was "What's the value of a pound of copper?"

"A pound of copper? Well, to tell the truth, I didn't give it much thought," I said.

"No? Wal, whattaya think?"

"Why, I guess it's worth whatever you can get for it."

"That's not bad," Frank said. "Most people would agree with you. But Marx says the true value is what it cost to produce, and the biggest part of that is the cost of labor. But the capitalist has to have his cut, which is much more than it should be, 'cause the workers compete for jobs and accept less than they oughta. And, a course, long after the capitalist has retrieved his cost and a profit, he continues to grind it out of the workers. That's what the union is all about, trying to get the men to quit cutting each other's throats to the benefit of the capitalists."

He sat on his bed, wearing only trousers and a threadbare undershirt, no shoes on his bony, discolored feet. His face was now black and blue with hideous yellowish splotches, but obviously healing. He got off the bed and knelt down to draw a scuffed leather suitcase from under it. He put it on the neatly made bed and riffled through the rumpled, dirty clothes, tossing them aside until he found what he was looking for. He brought it to where I was sitting on the only chair.

"This is just a short and simple version of Marx's basic ideas that some feller in London wrote up," Frank said, handing a well-thumbed pamphlet to me. "But it's pretty good to get started with. There's lots better stuff out, and I can tell you where to get hold of some, when you finish that. Go ahead, take it. I got it about memorized, anyhow."

I took the pamphlet and glanced at the thick, blurry print on cheap paper that seemed to have been made out of dried oatmeal. It looked about as inviting as the Big Ship's morning stirabout. I thanked Frank and looked around nervously. There was no sign of a gun, or much else. Obviously, Little kept everything he valued in the suitcase.

Little noticed my observations and said, "I'm a poor man, Goody. I travel light. And sometimes I have to leave in a hurry. Say, gotta fag?"

I gave him a Fatima. Little leaned over while I lit the cigarette. Then he sat back on the bed. He took a flat stamped tin out of his pocket and opened it. The lid served as an ashtray; the tin itself contained shreds of tobacco and cigarette butts. He passed the lid to me to use and knocked his own ashes into his pants cuffs.

"Marx says the capitalist has appropriated for himself the industrial improvements that increase production," Little said. "The fact is, they run the show, so they put a heavy value on capital, much more than it deserves." I nodded to show interest and Little went on in this vein for awhile, discussing the basic elements of the theory and applying it to mining, in a simple, practical manner. He admitted, for instance, that mining did require a lot of capital, just for starting up, but he insisted that the capitalists invariably tried to recover all of their costs immediately and began taking profits as soon as possible, at the expense of the workers' health and welfare.

"Still," I said, "a miner couldn't set up a mine by himself, or run it. That takes money, and education."

Little shook his head with an indulgent smile. "You allus hear that crap. You'd think all the operators were geniuses. They're just men. Workers. But they don't like to think of themselves as workers. You could run a mine. I could. It takes education, sure, but they learned it from someone. As for the capital, most of them inherited it. And only a few manage it very well. You could learn that, too. But the bosses like to let on that it's something they earned, that they got the loot because they're more noble, or more deserving. Shit! Most of the capital is borrowed, anyway. It ain't their own wealth at stake. And what Hearst and Guggenheim actually know about mining—well, that's why they hired Marcus Daly. He was just a poor Irish miner who learned his trade in the hole.

"But, I forgot: you ain't a miner," he said, "you're a writer, a journalist. So maybe the example is a little difficult to follow. Let's see . . . say you're the publisher of a big time magazine, like the *Smart Set*. Now, a big part of your expenses is paper and printing, that kind of stuff, and naturally you screw your suppliers as much as you can. But you can only go so far there. But then you've got all these reporters, journalists, and as it happens nobody can actually put a value on the written word. Oh, obviously a famous guy like Mencken or Lincoln Steffens sells papers, but what is the writing of somebody like Goodwin Ryder worth? Hard to say, since Ryder hasn't published anything before, not under his own name, anyway. So it'd be easy for a publisher to turn the screws on the journalist, so that the publisher can maximize his profit. Isn't that so?"

I didn't like the way this was heading. Frank's voice had an odd tone, almost sarcastic. But I had no choice but to agree with him.

"Unh-hunh. I thought so," he said. "Still, you must be doing all right, since I see you don't work but you get by purty good, buying the fellers beer and all. You make a pile in the stock market?" He grinned disarmingly.

"No, of course not! The stock market! You must think I'm one of those capitalists, one of the smart ones."

"Well, what does the *Smart Set* pay, if you don't mind me asking?"

"Well, it depends." My mind raced. Frank was onto something and I didn't know how far I should let it go. But I thought that, for now, it was best to go along the way I'd started. "Let's say, a hundred dollars."

"Let's see . . . that's about a month's pay for a miner. You make that much every month?"

"Per article. I'm doing it on acceptance, you see. If they don't buy it, I don't get anything."

"Jeez, I hope you write fast."

"Well, it beats shoe clerking. I could see there wasn't much future in Baltimore, clerking, so I 'lit out for the territories,' like Huck Finn."

"Them Finns are pretty good people," Little joked. "I wonder if old Huck was a Church Finn or a Red Finn."

I didn't know what he was talking about, so Little explained. Apparently, the Finns were very strong in the socialist movement. They'd had their own revolution in 1905, which was why so many of them had gone to mine copper in Michigan and Butte.

"Lenin says they're the most politically sophisticated people in the world," Little said.

"I guess Wuuri's a Red Finn," I said.

"Al? I guess you could say that. Whatta you know about Al Wuuri?"

"Nothing. I saw you talking to him, and some of the guys say he'll be a big man in the new union."

"Is that so? Wal, Al Wuuri's a true socialist. Most of the Finns are. They don't seem to believe in the Leader principle. No man on a white horse for them. I guess they had enough of kings and dukes and that kind of crap in the Old Country. So you don't find many of them in the leadership. Funny, eh? But they got the right idea. Brotherhood is what's needed, not a leader. The idea of the big man, the boss, is what we're against."

"You're a leader," I pointed out, relieved that the conversation had turned away from my fictional occupation.

"I'm an organizer. I'm not a boss. I don't tell anyone what to do. I tell 'em what I think and then it's up to them. It ain't up to me."

"Is that so?" I said. "I got the idea that whether Al Wuuri was the president or secretary-treasurer of the new union was probably up to you."

"Who says so?"

I shrugged. "Nobody in particular. I just got that impression. I figured you'd see to it that Al Wuuri was taken care of."

Little squinted at me, thoughtfully. "Al Wuuri is a 'Son of the People,' as the Finns say. They'll see he gets in."

"Especially if you say so," I insisted. "But what if the men like somebody else better? Will you have someone object to his nomination?"

Little reached for the tin lid, in which I had snubbed out my cigarette and did the same with his own. He carefully put the butts in the bottom of the container, then got up to dump the ashes in a wastebasket. He replaced the lid and put the tin back in his pocket. He stood looking at me, then said, "Wal, you remember what I said about revolutions and rosewater."

"Oh, yeah, some bird named Merrybull."

Frank laughed. "Mirabeau. You been talking to somebody about this?"

"No, I just heard some guys talking."

"What guys?"

"I don't know their names. They were just miners."

"What'd they say?"

I shrugged. I felt a peculiar sadness; it looked like Joe Davis' prediction was true. "They just said the Wobblies would fix the union vote, is all."

"We're not fixing the vote," Little said, impatiently. He sat down on the bed again. "The men'll vote the way they want. I got a lot of confidence in the wisdom of the common working man. But we got a right to be heard. Most of the men are sympathetic to the I.W.W. anyway, even if they don't call themselves Wobblies."

"But what if they don't vote the way you want?"

"Oh, I think they will. And I'm sure gonna do all I can to make 'em see their own best interest. The cause is too important to let some Company stooge steal the election. Lenin says . . ." Little checked himself and uttered a short laugh, ". . . wal, to hell with what Lenin says. Just another Russian, eh? You don't like hearing about Russians."

"You seem to think a lot of them," I said, crossly.

Little smiled. "I really don't just sit around reading Lenin and Marx, it just sounds like it." He gestured at a newspaper lying folded by the pillow. "I mostly read the funny papers and the sports. Jiggs and Maggie, that's my speed."

"I kind of like 'Krazy Kat,'" I admitted, happy to find a neutral subject, "but they don't seem to carry it in the papers out here."

"You do? That's my favorite! It's goofy as hell most of the time, doesn't make real sense. I'm not sure if it's s'posed to be funny, or not. But I like the drawings, and it's Western. I like that. It looks sort of like the desert, like Arizona. Seems like they'd carry it out here, but maybe it's too modern for 'em, or something. I spent quite a bit of time down in Arizona . . . wal, you know about that. Anyways, you get kind of tired of everything being about the East, New York and all. It's good to see the West, even if it's just in the funny papers."

He reached into his suitcase and rummaged around until he found a bottle of whiskey. He held it up. It was half-full.

"Whiskey?" he asked. "No?" He tossed it back among the socks and things. "I don't use it much, myself, but it comes in handy at times, on the road, and such."

"You must travel a lot," I said.

"I been just about everywhere in the country, and then some," Little said, with a trace of pride. "The capitalists have provided a great system for us, and it's free. 'Course, you gotta watch out for the yard bulls. Butte's not bad, but Cheyenne, now there's a hobo hell. You gotta get down when you come into Cheyenne. But I guess you don't ride the rods, do you?"

"Uh, not much," I admitted.

"Pullman is more your style," Little said. "I never rode in a sleeping car in my life. What's it like?"

I didn't reply. I looked at the floor. It was bare, but clean, just a film of dust.

"You meet a lot of people on the road," Little said. "They call 'em bums, but they're mostly working men, trying to find something a little better."

"A feller in the Big Ship says it's a 'feen in your blood,' swinging freights," I said.

Little laughed. "I've heard that. He must be a real boomer tramp, a hobo. That's a little different. A hobo isn't a bum, but he ain't much of a working man, either. Kind of a professional traveler, you might say. Their only ambition is to keep

145

going, seems like. Now you might be a professional traveler, Goodwin. Question is, what kind of goods do you travel in?"

When I didn't answer, Little spoke in an annoyed tone: "How's our old pal, McParland? Holding his own?"

"I don't know any McParland," I said, chilled.

"Wal, what's his name these days?"

"I don't know who you're talking about."

"The Op. The Denver Chief. What's he calling himself this time? Talk about the big man, there's a leader for you. He still slapping the boys on the back and buying 'em beer? Still chuckin' the kids under the chin? Maybe he's measuring 'em for future neckties." Little smiled maliciously.

I couldn't take this needling any longer. I decided to come right out with it. "Frank, you're in danger. They're out to get you."

"Wal, I know they're out to get me, Goody. They're out to get any man who has the dumbness, the low-down cussedness, to try to organize his fellow man. The question is: Who is it this time? McParland and his spies? Local thugs? More cowboys?"

I shook my head. "I can't say. I don't know. But, I heard . . . I heard from a guy who should know, that they're planning to rough you up and ride you out of town on a rail, and not a railroad rail, neither."

Little grimaced, his battered face causing him to wince. It was almost comic. "Jeeziss, I hate that," he said. I couldn't tell if he was being sarcastic or not. "I hate that damn tar. It burns and it's hell to get off, less you can get ahold of some gasoline, and then you smell like shit and don't dare to light up a fag for a week." He gave a short laugh.

"It's no joke, Frank."

Little sighed then and leant forward, elbows on knees. He stared at the floor for a considerable time, the silence swelling in the room. The noise from the Butte streets penetrated only distantly. At last he looked across at me and said, "I hate to see you getting into a mess like this, Goody."

"I'm all right. You're the one's in a mess."

"No, I'm about where I expect to be. This is my choice. My kind of game. A guy like me, you step into the batter's box you gotta figger they might throw at yer head. But you, you're just a young feller and you're not getting a very good start on things. It can make all the difference, how a young man starts out. These can't be very good people you're in with, Goody."

"I can take care of myself."

Little ignored this. "They probably seem like good fellers to you 'cause they got money and nice clothes and they travel in the Pullman. They know the cops and the people who count, the deacons and the Home Guard." He laughed bitterly.

"The Home Guard!" he snorted. "That's what the hoboes call 'em, the big boys who run everything. These guys here," he gestured over his shoulder with a thumb, "up the Hill. The thing is, Goody, they're the ones who should be the Home Guard, but they don't do much of a job of it."

I didn't understand and I guess my expression showed it.

"I'm talking about the fellers who have gained most of the benefits from this country," Little said earnestly. "The autymobiles, the big houses, the purty wives and healthy little kiddies, the private clubs and the servants. And they don't ever put anything back in. They take and take and take . . ." He pounded his fist on his thigh and his voice grew desperate and angry.

"And they should be the ones giving!" he declared. "Damn! They oughta be glad to give, to help out their fellow man. But they just keep takin'!"

I was shocked to see a tear glisten in Little's good eye. Frank blinked a couple of times, then cleared his throat.

147

"Wal," he drawled softly, sighing, "it gits to you, after awhile. You git so goddamned tired of fighting it."

Little suddenly pounded his fist on his thigh again, then he made a choking noise and seemed to sag, burying his head in his hands.

I was moved. I forgot my own misery and went to sit next to Frank, putting my arm around the thin, weary back. Little leaned his head on my shoulder. It was a strange moment, sitting in the quiet room, comforting Frank. I was not used to tenderness, giving it or receiving it. Not with a man, anyway.

"Thank you, Goody," he said, after a long time. "It's awful kind of you. You're a good feller." He patted my thigh and rested his hand on it. He squeezed my thigh.

I didn't know what to do. After what seemed a very long time, I shifted uncomfortably. I withdrew my arm from the older man's back and rested it on my thigh, nudging Frank's hand away. But Frank seized my hand, gripping it in a strong hold.

Little looked at me, his eye glittering. He seemed nervous, even ill. "Goody, I seen a lot, travelling around. I lived on the rez, too. I, uh, had some strange experiences." His voice was low and hoarse, almost pleading. "Do you know what I mean?"

I didn't know what to think or say. I was appalled. I wanted to run, but I wasn't dead certain what Little was talking about and I was afraid to enquire. What if it wasn't anything serious?

"A man needs . . ." Little spoke cautiously, but with an edge of desperation ". . . affection. I know that sounds foolish to you. But it's true." He looked at me pleadingly. "It wouldn't mean anything to you, but it'd mean a lot to me." He dropped his other hand onto my thigh again.

I felt sick to my stomach. I stood up, slowly disengaging my hand from Little's. I stepped away toward the door, but paused.

"I don't know anything about that kind of stuff," I said. "I just came by to tell you they were after you."

"Sit down, sit down," Little said, gruffly. He had a defeated look. He stared down at the floor. He waved his hand at the chair, peremptorily. I sat on the edge of the seat.

Little looked up, finally, and mustered a weak smile. His teeth weren't good. When his face wasn't pounded into a purple and yellow mess, he wasn't a bad looking fellow, but that was something I couldn't bear to think about at the moment. The bad eye was puckered and flaccid. You couldn't actually see what kept it shut, maybe it had just grown closed. There didn't appear to be anything there. But there was pain in his good eye.

"I beg your pardon, Goody," he said with dignity. "I truly do. I can't help myself sometimes. It didn't mean anything, I swear it." His voice was calm and assured, now. "No harm done?"

"No harm done," I said, not meaning it. I still felt sick, and angry, as well.

"Good. Good. It's just that you were so kind . . . comforting a feller like that. But, you're a kind feller. I saw that from the start. I shouldn't have taken advantage, and I apologize. I mean that."

He fell into a sombre mood, looking away, out the window. It had a flowery patterned curtain over it, a flour sack, evidently. It was thin enough that one could see the back of a house across the alley, though little else.

"Hah!" he barked, finally, seeming to gather himself together. "That was dumb. Wal, you never know." He might have been talking to himself. He looked up with a disarming grin. "You never know if you don't try. But, it doesn't mean anything, Goody. Believe me. I hope you won't think badly of me."

"I won't," I said. I tried not to think about it.

"Fine. I know you won't. You're all right. I guess that's why . . . why I was so bothered about you, about the people you're with, and so on. 'Cause you're a good feller. You're not like the rest. But, it's none of my business. A feller's got the right to do . . . but you're so young, and bright . . .." He looked at me intently. "You oughta be more careful." He laughed, suddenly.

I smiled. I felt better. It seemed that nothing serious had happened after all, though it could have. It was better to just forget it. At least I had gotten my message through. It was a great relief. I got up.

"No, don't go," Frank said. "Sit down, sit down. Uh, about these friends of yours, the ones you say are out to get me. Was . . . is one of them McParland?"

"I don't know any McParland. I told you that."

"Yebbut . . . is he about five-eight, five-nine? Dark hair? Likes a cigar?"

"I don't know," I said, uncertainly. "Lots of fellers smoke cigars."

"That's not much, I know, but I just can't think of any special features, or anything," Little said. "Does he wear glasses? Dresses like a rancher? You know, boots and hat?"

I shook my head, "No."

"Wal, how would you describe the bastard?" Little asked sharply.

I couldn't think what to say. "Ordinary," I offered lamely. "Just an ordinary guy. Kind of a talker."

"Just your ordinary killer," Little said sarcastically. Then, "Easterner? Maybe a little trace of a Scottish accent? Late forties, early fifties?"

I shook my head. "You must be thinking of someone else. The guy I heard it from is maybe thirty."

We looked at each other in consternation. Finally Frank said, "Ah, to hell with it. It could be anybody. It don't amount to a turd in a barnyard, anyway." He laughed helplessly.

"Well, I imagine it does," I said. "They're out to get you, Frank. But I don't know who all it is. Joe, I know Joe. Joe Davis, but . . . maybe it's not his real name."

"Joe, hunh? Jeeziss, I've known a helluva lotta Joes." Little laughed again, almost hysterically. "Too damn many Joes, if you want to know. But really, Goody, it doesn't matter."

"Frank! They might kill you!" I was immediately appalled at what I'd said. I had carefully buried the image of the gunman in the back of my mind, but now it surfaced.

Little shook his head. "No, no."

"Well, I didn't mean that, but they could. Anything could happen," I said.

"Oh, I suppose they could. Hell, they might."

"Well, then?"

"It doesn't matter," Little said, quietly.

I was suddenly angry. "Now, what the hell is that supposed to mean?"

Little looked up at me earnestly, his awful face rather endearing and innocently sincere. "It doesn't matter, Goody. You see, I'm going to die anyway."

I shrugged helplessly. "Well, of course, we're all going to die, some day . . ."

"That's it. That's part of it," Little said, as if encouraging me to get the rest of it out. But I just looked at him blankly, so Little nodded to himself and went on. "People allus say that,

151

but they don't really mean it. They don't really think they're
going to die. But I know I'm going to die, Goody. I could die
any minute. I've done enough, God knows. But that ain't the
point. The thing is, they can't really kill me. Oh, I mean they
can kill me – maybe, though I doubt it – but they can't really
be my killers. Here, siddown."

I wouldn't sit. I wondered if I was looking at a crazy man.

"You see, I've already killed myself, inna way," Little
explained. "That is, I've given up my life already, to be part
of . . . I belong to something else, to a bigger thing, an idea
that won't die. Can you understand that? I'm not just talking
about Communism, or Socialism, or the I.W.W. It's bigger
than that. It's Life, itself. It's a spirit of life, maybe. The idea,
the principle of life . . . and those things just are ways of
thinking about it. Are you listening, Goody? This is important.
This is crucial for you. It's what you have to learn. It's the
only thing I can tell you.

"You see, your friend Joe is already dead, too. But he's truly
dead. Not like I am. He's dead and he's of the dead."

"This is too thick for me," I said, impatiently.

Little stood up and laughed. He clasped me by the arms,
then hugged me.

Oh, god, not this again, I thought. But then I recognized
that this wasn't like before. This was not a hug of desire, but
of friendship. I laughed, too, then, if a bit uncertainly.

"You're all right, Goody." Little released me but held me at
arm's length for a moment, looking at me, then dropping his
hands. "I can see it in your face. You're a bit muddled, but
who ain't? No, I can see it. I'm never wrong about these things.
You're one of them people."

Little laughed again and sat down. He asked for another
cigarette. I handed him the pack. Little took one, then another,
with a questioning look. I nodded. Little tucked the extra one

behind his ear and put the other in his lips. He struck a kitchen match on his tin box and lit the fag. He puffed it and crossed one leg over the other in a casual, relaxed way.

"I had a buddy," Little said, "a kind of asshole buddy, you might say, who used to say that all the time. 'One of them people.' I knew what he meant. Same as you know. 'One of them people . . . going down the road.' That's what he'd say. I've come across them, once in awhile, on this road I'm on. I think I recognized all of them. Maybe not. But you're one."

Little drew down the cigarette, then went through the business of snuffing it out and storing the butt. He said, absently, "I've known a lot of them people."

He rummaged in the suitcase for a moment and came up with a little jar. He handed it to me. It seemed to be full of sand.

"What's this?" I asked.

"One of them people. Joe Hill."

I frowned. I didn't get it.

"Those are the ashes of Joe Hill. Wal, his real name was Hillstrom. You probably never heard of him. He was an I.W.W. They shot him, down in the Utah pen. It was a frame. He had his ashes sent out to all his old buddies. He wrote labor songs." He hummed a few bars. I didn't recognize the tune.

Frank took the jar back and held it in his hand, gazing at it. "Yeah," he said at last, "we had some times. Joe was one of them people." He looked at me. "You'll meet up with some of them, from time to time, Goody. You'll know them when you see 'em. At least, I hope so . . . for your sake."

He tossed the jar onto the bed, casually. "I don't know why I keep that. It's not Joe, not really. Oh, it's his ashes, all right, but the real Joe Hill is right here." He thumped his breast.

Then a smile crinkled his bruised face. "Silly, eh? Well, it's a hell of a thing to meet up with a real brother."

He shook my hand then, in a manly, comfortable way. "Thanks for coming by, Goody. I appreciate it. It was kind of you. And brave. You got sand. Oh, by the way. When?"

"When? Oh. Well, I don't know. They were kind of counting on me, I guess, but now . . . well, it'd have to be soon. Probably before the union vote, I reckon."

Little nodded sagely, as if considering some everyday matter. "Unh-hunh. That'd be about it. Wal, thanks again. I guess you'll be going on down the road, now. Is that it?"

"Something like that."

"Unh-hunh. Wal, good luck."

I opened the door. "Okay. Good luck to you, Frank. So long."

"Thanks, but I don't need it, Goody. So long." Suddenly, remembering something, he said, "Wait!"

He fetched the whiskey bottle and unscrewed the top, holding the bottle out to me. "One for the road."

I took a drink. It was warm and strong, some kind of cheap blend. But it tasted all right and stayed down. Little wiped the top with his hand and hoisted the bottle in a toast. "Here's to all our pals, all our Joes," Frank said and took a drink, then screwed the lid on.

"Don't forget me, Goody," he said. "But don't think badly of me . . . you know, for that . . ." he gestured with his head at the bed. "That was just a foolish little weakness."

"I don't think badly of you, Frank."

Little smiled. "No, I don't think you would. Just a word of advice, Goody: get out of the detective business. It's no kind of work for a decent feller and I don't think you got a calling for it. Wal, good luck. Don't let the bastards grind you down."

I smiled and stepped into the hallway. Frank closed the door softly behind me. I stood in the narrow hallway for a moment.

Suddenly the door opened again and Frank stuck his head out, the spare cigarette cocked behind his ear. "Oh, Goody, you forgot this." He thrust the Marxist pamphlet at me. "Something to read on the train. Think of me when you read it." He smiled. "So long."

The door closed. I looked at the pamphlet, then stuck it in my pocket and walked away.

CHAPTER THIRTEEN

"I don't get it, kid. Yesterday you were all set to go and now you say you're out. This ain't very mature of you. A man gives his word and sticks to it."

"But you said I could tell you for sure tonight," I protested.

Davis waved a hand contemptuously, "Sure, sure. You acted like you didn't know what was going on and I wanted you to be sure in your mind. But I never thought you'd go back on your word! What was it? You talked to Little and he wound you around his little finger, or something? Or are you one of his fancy boys?" Davis leered.

I was mortified. But then I got angry. So Davis had known that Little was queer! "I'm not a fancy boy," I snapped back. "For Frank or anyone!"

Davis smiled. "Sure, kid. Sure. I believe you." He seemed to imply that not everyone would. His face darkened then. "But that don't change anything. The point is, I got to move fast and now you got a stick in my spokes. I was countin' on you. I figgered you for a guy with a little sand in him, not one a these. . ." he gestured at the people sitting outside our usual beaded-screen booth, ". . .frickin' Butte hicks."

Strangely, Davis's irritation calmed me. "For all I know," I said, "this is just a deal you cooked up. Hell, as far as that goes, some of Frank's enemies in the union might have put you up to it. I'm not saying it's so, but how would I know?

You keep me in the dark, yet you want me to carry a pretty heavy load. And I can't even check with the Old Man. Well, it don't wash, Davis. I say let's ask him. If the Old Man says 'Go ahead,' I'm in. If he doesn't, I'm out."

"It's after ten, for cry-eye's sake! That's after midnight, back East. I can't get ahold of him tonight!"

"Tomorrow, then."

"Tomorrow's too late," Davis said. "I got to know now."

"Well, that's it then," I said. I felt relieved.

Davis sat there, staring angrily at me. He snatched up the whiskey bottle and poured himself a drink, downing it in one gulp. He continued to glare at me.

"Do you know a McParland, by any chance?" I asked.

"McParland? The Denver Op? Why? What do you know about McParland?"

"Nothing. I just wondered if you knew him."

"I know of him," Davis said. "You ever meet him? No?" He stared at me thoughtfully, drumming his fingers on the table. At last, he shrugged and said, "How about this? You know I can't get a word from the Old Man tonight, but how about if one of the higher-ups from the Comp'ny agrees to talk to you? He could explain things, maybe. Lord knows I've tried." He sounded aggrieved. "That do you? I can't do more than that."

I listened glumly. This sounded like a trap, just when I'd thought I was out of the woods. If Davis could get someone from the Company to vouch for him it would be hard to back out. Davis was grasping for straws, but at least this would bring the Company out in the open. If some responsible person approved the venture it didn't leave me out on a limb. Not all by myself, anyway. "All right," I said. "I guess that'd be all right. Though I don't know what he could say."

Davis smiled comfortingly. "You're smarter than I thought, kid. I don't blame you for being careful. I should of let you in more, but most of these birds I have to deal with," he waved his hand dismissively again, "if brains was leather they couldn't saddle an ant. Have a drink. I'll be right back."

He was gone for at least ten minutes. I had a couple of drinks but they didn't make me feel any better. I wished to hell I'd never heard of the detective business.

When Davis returned I could tell by his cheerful manner that he had worked something out. "Okay, kid," he said. "They didn't like it, but they'll meet." Davis took out a pocket watch. "We got a few minutes. Have a drink."

He poured us both drinks and after he tossed his back, he said, "You know, you kinda graveled me, but now I see you were smart. A man can't stick his neck out without he knows for sure just who he's dealing with. But this way you'll see you're dealing with people you can depend on, people who are somebody in the world."

A half-hour later, we walked up the hill along dark streets for ten minutes. I figured we must be near the Anselmo mine, which I'd passed on my walk with Frank. Davis stopped and we waited by a wooden fence. Shortly, a large saloon car ground up the hill and stopped before us. Davis opened the rear door.

A mild voice from the interior said, "You get up front, Mr. Davis. The young man can join me."

We got in and the car bounced along the rutted dirt street. "Good evening, Mr. Ryder. How do you do?" the man in the seat said, a soft burr lingering on my name. I could not see him clearly in the darkness, but he had a warm, confident handshake. Nothing more was said for the time being. We drove away from the houses and mines and took a road that led around the big, pyramidal hill known as Big Butte. On

159

the other side, we drove for some minutes into black country-side until, finally, we stopped on the empty road. A distant, yellow light gleamed. A kerosene lamp in a lonely ranch house, perhaps.

Nobody got out. There was a glass between the back seat and where the chauffeur and Davis sat. The man offered me a cigar, which I declined. The man lit it up himself and by the light of the match I saw a middle-aged fellow wearing gold-rimmed glasses, a homburg hat. He had a pleasant, clean-shaven face, like a banker, or a lawyer. He looked like the kind of man who probably had daughters in a fancy finishing school; a man who served as a deacon in his church.

"They tell me you're a very fine young man, Goodwin," the man said, drawing on the cigar. "I have no doubt of it. I'm sure you're wondering who I am, but you'll have to appreciate that, under the circumstances, it's as well that I don't formally introduce myself. Suffice it to say, Goodwin, that I represent the Company in a very influential way and that I have full authority to deal with this, ah, unusual situation. Are you satisfied that this is so?"

I considered for a moment, then said, "With no disrespect to you, sir, but I feel like I'm the one in the unusual position. You know who I am, all right, but I don't know you from the King of England. Why couldn't we meet in your office?"

The man chuckled. "You're as smart as I was told. And you've got spirit, too! Good. I'm no friend of the English king, Goodwin." He chuckled. "We could meet in my office, but the hour is late and I understood there was some urgency. At any rate, it's not important to your mission. I've come straight from my home, you understand. I'm not trying to trick you, Goodwin. I'm here to help you and Mr. Davis, not hinder you. I'm not, for instance, the District Attorney, if that's what you're worried about."

160

The idea had not entered my mind. But now that it had, I was alarmed.

"The District Attorney is not chauffeured in a Packard, Goodwin. But if that doesn't convince you, perhaps this will. Would you strike a match, please?"

I did as I was asked and watched as the man picked up a satchel from the floor, opened it, and took out several packets of new bank notes. The match went out. I struck another. The bills appeared to be in denominations of tens and twenties, amounting to several thousand dollars. I couldn't be sure. I had never seen so much money in my life. It looked like a lifetime's wages.

I glanced up at the man, the matchlight glittering on his glasses. He smiled and drew on his cigar. It was a very large cigar. The match went out and the man spoke in the darkness. "This is no proof, admittedly, but you'll have to concede that few people in Butte, unconnected with the Company, could put their hands to this much cash on short notice. It will have to suffice for my bona fides."

I had no idea what bona fides were, but I was convinced that the man was a Company man. With the image of all those dollars—"Spondulicks!" I thought—still dancing in my eyes, I completely forgot any questions I should have asked.

"This money is yours, Goodwin, or at least a significant portion of it. I don't know what your arrangements with Mr. Davis are, but you can have your share right now, if you like. All I require is your assurance that you will undertake the mission that Mr. Davis has outlined to you. Mr. Davis tells me that he needs you especially, that you are uniquely competent to carry it out. Are you, Goodwin?"

"I don't know about that, sir. I guess so."

"Fine. Mr. Davis informs me that you are an honest, decent and trustworthy young man, that you are reliable and under-

161

stand the urgency and necessity of this otherwise regrettable action. I trust Mr. Davis's judgement and from what I have seen of you, I feel that you are our man. Are you our man, Goodwin?"

All of this was delivered in a calm, matter of fact tone. It was logical and reasonable, reassuring and even comforting. It made me feel in some way beholden. The cigar end glowed in the dark interior of the limousine. It was very still. The man waited for me to answer, but all I could do was cough. The man opened a window slightly, to let out the smoke.

I thought I could hear a coyote yapping in the distance. My throat was dry and I couldn't speak.

At last, the man said, impatiently, "Well?"

"I, uh, I don't know, sir. I'm not sure," I rasped.

The man drew on the cigar. At last he said, gently, "I can understand that, Goodwin. The enterprise is of some moment, for all of us. Goodwin, do you appreciate the kind of man we're dealing with, this Little? He attacks the very fabric of our society. He attacks our flag, our public servants, our traditions and our democratic ideals. He . . . Goodwin, are you a Christian man?"

I hardly knew what to say. "Why, sure, of course," I managed. "As much as most, I guess." I was very conscious of the fact that I hadn't been to church in several years, not since my mother had died. I wondered, fleetingly, how much this man knew about me. Surely, he couldn't know about that, although he seemed as omniscient as the principal of my old high school.

"I see," the man said, as if he did, indeed, see everything in my sinful mind. I almost panicked, wondering if the man could know about Sheila. It wasn't likely, I decided.

"Frank Little," the man said, "is not a Christian man, Goodwin. Frank Little is an atheist." The word was hissed, as if it could not be spoken outright in polite society. "Frank Little doesn't believe in anything, not even God the Father, or Jesus Christ Our Savior."

"Sir," I managed to speak up, "Joe and I have been through all that, about Frank."

"Good, good," the man said, almost heartily. The silence descended again. It became a straining influence. I listened for the coyote, but couldn't hear it. When the man spoke again it was in a more casual, man of the world manner.

"You might look upon it as just a job, Goodwin. A job we're asking you to do and for which we're willing to pay very well. Not a pleasant job, admittedly, but a necessary job. It's a job that demands a special kind of man, a tough man. They tell me that there are plenty of tough men in Butte, men who would do this job for nothing. Butte men have courage, I know. But many of these men are careless men, men of no great integrity, willing to take the wages and perhaps botch the job. Or it may be that they'd get drunk and boast, later, which would not do. You aren't a drunkard, are you, Goodwin?"

"No sir! Oh, I don't mind a drink now and then . . ."

"Fine, fine. Yes, what is needed is a special kind of man. A soldier, one might say."

"A soldier, sir?"

"Why yes," the man said, detecting my interest. "Are you a patriot, Goodwin?"

"Why, sure! Of course, sir!"

"Of course! And you've heard of Nathan Hale, I'm sure."

"Oh, yes. We had him in school."

"Nathan Hale gave his life for his country, Goodwin. I have seen a memorial to that great patriot at Yale College. Do you know what it says?"

I seemed to remember something about giving one life, but I knew I wouldn't get it right, so I said, "No sir."

"It says, 'I wish to be useful.' Those are the words of a great man, Goodwin. We're not asking you for Nathan Hale's kind of sacrifice. Indeed, we are willing to reward you handsomely. But we are asking you to be a patriot, a soldier; a soldier of justice and decency. A sergeant of virtue, one might say."

He seemed to like this phrase and lingered over it. "A sergeant of virtue is the kind of chap who, when he's asked to take on a special mission, simply goes out and does it. He gets paid, and well, but what is uppermost in the sergeant's mind is the proper completion of his mission. The glory and the rewards are for later. His chief reward is the incomparable satisfaction of having completed his mission, however difficult or unappealing. That's the kind of man I'm looking for, Goodwin. A sergeant of virtue." He relished the phrase, his tongue lingering on the "r's" of sergeant and virtue.

"There are damned few sergeants of virtue around," the man said regretfully. "Please excuse my language. But I suspect that you are just such a man. Am I right, Goodwin?"

I wanted nothing more than to declare a strong, unequivocal, "Yes, sir!", to this exhortation, but to my dismay I found that I could not. Miserably, I could only utter, "I . . . I'd like to think it over, sir."

"Goodwin! The hour is late! Remember Nathan Hale! 'I wish to be useful.'" He whispered the last words, almost reverently and they hung in the air of the closed car.

"I know, I know, but. . . . " I couldn't quite see what Nathan Hale had to do with running Frank Little out of Butte.

"Goodwin, we are asking you to help save your country from this scourge, this present danger. What the Republic needs now is strong, forceful and immediate action, in an

164

hour of growing peril. I must know now if you intend to aid your country."

I was overwhelmed. "My God, sir! Of course, I want to help my country, but . . .."

"Goodwin, Goodwin . . . you are a fortunate young man. Very few of us are pressed to the front of our nation's battles. Very few are given the opportunity to strike a blow for freedom and democracy. What a grand opportunity!"

My mind reeled. I was, after all, just a kid from the slums of Pittsburgh, tossed up here in Montana, a pawn in an enormous industrial struggle. With one part of my mind I began to see myself as a hero, a man of potential greatness, with greater to come. But another part of my mind, the wariness of a Pittsburgh street kid, I guess, held me back.

The man tried to give me an inspirational nudge. "There is a tide in the affairs of man, Goodwin, which if taken at the ebb. . . . " The man stumbled. "Er, I mean at the flood. . . . " And then he didn't seem able to remember the rest of it.

I listened, puzzled at first, then tried not to grin while the man lamely finished, saying, "What it means is that a man must strike while the iron is hot. This is such a moment. What is it to be?"

Well, this is it, I thought. In or out. It would be a relief to just say yes and get on with it, but somehow I couldn't do it. For one thing, I couldn't help wondering why I was so important to this deal. For another, all this heavy pressure was getting on my nerves. I felt like telling this fancy joker to go to hell, but I have to admit I was scared of the consequences. What the hell, I was sitting in a car out in the middle of nowhere, in the pitch dark, with guys I didn't know anything about and couldn't really trust. One of them for sure was carrying a gun.

"I know what you're saying, sir," I finally blurted out, "but would it be okay if I slept on it? I could tell you for sure, yes or no, in the morning. I promise."

The silence was very long this time. The cigar end glowed on and off. The men in front shifted their positions, causing the car to rock gently. No further comment from the coyote, though. Finally, the man leaned forward and rapped on the glass partition.

"Take us back," the man said, coldly.

Not a word was spoken on the return. The car stopped where it had picked us up and Davis got out and opened the door. The man sat coldly, not speaking even when I said, "Good night, sir."

Davis told me to go off a ways and wait while he talked to the man. I stood in the darkness, smoking a cigarette, occasionally glancing back. I got the impression that Davis was hot, but I couldn't be sure. Voices were raised, but I couldn't make out what was said. At last, Davis closed the door of the car and it drove away.

Davis set off toward the lights of the district, not speaking. I hurried after him.

"Joe," I said, "what'd he say? I didn't know what to say, Joe. He kept talking about Nathan Hale."

Davis stopped. "Who?"

"Nathan Hale," I said, puffing to a halt. "You know, the patriot."

"I know who Nathan Hale is. You think I don't know who Nathan Hale is? Jeeziss!" He looked back up the hill and shook his head.

"I just couldn't tell him, yes or no," I said.

Davis strode on again until we reached the edge of the street-lights. He stopped and pulled a packet of bills out of his coat pocket. He counted out $500 and thrust it into my hand.

"That's for nothing," Davis said. "It's yours. Maybe it'll help you think. I'm moving on Little t'marra. If you decide you want in, you can get me at the Finlen Hotel. If not, you oughta be on the train to Spokane. And kid . . . don't get any dumb ideas about going to the cops. The cops are in here." He thrust the rest of the money back into his pocket and patted it emphatically.

"Joe. Joe? Who was that guy?"

"Till you make up your mind," Davis said, walking rapidly away, "you don't need to know."

CHAPTER FOURTEEN

"Hey, what's dis? Yiz leavin' awreddy?" Dewey looked up from his stirabout. I was dressed in suit and tie, carrying a bag.

I nodded. "The jernt is perzin. I'm gonna jern the Army."

Dewey laughed. "Butte is perzin, but it ain't dat bad. Which way yiz headed? Maybe I'll jern up wid yiz. Wait up, I gotta buy yiz a beer."

Dewey wolfed down the rest of the stirabout and we walked uptown to the M&M. Several guys came round to shake my hand and agree with me that, the way things were going, it was a good idea to join up. Many Butte men had already been drafted and expected to leave within thirty days. It was a grand thing. Dewey bought me a beer and accepted two or three in return, before slipping away, presumably to discuss Zack Wheat's batting average with a "Gi'nts" fan.

I was actually out the door when I bumped into Sean Paton.

"What's this?" Sean said, alarmed to see my suitcase. "Doc, you can't leave, now."

I explained that I'd gotten fed up with all the union fuss and that I was off to the Army. I couldn't afford to wait it out.

"Jeez, and I ain't got that sawbuck you lent me," Sean said. "If ya just stuck around for a week, maybe we'd get back ta work. Or I could borry it off one a the guys. . . . "

"Nah, forget it," I said. "I'll bump into you one of these days and you'll buy me dinner."

"Jeez, yer a pal. I'm gonna miss ya, Doc. Say, did ya hear about Frank?"

My blood chilled. "No. What?"

"He broke his fool leg! How about that? The dern idjit jumped off a trolley and landed wrong, er sump'n. Anyways, he's laid up fer a week, er so. I jist seen Al Wuuri an' he told me. Frank was restin', Al said, an' din't wanta see nobody. But I bet he'd be glad to see ya, if yer leavin'."

I couldn't believe it. "He broke his leg?"

"Or his foot. I dunno which. Al sez it's in a cast."

"What about the union meeting?"

"I dunno. I guess Frank'll be there, if they gotta carry him in. Say, the old lady's gonna be sore if you slip away without saying goodbye. Why doncha run by there on the way? It ain't far outta yer way."

I looked around. There was a clock on an ornate post halfway up the block, on Park Street, in front of Young's Jewelry, but merchants had already lowered their awnings against the glare of the sun and I couldn't quite make out the time.

"I gotta run, Sean. I'll miss the train."

"The Milwaukee? Don't worry about it, Doc. Ya got lots of time. The old lady'll kill me if ya don't stop by. Besides, ya promised me y'd give her a little chat, about married life. Ja fergit that?"

"No, I didn't forget. But you said everything was fine, now." I'd thought of Sheila the first thing, on awaking, but I'd told myself that it was no good. The fact was, I was afraid of her. If I went to see her there was no telling what might happen. She might insist on going with me and there was no time to argue about that. She couldn't go. It was absurd. She had a

170

husband, whom she cared about, I knew, as much as it appalled me. And she had four kids. It wasn't in the cards.

"I'll go down and get my ticket," I waffled, "and if it looks like I got the time, I'll run by there."

"Say, that'd be swell. Uh, you wouldn't have time for a beer, wouldja?"

"No, I don't. But, I'll tell you what . . ." I set down my bag and pulled out a bill from my pocket—as luck would have it, a fresh twenty. I sighed and pressed it on Sean. "Here, have one on me and buy a round for the boys. You can pay me back some time."

Sean was too astonished to say anything until I was across the street. "Doc!" he yelled, "I'll get it back to ya! I promise! Drop me a line! I'll wire it!"

I waved and began to half-run down the hill. I was in plenty of time. An agent told me the train had just cleared Homestake, up on the pass. It wouldn't be in Butte for twenty minutes and then it would probably stand for at least ten, though the agent said it wouldn't stay long because it was behind schedule.

I walked away and slumped onto a bench on the platform in relief. I was glad to be leaving. I felt bad about running out on Sheila, but that was balanced by the relief I felt concerning Frank. A broken foot! A good break if there ever was one, I told myself, and almost laughed out loud. I wondered if Davis had done it. It didn't sound like it. Still, you never know. If so, well, a broken foot wasn't a bad deal compared to what I'd imagined. Whew! What a lot of soul-searching and brain-busting over nothing! And the best part was, I wasn't involved. I was free! Now I did laugh.

"What's the joke, kid?" Davis asked, looking down at me.

The laugh died in my throat. "Oh. Hullo," I said. But then I smiled. "No joke," I said, "it's just funny how things work out."

Davis frowned and kicked my bag, lightly. "Taking off, kid?"

I looked around. We were alone on this portion of the platform. "Just following orders," I said.

"I thought you were gonna stop by the Finlen."

"That wasn't what you said," I reminded him. "You said, If I changed my mind. I haven't. Anyway, you don't need my help now."

Davis frowned. "Whatta you talkin' about?"

"Frank's busted leg."

"Little's got a broken leg?" Davis swore. "So that's what that bird was jabberin' about! Where'd you hear this?"

I told him. "You didn't do it?" I asked.

"I'd like to bust his frickin' neck," Davis said, "but I didn't know anything about it. A trolley, you said?" Davis looked thoughtful.

"Listen, kid," he said, at last, "this changes everything. I gotta check it out. You better get yer ticket changed for t'marra and come up to my room in the Finlen. Make it in an hour. I gotta talk to some people."

"But, what for?" I hated the whine in my voice, but I couldn't help it. "Frank's laid up. You got what you wanted and without any trouble."

"You must be kiddin'. Little has put out the word he's got a broken leg, but does he really? Anyways, even if he does, that won't stop him from nothin'. I can just see the bastid stumpin' along on a crutch and rallyin' the troops. Hell, they'll be carryin' him on their frickin' shoulders!"

"Well, I'm out," I said, stubbornly.

"No, you ain't out," Davis said, menacingly. "Do I have to remind you about the cops? Think they can't hold you for vagrancy, or something? Anyways, I have to wire the Old Man and let him in on this. He'll want to know what you're doing. If you want, I can tell him you want out."

"All right, all right," I sighed. "I'll put it over until tomorrow. But ask the Old Man if he has any special instructions for me."

I put the best face on it that I could. I reckoned that nothing had really changed, except the date of my departure. Frank was lying low. He had been through this before. He'd lie low, then get up and fight again, just when they thought he was out of the way. But I'd be gone.

I heard the whistle of the Milwaukee's "Hiawatha", approaching the station. I hurried in and changed my ticket. I considered going to see Sheila, but decided against it. Maybe later, after I talked to Davis and heard what the Old Man had to say. I went out and watched the enormous steam engine puff into the station. It was impressive and I was reminded of Joe Davis' taunt: "Do you know how to run a railroad?"

There was no doubt about it. As competent as the engineer and the fireman and the brakemen looked, it was clearly an enormous enterprise to get something like this built and operating. Certainly beyond the capability of these mere workers. They were just cogs in the machinery, despite what Frank would say.

The Finlen Hotel was very fine and Joe Davis had a room on the fifth floor, overlooking Broadway. He welcomed me in and offered Guckenheimer's Rye. I told him I couldn't bear rye and he promptly sent out for a bottle of Old Taylor. I sat in an easy chair and couldn't help contrasting this interview with the one in Frank Little's room.

"It looks like Little's broken leg is the genuine goods," Davis said. "They say he jumped down off a Broadway trolley and either broke his ankle or sprained it so bad it's the same thing.

173

He'll probably be laid up for at least a coupla weeks . . . they say. But don't bet all yer simoleons on that nag."

"Did you wire the Old Man?" I said.

"Yeah, and got an answer straight back. He's leavin' the situation up to me, as usual."

"What did he say about me?"

"Hunh? Oh. You're supposed to stick around. Listen, I gotta think this through. Help yourself to the booze, but don't make a pest of yourself, okay?"

For the next couple of hours, I sat and watched while Davis alternately sat in a chair by the window, gazing out at the mines up the hill or jumped to his feet to pace back and forth, frowning, muttering, puffing on a cigar, relighting it. I smoked cigarette after cigarette, occasionally drinking some whiskey with a water chaser. It was getting dark. I was about to give up and go out to eat, when Davis stopped his pacing and pronounced himself satisfied that he had a plan.

"Swell," I said. "What is it?"

"It's just as good as my original plan, except it's a little more risky. Not much, but some. Well," he shrugged, "can't be helped. You see, I kept thinking, how was I gonna get Little to come out? He's gotta come out t'marra for the vote, and all, but he'll be surrounded with his gang. The rest of the time, he'll stay in the boarding house and if his guys need to talk to him, they'll go to him. It's a tough nut to crack. He couldn't be better off if he'd planned it."

Davis paused for a second, as if struck by a new thought, but he shrugged it off and went on. "Anyway, it finally came to me."

I looked at him expectantly. Davis savored the suspense for a few seconds, then blurted out: "We go to him!"

"We go to him? That's a plan? That's nuts," I said.

"Listen to me. His guys are going to him. Right? That's what give me the idea. The old lady in the boarding house is used to guys tramping in and out all hours a the night. We'll go to see him, only it'll be late. Very late. Say three in the ayem. We walk in, knock on the door, and take him! What's to stop us?"

"But he's got a broken leg! He won't want to go out!"

"He won't want to, sure, but he's gonna."

My spirits slumped. But then I saw a sliver of daylight for me in this plan. "And what if he's got a bunch of his guys hanging around Mrs. Byrne's?"

"That'd be bad," Davis conceded. "But I bet he won't."

"Well, you won't be needing me," I said. "If you're just gonna snatch him, where do I fit in?"

"Oh, don't worry," Davis said, evidently thinking that I was disappointed not to find a role for myself in this fabulous scheme, "you're the key to it all. You've been there and besides, Little'll think you're coming by to see him. If his pals are there you can get the lay of the land. If there's too many and they're armed, we'll have to come up with something else."

"Why on earth would I go to see him at three in the morning?" I said. "Kind of late for visiting a sick friend, isn't it?"

"You can go over about ten or eleven," Davis said. "I'll have someone watching the place. His friends'll probably leave by then, unless they're staying. That's what we need to know: is everyone out of the joint, or not? Is he really alone? That's where you come in."

"And what's my excuse? I'm visiting him at ten or eleven, when everybody else is gone home? It's silly. He'll be suspicious."

"Why else? You thought it over and decided he wasn't such a plug-ugly after all." Davis made an obscure gesture with his thumb at his pants seat that was obscene. He grinned lewdly. "You know, whatever guys like that do."

"Oh no," I said in horror, starting up.

"Now don't get your knickers in a tangle," Davis said, placatingly. "I know you ain't that way, but guys like Frank . . . well, hope springs eternal for them sods. They can't get enough of it. I seen a lot of them, in prisons and such. They're like hooers, they can't stay away from it."

"No," I said firmly. "That's it, and that's final." I picked up my cap and put it on.

Davis looked at me as if amazed. "Now what the hell is this? You afraid? Or maybe you *are* one a them. You and Frank. You can't bear to see your precious Frank get hurt?" His voice took on a nasty, sissy intonation.

"You're a goddamn lunatic," I said, as calmly as I could. I was seething. "I'm sending a wire to the Old Man. This is going on the report."

"Hey, calm down, calm down," Davis said. He grasped me by the elbow, but I shook him off. "Hey! I was just needling you! Trying to get your goat. And I got it!" He laughed. "No kidding, kid, it was just a joke. Calm down. Here, have a drink." He held out my glass and poured bourbon in it.

I took the glass and sipped. It calmed me.

"You're right, a course," Davis said. "I never meant that at all. It's a loony idear. Just a little joke. Say, do you know how to drive?"

"As a matter of fact, I do," I said, proudly.

"Well, that's it, then! You can drive the car," Davis said.

"What car?"

"Why, the car that we'll use to drive Little down the road a ways and kick him in the butt. You won't even have to go in the joint. We'll bring him out. And you can wear a mask. We'll all be wearing masks. But I can't drive and neither can none of the other guys."

"And what if he's got friends in there with him? What about that?"

"I'll deal with that," Davis said. "If he's got some muscle, then we just go away quietly and that's that. No need for you to go in at all. You're right, it'd be nuts to send you over there ahead of time. It'd put him on his guard."

I grasped at this straw. Maybe Frank would be wise enough to keep some of his cohort around him, the night before the union vote. But if not. . . . "That's it?" I said. "You're not gonna hurt him?"

"Tar and feathers ain't no picnic," Davis said, "but the only thing it'll hurt is his pride. See, we tie him to a telegraph pole by the road, where they'll find him in the morning. Everybody'll see him. He'll look like a frickin' tar baby," he crowed. "He'll be such a laughing stock all he'll want is to hightail it for the boondocks and nurse his pride."

"That's all there is to it? You swear?"

"Aw, maybe we'll stick a vigilante sign on him. You know, the ol' '3-7-77' I told you about. You don't even have to go in when we roust him out. Somebody has to keep the car running. Little'll never know you're along, and in the morning you'll be on your way to Spokaloo. Whatta you think?"

We discussed it and argued for another hour, but at last I gave in. "I'll drive the car," I said, "but nothing else. No rough stuff."

I told myself that I was doing it for Frank. If I was along, I figured, I could head off any real rough stuff. It was a dumb plan, and I figured there was a good chance it'd never come off. Even if Frank were alone, Mrs. Byrne might not let Davis and his bully boys in, for instance. But if it did go as Davis

177

hoped, it would be better for Frank if I was there to see that things didn't get out of hand.

"You hold up here," Davis said. "Your buddies think you're gone, anyway, so it's best to stay put. I'll order up some grub, then I have to go out and round up the lads and arrange for the car. I'll be back after midnight, probably."

I hid in the fancy bath when the boy brought up the food, then Davis left. For the rest of the evening I lay around, smoking cigarettes and trying not to think. At one point I tried to read the Marxist pamphlet Frank had given me, but it was impossible. I gave it up and turned my attention to the whiskey. When Davis returned after midnight the bottle was more than half empty.

"Jeeziss, kid! You're not drunk?" Davis said, alarmed.

I was drunk, but mobile. Davis got me into the shower and when I came out there was a fresh pot of hot coffee and some sandwiches. I wolfed them down hungrily. I wasn't sober, but I had a grip on it.

"Damn, kid, that wasn't smart," Davis scolded. "You coulda messed the whole thing up. I got the boys all set. We'll meet them in a hour or two. Come on, I want you to see the car and drive it around."

We slipped out the back way. The car was parked on a side street, over toward Finntown. It was a large, open vehicle, a Reo touring car. I got it started and we drove up toward Walkerville. We returned on Excelsior, then went over to Wyoming, past Mrs. Byrne's boarding house and down to the Milwaukee Road trestle on the edge of town. That would be the route, Davis explained. After that, we returned to park a couple of blocks from the Finlen. There we waited for another hour and Davis produced the remnants of the bottle of Old Taylor.

"It's better if you got a little jag on, instead of just being hung over," Davis explained. "You won't be so nervous." A couple of drinks made me feel much better, a curious mixture of recklessness and passivity. Whatever happened was going to happen, I told myself. Just go along. Let Joe do the worrying.

"Well, it's about time," Joe said, presently, checking his pocket watch. He explained that the men would meet us outside Mrs. Byrne's rooming house on Wyoming Street precisely at three o'clock. If the coast looked clear, Davis and the men would enter the house, bring Little out, and I would drive them all down to the trestle. Davis had stashed tar and feathers down there, he said.

"How will we all fit in the car?" I asked.

"It's a big car," Davis said. "It won't be as crowded as you think. If they have to, the guys can stand on the running boards."

Davis and I walked to where the car was parked. We shared a jolt of whiskey, then started the car. I drove to Wyoming Street. There was no sign of the men. Davis drew his pistol and got out.

"Joe! You're not going to use it?" I said.

"Just to keep any nosy parkers out of the way," Davis assured me.

Five men appeared out of the darkness. They wore black party masks, the Lone Ranger kind. They were clowning and joshing one another, roughhousing. They were drunk, or close to it. One of them said that several men had left before midnight and no one had come in or gone out since.

"Joe! My mask!" I called out.

"Hunh? Oh forget the mask, kid, nobody'll see ya." He turned on the men, snarling, "Cut it out, you birds. This ain't no frickin' party."

179

"Oh yeah?" one of them retorted. The others guffawed as they followed Davis up to the building. It was more like an apartment building than a house. A light was on and the door was unlocked. Davis and the men simply walked in. I heard some voices and some pounding. I sat in the car sweating, my reckless mood gone. If only some of Frank's friends were still there, I hoped, but it didn't sound like it.

Suddenly, one of Davis'es thugs came to the door and called my name, quite loud. "Hey, Ryder! They want you. Inside."

I was dumbfounded.

"What does he want?" I tried to whisper.

"Can't find the room," the man said loudly.

"But I don't have a mask," I said.

"C'mon, fer chrissakes," the man said. "We ain't got all night!"

"Good lord," I said. I set the idle and went in the house. The men milled about the hallway like cattle. Davis was fuming.

"Where the hell is he?" he demanded.

They were standing right by Frank's door. I pointed to it.

"Jeeziss! All right. You go keep an eye on the old bitch," Davis said. "See she doesn't try anything."

I went to Mrs. Byrne's room. She had evidently dragged a bed across the door, but a couple of the men forced it aside. I went in and stood by her. She was a frightened woman, wearing a housecoat and slippers. She looked to be about forty.

"What do you men want?" she asked me, fearfully. "That other fellow said you were police."

I nodded without saying anything. I could hear the men battering down Frank's door.

"They're damaging my property," Mrs. Byrne complained. I hushed her. "Why are they wearing masks, if you're police?"

"Is there anybody else in there?" I asked her. She shook her head. She fell silent.

Shortly, the men clattered out half-carrying and dragging Frank Little, still in his threadbare underwear and wearing a cast on his leg.

"He doesn't even have his crutches!" Mrs. Byrne said.

"Shut up!" Davis snarled, brandishing his huge automatic pistol. He pulled me out of the room and closed the door violently. "Get in the car," he told me.

I ran out past the men and got in the driver's seat.

Davis pushed Little into the back seat and jumped in beside him, along with another man.

"Let's go!" he shouted. The others jumped on the running boards or piled into the front seat. I let out the clutch. Frank did not utter a word. In the darkness and turmoil I hadn't been able to tell if he was injured or not.

I drove the car down past Park Street and over to Silver Street until suddenly, one of the men yelled, "Stop the car!"

Thinking one of the men had fallen off, I pulled on the brake and the big car lurched to a halt, the engine nearly stalling. I nursed the engine back to a roar.

"What's the matter?" I yelled.

Nobody paid any attention to me. They dragged Little out of the car and one of them produced a rope. They tied one end around Little's wrists and the other end to the rear bumper of the car.

"Let's go!" they yelled, piling back into the car and onto the running boards.

"You can't," I protested. "He'll be killed."

A gun barrel pressed against the back of my neck. My hair rose. Davis said, "Drive, Goodwin."

I released the clutch and we moved off slowly, with Frank hopelessly hobbling along behind.

"Faster!" Davis snarled.

I sped up. I did not look back, but I felt a jar as Frank fell and then began to drag. I slowed down but the gun jabbed painfully against my skull and I advanced the throttle. But after a hundred feet I could no longer go on. I pulled to the side and stopped.

Davis jabbed again, but I turned and looked at him. "I can't go on, Joe. You'll have to drive."

Davis gave me a long, hard look, then said, "All right, fellers, get him back in the car."

They hauled Frank into the back seat. I could see he was bleeding from awful scrapes, his underclothes in shreds and the cast dangling. He looked dazed, his already bruised face scratched and bleeding. He tried to suppress his groans, gritting his teeth. He slumped between Davis and another man.

I drove quickly to the railroad trestle. When we got there, I got out of the car and walked off to one side. I stood in the darkness, away from the lights of the car. I felt choked, paralyzed.

The men pulled Little out and tied his hands behind his back. Then one of them produced a noose and slipped it over Frank's head. Frank sagged in the grip of two men who held him. He was in awful shape, bleeding and having trouble standing. His underclothes were no more than rags and he shivered in the chill mountain air. He could barely lift his head. I don't believe he could see me, standing outside the headlamps' glare.

The men were insane, laughing and yelling and punching Frank, or kicking him. They capered in the light of the car's big headlamps like maniacs. They all were armed with guns or knives, and one of them brandished a hatchet.

They seemed to have forgotten me, even Davis, who stood to one side, his gun hand hanging down, looking on in a calm, matter of fact way. Frank struggled erect as one of the men danced in, swinging a knife and exclaiming, "Let's make a steer out've 'im!" Frank lashed out with his broken foot and caught the man full in the crotch. The man howled with agony and doubled over.

The pain of the blow was felt by Frank as well and the effort made him slip. But the men bore him up. Now another, larger fellow shouldered in, waving a hatchet and crying, "Here, this'll fetch them oysters!"

"No!" I cried out and started forward. Something hard and heavy crunched my right ear against my skull. I pitched forward onto my face on the gritty wooden platform of the trestle approach. I shook my head to clear it and when I looked up, Frank stood above me, a few feet away, his head bowed. He seemed to frown, as if in thought.

But suddenly he lifted his head and opened his good eye. He looked at me, but I don't know if he recognized me. He seemed to be looking for someone else. Finally, he focussed on Joe and squinted, frowning. He said, "Is it you?"

Joe didn't answer.

A ghastly grin contorted Frank's face and he spewed out the words, "No. You're nobody. A minor devil. That's who they send." He laughed an awful, mocking laugh.

One of the men struck him, either with a fist or a club, I couldn't tell. Frank slumped down again. But then he made a final huge gasping breath and spoke, clearly, "You are dead."

Joe Davis turned away and gestured with his head over his shoulder. One of the men leapt forward and stabbed Frank with an enormous knife, a swooping upward thrust into the chest. That was all for Frank.

Now the others crowded in, swinging and slashing. There was nothing I could do, I saw. I edged backwards on my hands and knees, out of the light, then scrambled to my feet and began to run away. Within a dozen steps, however, I ran smack into another parked car, a huge black sedan. I bounced off and fell sideways onto gravel. Someone in the car yelled out, "You fools! Over here!"

"Stop him!" Davis yelled. "You stupid bastards! Get him! Don't let him get away!"

I scrambled to my feet and ran into the pitch blackness only to fall headlong, tumbling down the railroad grade, scratching and banging myself on the sharp stones of the ballast. I leaped to my feet and raced wildly away along the bottom of the grade, weeds whipping at my legs. I could hear shots behind me, but whether aimed at me or at Frank, I had no idea. And then I ran full tilt into a telegraph pole.

CHAPTER FIFTEEN

I was knocked out when I ran into the pole, I don't know how long. Maybe that saved me. I don't know. When I came to I crept away, hiding in the weeds, moving along the riptrack. There were a lot of boxcars there. At one point I heard the killers coming for me. Two of them walked by so close I could have touched them. One of them said you couldn't see a white cat in this dark and the other complained that they were missing out on all the fun—I guess he meant Frank . . . back on the trestle.

When they were gone I slipped from one string of boxcars to another and worked my way back toward an overpass. I came out on a dirt street that I realized ran up to the Cabbage Patch.

It was getting toward dawn by the time I got to Sheila's. A few dogs had barked at me, but I had seen no one. I knocked softly. There was no answer. I knocked louder, then louder.

Suddenly, the door opened and I fell inside. Sheila held a little kerosene lamp. She was dressed in a long, flannel nightgown. She recoiled in surprise, then peered at me.

"My Saints, it's Goody! You didn't leave!" She set the lamp on the parlor table and hugged me.

185

"You're hurt!" she cried. Three of the children were asleep on the floor, rolled into their blankets beyond the table. One of them lifted her red head and gazed at us stupidly.

"Hush!" her mother said. "Go back to sleep, Moira." The little girl obediently laid her head down.

Sheila led me back into the kitchen and held up the lamp again to inspect me. "Oh, my poor laddy, you're a bloody mess! Have you been drinking?" She sniffed and made a sour face. "Indeed you have. You rogue, you. But you've come back to me." She hugged me again.

"What the hell?" a voice mumbled. Sean leaned on the door jamb, his hair tousled, barefoot, wearing a saggy union suit. He rubbed his bleary eyes.

I cautiously drew apart from Sheila. "It's not what you think," I said. My voice was dry and rasping.

Sean shook his head to clear it. "Not what I think? What the hell should I think?" His eyes suddenly cleared. He gawked at his wife, then me. "You! So it was you!"

"No, no, you don't understand," I croaked. "Frank's dead. They've killed him."

"What?" Sean was completely at sea. Then his voice grew soft and wondering. "Frank? Dead? Who?"

"Blessed Saints," Sheila whispered, understanding everything at once. "And you tried to tell me . . .."

"Frank's dead?" Sean said again, his brow knitted in effort. "You saw him? Where?"

"At the trestle," I said. I turned to Sheila. "Have you got any whiskey?"

"You want whiskey, at this hour?" Then she understood. "Yes, of course." She pushed Sean before her, into the bedroom.

I stood teetering in the kitchen, looking about me foolishly, hearing their muffled voices in the bedroom. There was a coal-fired range behind me. It was still warm, against the chill of the mountain air. Through a shabbily curtained window I could see the daylight growing in the backyard.

Shortly, Sheila came out carrying a pint bottle. She handed it to me. I opened it and took a deep, satisfying draught of burning liquid down my throat. It tasted like cheap brandy. I took another, then Sheila took the bottle from my hand.

"Tell me what happened," she said, calmly.

"They murdered Frank," I said. "I didn't know they were going to do it. I thought they were just going to run him out of town." Somehow, my voice was calm.

"Were you there?"

I nodded. She looked at me grimly. I turned away from her gray eyes. Sean reappeared in the doorway, listening.

"Here," she said, pressing the bottle into her husband's hands. "Drink that."

Paton gulped down a prodigious quantity. He gasped and then said, "What's this, now? You saw Frank dead?"

"Yes," I said wearily. "No. I didn't actually see him dead. But he's dead. I'm sure of it."

"Who was it?" Paton demanded.

"Pull yourself up," Sheila commanded. "It was the spies. Goody, here, tried to stop them but he couldn't."

"You couldn't stop them?" Paton asked. "Why not?"

"I couldn't," I said.

"Why couldn't you!" Sean roared.

"Shush, you bloody fool," his wife said. "You'll wake the little ones." From the sound of stirring, they were already awake. "Goody couldn't stop them because they were too many. You can see they tried to kill him, as well."

Paton peered at my torn clothing. "They tried to kill you?" he said. Then he groaned and disappeared into the other room, saying, "They killed Frank! They killed our poor Frank. The bastards, the fuckin' bastards!"

Sheila hurried after him.

"They never let us have nothing!" Sean moaned. "The fuckin' bastards!"

Sheila's voice mumbled and Sean fell silent. The springs of the bed creaked. Presently, she came out, carrying the bottle. "Drink the rest," she said, "quickly."

I drank it down.

"Now, what's to be done?" she said, more to herself than to me. She stood in thought. Then she glanced at me and said, "We'll have to leave on the morning train."

"You're crazy," I said. "They'll be waiting for me. They'll have me arrested, and then, in jail, they'll murder me."

Sheila nodded. "Perhaps. But it's your only chance. They may do nothing, if you do nothing. Here, sit and eat." She pushed me into a chair at a tiny wooden table and stepped out onto the back vestibule. She returned immediately with a loaf of bread and a lump of ham. She sliced them and set them before me.

"Go ahead, eat."

I put the food in my mouth. It tasted good, to my surprise, and I gobbled the rest of it down.

In the meantime, Sheila fetched water and calmly began to make tea. When it was ready, she poured mugs of it for both of us, heavily sweetened. "That's nearly the last of the sugar," she said, resignedly. Then, "Ah well, we won't be needing it."

When I had drunk enough tea and recovered my senses a bit, I said, "This is crazy, Sheila. You can't get involved. I'm leaving." I got up.

"And where will you be going, in those clothes and your face such a bloody mess? Ah, your poor handsome face."

She got out a basin and began to bathe my face with soap and warm water from the kettle. I sat patiently, letting her play nurse.

"Now we must plan," she said, when she'd finished. "Do you have any money?"

I got out my wallet and showed her. I don't believe she had ever seen so much money. Her eyes grew wide, but she didn't say anything, then or later. She only nodded and began to lay out the plan. I protested almost every element of the plan, but to no avail. I was too tired, too confused, to seriously resist her. She went into the bedroom then and I sat miserably while muffled voices discussed and argued. At last she came out, carrying a rough woolen suit and a white shirt. She laid them on the table.

"Put these on," she said. "And you must shave off that silly mustache. I never liked it anyhow."

"You didn't?" I was surprised. I had thought that all women were crazy for mustaches.

She provided warm water and Sean's shaving gear. I sat before a mirror and shaved off the mustache that had taken weeks to grow. While I dressed she went into the bedroom and quickly returned in her usual skirt and blouse, with a shawl. She took my money and ran out the back way. She was back almost before I'd finished dressing. She handed me several train tickets.

Sheila bustled about, waking the children and preparing stirabout for them. I went into the parlor and lay down on one of the pallets. Sean did not stir out of the bedroom. I must have dozed off for awhile, because it was mid-morning before I became aware that the children were quite excited. They were dressed in their church clothes, a dress for little Moira and clean trousers and white shirts for the two boys. They were talking about taking a trip.

I could hear Sheila and Sean talking in the bedroom. Shortly she came out, dressed in the clothes I had bought for her, for the trip to the Hot Springs. She looked quite fine in the dark green dress. Her hair was up and she wore a hat that she'd put together from unknown sources, with a low crown and a wide brim, flowers around the crown, together with a long pheasant feather and even a bit of a veil. It was amazingly attractive, but then I was annoyed with myself for even noticing it.

She looked the children over. I got up stiffly, aching in every joint. Sheila turned back to the bedroom.

"Sean, lad," she called softly, "we're going now. You'd better come out and speak to the children."

There was a muffled reply, then Paton came out in an undershirt and trousers. His face was puffy and his reddish-blond beard was rough; he looked ten years older. He passed me without a word or even a glance. He went into the front room and knelt down before the three oldest kids, drawing them all into his arms.

"Ain't you coming too, Pa?" the oldest, nine-years old Moira, said.

"No, honey," Sean said. "You ain't going away forever, you know. Just a visit."

"Who are we visitin', Pa?" one of the boys asked.

"Some a yer Ma's folks," Paton said. He hugged them all separately then and kissed them. "You kids are lucky ducks!" he said. "You'll ride on the train and have a grand time and then come back and tell yer Papa Sean-O all about it."

"We will, Pa!" they said, eager to be off.

Paton stood up then as Sheila entered, carrying the youngest, a boy of two. Paton took the child from her and carried him back into the bedroom. Sheila was taken by surprise. She stared at me, then went into the room.

"Sean, what do ye think ye're doing, ye daft man?"

"Yer not taking him," Sean said, from the dark interior of the room. "Get off with yer fancy man and the others, but he stays. He's mine!"

Sheila came to the door and looked at me as if for help. What could I say? I shrugged. She bit her lip. She started to say something, then turned back to the room. "You take good care of him, Sean," she said, her voice choking. "I'll be back."

"I know," he said.

She came out then, carrying an old leather-bound suitcase, which she handed to me. On my head she placed Sean's old derby hat, which fit very nicely.

"Ain't Seanie coming, Ma?" the kids asked.

"Not . . . not presently," Sheila said.

"Seanie don't git to go!" the littlest boy crowed.

"Come," said the mother.

We marched out of the Cabbage Patch as boldly as soldiers, nodding to neighbors but not stopping to chat. The neighbors were out in great numbers, obviously excited about the news of Little's murder. They were concerned about what would happen next, it seemed, and they hardly noticed us except to call out and wave, only a few asking "Where to?"

"On holiday!" replied Sheila, gaily. "Visiting friends!" We simply walked away, down toward the station, Sheila and her kids with me at her side, the brim of the derby hat pulled low on my brow. The kids could see the train approaching the station as we descended the hill and they became wildly excited. They pleaded with their mother and me to hurry, but we ignored them. At least, Sheila did. For my part, I was as anxious to be on the train as the kids were.

"We'll be left! We'll be left!" they exclaimed.

"Oh no," their mother assured them, "they shan't leave without us. We have the tickets."

With excellent timing we strolled into the station, paraded the length of the platform and stepped up into a Pullman car. I noticed several men who, although I didn't recognize them, I knew had to be detectives, but I didn't look at them and they ignored us. A porter assisted us into the car. A negro in a white jacket showed us our seats, then advised us that breakfast was still being served in the dining car.

We traipsed through the cars to the dining car, with its white napkins, heavy silver and a single rose in a vase at each table.

I sat among the children, who seemed quite indifferent to me, just as if I were a real father. I gazed out the window at the people on the platform. There was no sign of Davis or any of the men of the night's heavy work, but there were unmistakable lawmen loitering about, their eyes sharp for any tall, young man with a mustache.

The train sat there. And sat there. The damn thing would not move. I got more and more nervous. Obviously, they weren't going to let it depart until they found the fugitive that Davis had tipped them about. Any minute now a party of officers would enter the dining car, thoroughly checking every passenger. I thought it might be a good idea to go to the toilet, but as in a nightmare, I couldn't budge.

At long last the whistle sounded, the conductor yelled, "All abooooooard!" and the train gave a lurch, then the station began to slide backwards in a billow of steam. A waiter came with menus.

The train rolled out of Butte, trundling slowly among the standing freight cars, sliding across sidings where barriers stopped a trolley and a rare automobile, or a horse-drawn wagon loaded with fresh vegetables, enroute to the neighborhoods. People waved at the train and the children waved back.

At the edge of town the train slowed as it approached the trestle. There was a knot of men, including a handful of uniformed policemen standing about, gesturing and talking, but no visible evidence of the night's outrage. The engine whistled and rolled ponderously onto the trestle, drawing the long, gleaming cars after it. I stared at the spot where I'd drawn up the Reo.

"An accident," a man at the next table opined to his wife, sipping his coffee. He asked the waiter about the crowd.

"Somebody said a man was killed," the waiter said. "But they don't seem to know nothing 'bout it."

"Hobo," the man said, knowledgeably. "They ride the rails, under the cars. Sometimes they get drunk and fall off."

"Mus' be," the waiter said, affably.

I got up without a word and passed a few bills to Sheila. I walked back through the cars. When I passed the conductor I showed our tickets and asked where the club car was located.

"It won't be open yet, sir," the conductor said.

"I need a drink," I said. "Bad."

The conductor looked me over. "From Butte, eh?" He smiled sympathetically. "Well, you can find the attendant in the last car. Maybe he'll fix you up."

I stayed in the club car most of the day and got soaking drunk. At Deer Lodge, and again at Missoula, I felt unbearably tense as the train approached the station. But there was no sign of police or sheriffs at either stop and after that the train did not stop again until Sandpoint, Idaho.

There were Missoula newspapers in the club car, but they had evidently gone to press before hearing any news from Butte. The conductor and a carman came in at one point and said there was trouble of some kind back in Butte. They thought it had something to do with the strike, but they weren't sure.

The talk in the lounge was mostly about the baseball pennant race and the War. I didn't join in. I just drank and watched the mountains and forests drift past.

About ten o'clock that evening, after putting the kids to bed in the sleeping berths, Sheila came to find me. Somehow, I got to our compartment, with her help. In the narrow bed she hugged me. I clung to her as we rocked down the Columbia River gorge toward the sea.

The following morning, still on the Columbia, I read the Spokane papers. They were full of the lynching of Frank Little. There was talk of riots in Butte and speculation that the Army would be asked to intervene, "to bring peace to the strike-torn city." The newspapers editorialized on the need for a sedition law. The governor of Montana appeared ready to call a special session of the legislature for the purpose of passing such a law.

In the lounge, the businessmen and salesmen discussed the murder, but I didn't take part. The consensus seemed to be that "it served the Reds right." One man even declared, "These Butte fellers got the right idea. The sooner we string up all these traitors, the quicker the war'll be over and our boys'll be home."

At one point, somewhere west of The Dalles, a salesman observed that "It's too bad. Butte's a great place. This is a black eye for Butte."

"You ever spent any time in Butte?" I demanded thickly.

"Why, of course," the salesman said. "Great town. Mercury Street, eh?" and he winked.

I nodded, about twenty times. Finally, I said, "S'a helluva town."

PART TWO

Local Leader of I. W. W. Taken From His Room by Masked Men and Strung Up—No Clew to Identity of Perpetrators. Seditious Utterances of the Man Fail to Draw Him Into the Clutches of the Law—City Wrought to High Pitch.

Frank H. Little, executive board member of the national I. W. W. organization, who had made many seditious speeches openly in Butte, called American soldiers "scabs in uniform," denounced the government and the president, threatened governors and other legal authorities, gave warning of rebellion and armed revolution, the frankest exponent of direct action and slugging tactics in the present labor troubles in Butte, and who was even under suspicion, by some of his associates as being a detective, was taken from his room in the Steele block on North Wyoming street early yesterday morning by masked men and hanged from a railroad trestle south of the city.

The lynching, first that has ever disgraced the city of Butte and brought shame to its good name, a travesty on law and order, followed the failure of federal, state, county and city authorities to properly deal with the case of Little and his fellow agitators. The authorities were repeatedly informed of the destructive action and violence advocated by Little and his fellows. Written official reports were made to the authorities about the conduct of Little, and citizens expressed fear of results if the outrages were not curbed.

The plea of the authorities was that there was no expressly written and worded law that would warrant them in interfering, although on previous occasions sufficient excuse was found for police interference with disturbers not half so violent as the unfortunate and irresponsible Little and his more responsible associates were guilty of.

The result: A crime that will forever be a blot on the name of Butte and a shame to the whole state.

Last night the authorities were without a clew to the identity of the men who participated in the lynching, though the federal, state, county and city authorities come with the promise that their utmost efforts and resources will be employed to apprehend and bring to justice the lynchers.

Early in the Morning.

Little was taken from room 32 at the Steele block on North Wyoming street, near Finlander hall and only two blocks from the Thornton hotel, shortly after 3 o'clock yesterday

FRANK H. LITTLE.

ers who had been awakened by the noise advised her to make a report. Within five minutes detectives were at the house and they informed Mrs. B that Little had evidently been deported. Efforts were made to trace the automobile.

From the Milwaukee Trestle.

The first report of finding the body was received at the police station. The body was found about 6 o'clock hanging from the north side of the Milwaukee trestle, just on the outskirts of Butte and near the Centennial brewery. The ties are about 14 feet above the ground, and Little's feet were about five feet from the ground, the rope giving a drop of only a few feet. It was thought that Little had been bound and a towel placed over his mouth to prevent an outcry as he was taken from the rooming house, but no gag was found at the scene of the hanging.

Wynne, whose father was one of the men who figured in the "clean-up" days in Alder gulch.

The body was brought to the city and taken to Sherman & Reed's undertaking rooms. Soon members of the Metal Mine Workers' union heard of the lynching and they had the body removed to Duggan's undertaking rooms and before the body could be prepared for burial hundreds of men wanted to get a glimpse of it. Many of these were attracted to the morgue out of morbid curiosity.

As soon as the body was brought uptown the investigation began.

Hit Over the Head.

An autopsy was held and it was found that death was due to strangulation, the neck not being broken. There was a mark on the back of the head, probably inflicted with some blunt instrument, perhaps a gun. Blood had run down over the shoulder. There were marks on the left shin and leg.

One of the first men to arrive at the spot said the body had the appearance of having been placed there after Little had been knocked unconscious by the blow. There was no evidence of a struggle. The mouth was not open and there were other evidences that the lynchers had struck their victim so that his death struggle was not a lingering one. Little was a slight man, weighing about 155 pounds. He was 5 feet 11 inches tall. The body was clad in a very tight suit of summer underwear cut short at the knees and shoulders.

Body Pulled Up.

Evidence gathered at the scene of the hanging showed that the automobile was driven under the trestle which is 200 feet from the regular highway and in an open space, where every move could be seen if any one was about. The rope was evidently placed about Little's neck as he sat or stood in the machine. It is apparent that he was not taken on top of the trestle, hit over the head and the body pulled up by men who held the rope on the other side of the trestle. The rope was 25 feet long.

The automobile then turned around and went back onto the country road. There were no tracks were left. The autopsy report showed that there were no bullets fired into the body.

Coroner Lane took Little's effects from the Steele block. He had a few dollars in change in his clothing. His suitcase contained I. W. W. literature and membership books with letters from various organizers in the coun

CHAPTER SIXTEEN

Groundhog Day in 1951, in Butte, was brilliantly sunny. Any stupid little rodent would need sunglasses if he ventured out of his burrow today, plus an extra fur hat and coat. This was the view of Special Agent Senkpiel. If *he* had a nice warm burrow he was darned if he'd go out, hungry or not. It was brutally cold, –27 ° F at one P.M. Senkpiel tugged on galoshes, wrapped about his neck a woolen muffler that his fianceé had knitted, turned up the collar of his heavy tweed overcoat, pulled on rabbit fur-lined gloves and arranged earmuffs under his felt fedora before he dared step outside the regional office of the Federal Bureau of Investigation. By the time he reached his government Ford, his bones were cold and even his *eyes* were cold! This was the eighth straight day that the mercury had not risen above minus ten, and Agent Senkpiel was getting nervous about it. It got cold in Michigan—he was from Grand Rapids—but it never got *so* darn cold and it never stayed this cold for so darn long. People around Butte liked to say it was a dry cold, not that nasty damp cold of the Midwest. But at twenty-seven below, what the heck difference could it make? He had begun to feel an edge of panic: maybe it would never get warm again.

It occured to him that many Butteants were like groundhogs, anyway: they went down into the warm copper mines every day. It was said to be hot down there, that the men worked in their shirtsleeves, or even bare to the waist, glistening with sweat. The very thought of bared flesh sent a chill into him. It was the first time in his life that Arthur Senkpiel had ever thought of mining as a desirable trade.

Somehow he coaxed the frozen car to reluctant stuttering life and heel-and-toed the brake and accelerator down Montana Avenue to the "Flat," as Butteants called the residential area that lay below the Hill on which the old part of the city was built. It was even colder down here, he thought; the cold oozed down, like frigid oil, a kind of semi-solid seepage. He found the street he wanted and parked slightly atilt on a hard drift of frozen snow in front of a small, white clapboard house. He turned off the ignition reluctantly, fearful that the engine would never revive.

He took a brief moment (a very brief moment since the temperature in the car rapidly sank) to mentally review the request he had received from FBI headquarters. Evidently someone very high up was interested in Goodwin Ryder, the famous mystery writer. The woman he was about to interview was either Ryder's wife or ex-wife, the memorandum hadn't positively declared. This was by way of a fishing expedition, one of a kind with which most FBI agents were becoming familiar in these early days of the cold war: a casual exploratory scan for possible communist sympathies and/or affiliations. He supposed that Ryder was up for some government post, or something. The memo wasn't explicit. It did mention a single name, Frank Little, that the witness should be sounded on, particularly concerning Ryder's acquaintance or knowledge of said Little, a name which meant nothing to Agent Senkpiel. And now it was too bitterly cold in the car, his breath forming ice on the inside of the windows. He crawled out.

The woman who answered the door was wearing a heavy hand-knitted wool cardigan sweater that didn't begin to obscure an enormous bosom. Steamy clouds billowed out the door bearing a cloying odor of fuel oil, tobacco smoke and perfume. She was a stout woman of about sixty, with red hair that was trying to turn gray but not succeeding, thanks to copious applications of henna rinse. To say that Agent Senkpiel found her unattractive was inaccurate: he thought her repulsive. She might have been a beauty, a long time ago, but Senkpiel was too young to see it. To him she was old and fat and ugly. She wore too much makeup and wasn't at all tidy. There were ashes scattered all across her immense bosom and the agent thought she shouldn't be allowed to wear slacks. Not unless she lost thirty or forty pounds.

The woman brought in tea and then seated herself in an upholstered platform rocker next to the heater. The windows were frosted to mere luminosity with thick, fantastic crystalline patterns. She rummaged in the enormous bosom of her sweater and drew out a pack of Lucky Strikes. She offered them to the agent. He declined. She lit up and began to puff the first of ten or so that she would smoke during the interview. She poured tea for both of them, and then, to the agent's amazement, produced a pint of brandy from a handy bookcase and offered to "sweeten" his tea.

"No thank you," he declared emphatically.

She shrugged and poured a generous amount into her own teacup.

Agent Senkpiel explained that he had been asked by a Federal agency, which he would not specify, to make certain inquiries. Mrs. Ryder was under no obligation to answer the questions, but he was obliged to record all of her answers for his report, including refusals to answer.

Mrs. Ryder uttered a little barking laugh, said, "La-de-da," with a flutter of pencilled eyebrows and asked what the hell it was all about. She had a hint of an Irish accent, which Agent Senkpiel had found to be not uncommon in Butte.

Agent Senkpiel said he was not at liberty to say, for the moment, which was approximately false: he didn't really know, but if he had known, he supposed he was probably not to say. For now, he was simply required to ask several questions. Could they begin?

Mrs. Ryder took a hearty sip of her "tea," smacked her lips, which were painted a little larger than reality, and said, "Fire when ready, Gridley."

She caused him consternation right away, by denying that she was the estranged wife of Goodwin Ryder.

"We never really got married," she explained cheerfully. "I was married to Mr. Paton, you see. But I ran off with Goody and we had a kid and Sean—Mr. Paton—refused to let me put his name down for it. I didn't want the kid to be a bastard, so me and Goody just said we were married. Nobody ever questioned it."

"He listed you as his wife on his military records," the agent protested. "You were paid his Army allotment."

"So sue me," Mrs. Ryder said.

"It could be more serious than that," Agent Senkpiel said, mustering maximum severity—it was well to put witnesses at a disadvantage early on. "I don't know the statutes right off hand, but I'm sure it's a Federal offense."

She thrust out her thin wrists, jangling with hoops of silver and brass, as if eager to be manacled. Then she laughed and puffed her cigarette. She went on like this, throughout the interview, clowning and carrying on.

Agent Senkpiel had never conducted such an interview, although he hadn't done many. He was a very young agent. He was irritated, almost infuriated, but he was a stolid sort and he kept his temper admirably. He never perceived her anxiety, especially whenever he touched on the events surrounding Goodwin Ryder's initial visit to Butte, in 1917, or whenever he mentioned Frank Little.

Mrs. Ryder staunchly maintained that she had never known Frank Little, although she'd heard about him, of course. She had never heard Goody mention Mr. Little, she averred, and as far as she knew Goody had never met the man.

"Goody was a detective, like you," she said. "He worked for the Pinks. The Pinkertons, or one of those agencies, I was never sure. I don't know what he did—strike-breaking, I guess —but I'm sure he never came into contact with Frank Little."

The agent was at a disadvantage here because he had no idea who Frank Little was. He hadn't had time to find out, but he presumed that it didn't matter that much or the Bureau would have informed him. He made a mental note to check out Little in the files. For her part, Mrs. Ryder, or whoever she properly was, did not enlighten him. And gradually, at first to her relief, but finally to her surprise, she realized that the FBI was not interested in Frank Little. They were only interested in Goodwin Ryder, though it wasn't clear why.

So what was the FBI on about, she wondered? She decided that this must be something to do with the Army. Goody must be doing something for the Army, a movie perhaps. This was a whatchamacallit, a security check, she thought. Security checks were a fact of life, anymore. It was a big thing since the War, since the Iron Curtain and the cold war, Senator McCarthy and all that silliness. Pretty much nonsense, of course.

At this point, she began to relax and have fun. She had a lot more brandy and lapsed into misty nostalgia about Goodwin Ryder. "Oh, he was a lovely boy," she said, more than once, shaking her head. "He was good for all night, that one."

As for communism, she couldn't remember him ever mentioning it. "He was more a bosomist, if you ask me." She pronounced it "boozumist", with a flirtatious Irish wink and a ringing laugh.

Young Arthur Senkpiel tried to restrain a laugh and failed—it came out as a kind of half-choked snort that forced him to hastily snatch out his handkerchief and wipe his nose. He had gotten over his irritation and was amused, despite his professional misgivings, his apprehensions about the astounding cold, his general unhappiness.

Senkpiel didn't enjoy being an FBI agent in Butte. He was twenty-five years old and had expected to be in Washington, D.C., by now. He'd been in the Bureau for two years. Things seemed a little tight, promotion-wise, but the post-war communist conspiracy augured well. He had decided that if he hadn't moved up the ladder by the end of the fiscal year, he would go back to law school.

Another side to Agent Senkpiel's character was a certain Mid-western romanticism. It was why, in fact, he'd joined the FBI. He'd actually believed the "gang-busters" stuff he'd read in pulp magazines and heard on the radio—Mr. Hoover's endorsement and authorization of these stories led him to accept them as essentially factual. But he also appreciated the fictional depiction of crime fighters: one of his favorite radio shows was "Damian Knight," in fact, a mystery show based on Goodwin Ryder's detective stories. He also strongly believed in J. Edgar Hoover's public campaigns against communism. But, when he joined the bureau he soon discovered that the FBI was nothing like it was portrayed. Of course, one doesn't really expect it to be, but there was no gang-busting, no running down of spies, none. It was boring. Especially in Butte, so far, anyway.

Thus, he was entertained to discover that Sheila Ryder/ Paton actually was acquainted with the actors Edward G. Robinson and George Raft.

"Eddie is a wonderful guy, a real gentleman," Sheila told Senkpiel. "He's an art collector, you know. Mmmhmm. You wouldn't think so. An Irish Jew, if you can believe it, although I think his mother was Hungarian. And the sweetest manners. Not a tough guy, at all. He's not what you'd call handsome, but oh! those bedroom eyes! That 'Rico' stuff is all malarkey. Tiny little feet he has, and lovely toes. A perfect gentleman. Now Georgie I didn't like at first. He tried to get in my slacks within the half-hour! But we soon got that straightened out and he's still a good friend. He was a hoofer, you know. A dancer. I think it was Jack Warner, or one of those cretins, who thought he'd make a good gangster. Of course, we didn't know any of these chaps when we first went to Hollywood, but Goody soon was chumming around with Coop and Clark and–"

"You don't mean Gary Cooper and Clark Gable?" Senkpiel interrupted.

"Who else? Coop's from Montana, you know. Over around Helena, or someplace. Myrna's from over there, too."

"Myrna Loy?"

"Who else is named Myrna? God, I hated her! What a snoot, and yet she's naught but a high school lass who ran away from Montana. I'm almost certain that 'Loy' is just a clever shortening of Malloy, which after all, is as common as my own Callahan, in Dublin. Anyway, Coop used to come over and we'd gab about Butte. He's crazy about hunting and fishing and he's forever on about getting back up here–he loves the Big Hole country. I dare say he does get back, once in awhile, but I never see him. Goody played poker with him and Clark and Papa till all hours. I'll tell you one thing, that

Hemingway is an awful shit. He was a horrible influence on all of them. Except Goody. You could put Hem in a room with a bunch of Fuzzy-wuzzies and they'd all come out talking like Papa. But not Goody. Goody saw through him. But they all drank too much anyway."

Senkpiel was enrapt. The next time she offered the brandy he cautiously accepted "a wee splash" in his tea. It didn't taste so awful. Besides, it was so darned cold out and so warm and cozy inside.

She told him how she and Goody had spent the early years of their so-called married life in San Francisco, after Goody had gotten out of the Army. "He got gassed, you know. In the Great War. It affected his lungs."

Senkpiel wondered how Ryder had gotten gassed, but he didn't say anything. He'd been sent a flimsy file on Ryder that included his military record: two stints in the Army, 1918-1919 and 1942-1944. Ryder had been given a medical discharge in 1919, for influenza but somehow he'd gotten back in the Army in 1942, at the advanced age of 44. Ryder had never left the States during the first war and never been in a war zone. In the second war he'd been a company clerk at Ft. Ord, in California—pretty easy duty. But the agent let it pass. It wasn't his business to inform informants.

"I worked as a waitress to support him, while he wrote," Sheila told him. "It was quite a strain, with all the kids. Goody wasn't awfully good with them, I'm afraid." She sighed and took a gulp of spiked tea. "I'd come home from the restaurant and find Jean and Devvy running up and down Post Street at ten at night! And the little one, Alex, crying in his crib with shit all over his little ass! And Goody typing away and smoking, which he shouldn't have done—because of his lungs, you see—and blind to it all! None of them would have eaten a scrap all day."

"Did he have any communist friends in San Francisco?"

"Communists? My God, no. The man was trying to be a popular writer and the only work he had, when he would work, was as a fly cop! He hung about with cops and bums and crooks, and sometimes he did a little job of work for the Pinks—the Pinkertons, not the commies. You know, a stakeout, or following somebody, maybe looking up records at the Hall of Justice. He was very good at following, one of the best. It didn't pay much, though."

She shook her head, ruefully. "Still, it was the best time. People always say that about their time of struggles, when they were poor and all, I know, and it does sound silly, but it was the best time. Later on, when he got famous and we had lots of money, it wasn't nearly so much fun. Goody was having it off with all these young girls—starlets, they call themselves, but they're no more than whores—and was never home much. By then we'd had Molly, Goody's only child—the others were Sean's. I finally got fed up and came back here."

Senkpiel ignored her risque language, although it would have shocked him, a teapot earlier. "Why'd you come back here?" he asked. "You're not a native of Montana." Butte was not a place to come back to, in his mind. He was constantly astonished by the ferocity of the locals' devotion to the place.

"My God, I wasn't going back to Ireland, was I," she said. "My boy lives here. Seanie's a poet, you know. He writes lovely poetry about the mines, and bootleggers. He'll not leave Butte."

"It was your first husband who was a communist, then?" Senkpiel asked, struggling back to his task.

"Why do you go on so about the communists? Nobody in this whole bloody country is a bleeding communist! Why would they be? Oh, it's true Sean belonged to the I.W.W. Is that communist? I thought it was before communism. It was

205

supposed to be a labor union. Poor Sean-O, he thought the sun rose and set in Frank Little's ass–" she covered her mouth with her hand, in mock embarassment, adding "–not that my Sean was queer, or anything like that. Why he was as straight as a poker. And as hard–when he wasn't drinking." She laughed, girlishly.

Senkpiel smiled, but doggedly pursued what appeared to be a promising vein of information. "Were Ryder and your husband associates? I mean, were they good friends?"

"They were bosom buddies. Well, they fell out over me, of course, especially when Goody and I ran off to California. But they made it up. You know how men are: they might be crazy about a woman for a while, but friendship is more durable, in a way. Sean came out to stay with us, after a bit, from time to time. It was Goody who got Sean into the movie business."

Senkpiel perked up. "So Mr. Paton was also in the movies," he said. "In what capacity?"

"Sean was a rigger. The poor man passed away in 1940. Liver problems. Oh, he was famous! Probably the best rigger in Hollywood."

Senkpiel had no idea what a rigger was and rather than expose his ignorance he passed that over for a few questions about the curious relationship between Mrs. Ryder (or Paton, as it were) and the two men. "Wasn't Mr. Paton jealous?" This was irrelevant to his inquiry, of course, but he was intrigued.

"At first," Sheila admitted. "But he saw how it was. I was just crazy for Goody and Sean-O admired him, of course, saw that he was a superior sort of chap. And then, well me and Sean, we had a kind of private arrangement ourselves." She smiled slyly.

"Did Ryder know about this, uh, private arrangement between you and your, uh, husband?"

"Not likely! Goody would've blown his top. He was very jealous . . . though it was all right for him to go out and screw every slut in Hollywood, and I wasn't to say a word! Well, two can play at that game. I made it a point to have it off with every single friend of his—Coop, Georgie, Bogie, all of them. Well, not Eddie. Eddie was too much of a gentleman."

Senkpiel was flabbergasted. "You mean you, uh, *went* with Gary Cooper? And the others?" When Sheila smiled knowingly, he pushed on. "With Clark Gable? You did?"

"He has false teeth, you know, and his breath is not too lovely."

Senkpiel believed her. Although, he was sure she was lying about something, but not this. Something else. He tried to visualize her with Clark Gable and, surprisingly, it wasn't too hard. A big, laughing, red-haired Irish lass with a terrific figure. She must have been something to see, he thought, and not so very long ago, after all.

"Did Mr. Ryder realize this was going on?"

"I didn't exactly advertise it in *Billboard,*" Sheila said, with a lascivious grin, "but I know it got back to him. There are no secrets in Hollywood, that's for sure. Your reputation's more secure up on Mercury Street, in Venus Alley," she gestured toward the Hill. "And that is surely why I'm sitting here in this wretched hovel in Butte, instead of the beach house in Santa Monica. Not that I mind Butte—I've always loved Butte . . . Butte people are real people. But I could be better situated —up on the Hill, perhaps, on Excelsior—or out by the Country Club."

Agent Senkpiel unconsciously rubbed his ears. Was she making this up? His limited experience had not prepared him for this kind of blithe rhapsody. He concluded she was

207

telling the truth. The lives of people like Ryder, and Sheila, were simply different from those of ordinary folks. She probably didn't think it was extraordinary. He wanted to ask her about Bogart, but he couldn't. It wasn't in him.

"This friendship between Mr. Paton and Mr. Ryder," Senkpiel said, "did your husband influence Ryder toward communism? Did they talk about socialism and that sort of thing?"

"Sean? Influence Goody?" Sheila snorted. She poured herself more tea and brandy and offered a refill to Senkpiel. He accepted it—"just a little." She slopped his cup full.

"Sean could never influence Goody," she said. "They were just pals, the way so many men are in America." She eyed Senkpiel shrewdly. "They're like boys, aren't they? Though, I must admit, Goody is more of a man than any of them. Or was. He's not in good health, they say."

"Did Mr. Ryder ever talk about the Communist Party or any such organizations, maybe with Mr. Paton?" Senkpiel asked doggedly. "No? Did you know other people who were communists?"

She shook her head with a look of mixed disgust and disinterest. "Sonny, I wouldn't know a communist if he pinched my leg," she declared. "What do they look like?"

"Do you still communicate with Mr. Ryder?"

"Oh, sure. Well, now and then. It's not like we're bloody neighbors, is it? He's living in New York, now, shacking up with that what's-her-name, the playwright. But sure, he writes, now and then. And the girls always hear from him. And Molly writes me everything he says. Molly lives in Seattle, you know. Jean is just over here in Anaconda." Like so many Butteants, she pronounced it "Andaconda."

"I would think you'd resent Ryder, now. After having supported him during his struggle, to be. . . . " Senkpiel gestured at the surroundings.

"Not so much as some might," she said. "We Irish have a great regard for artists. He wrote the stories, after all. I couldn't have written them. You couldn't. I don't think even Goody can write them, anymore. But I shouldn't say that. He's surprised me all along. I never thought we'd go so far and do so much. I knew it was going to be better than stopping with Sean, but I'd have gone anyway. And I had a bloody good time. Goody supported us well when the money came and he still sends money. He's been real good about Molly and Jean. Devin works in Hollywood. And now, I still have Seanie. He's a comfort."

"But Ryder has treated you so shabbily, it seems," Senkpiel protested.

"He's a lovely man," she insisted. "Goody isn't exactly a Milord Percy, but he's got guts, when it comes down to it. He is generous, by his own standards. He never asked for a lot, but he took whatever was given and enjoyed it. It's not a bad philosophy, such as it is. If I asked for more, I'm sure he'd give me more, whatever I asked. But I don't ask."

Senkpiel poked around a bit more, inquiring about possible communist influences and associations of Goodwin Ryder, but finally he gave it up and they whiled away the afternoon with Sheila's ribald reminiscences of Cooper and others. There was a wonderful story about Groucho Marx that came in response to a last feeble question about "Marxist influences." Groucho had once goosed her at a party at David Selznick's and Sheila had elbowed him into the pool an hour later.

About four o'clock, Sean Paton, Jr., the poet, came home from the bars. He was a huge fellow in his late thirties, a little thick in the hips and red of lip, and more than a bit tipsy, but pleased to find his mother and a friend in like condition. The three of them sat down to a little serious drinking and Senkpiel had to be driven home, ostensibly because his car wouldn't start.

The next morning it was warmer. The cold spell had broken. But Senkpiel's head felt broken, as well. Like a good FBI agent, however, he struggled down to the office and began to draft his report.

"The subject," he noted, "seems to have an active fantasy life and is clearly an alcoholic, however a few comments emerged that may be of significance in this investigation . . ."

A cable came back the next day, from Headquarters. "Ask informant about John J. McParland, former Pinkerton official, special reference Aug. 1917. Did subject know McP? Also, get more background re Loy, Gable, Fonda, et al. Other info welcome if informant seems open. Special reference subject's Communist Party affiliations. File to follow." The file was more enlightening than previously. Apparently, Headquarters was keen. Ryder was strongly alleged to be a member of the Communist Party, USA.

Well, Senkpiel was willing. Butte seemed a nicer place all of a sudden. He'd relayed all the gossip to his fiancée, a very pleasant young woman from Grand Rapids, and had hinted that maybe things were looking up in Butte.

By now he was a great favorite at Sheila Ryder's. He knew enough to bring a fifth of Jim Beam whiskey when he came calling. Sean, Jr., was sitting in on all the sessions. They tended to go on until the Beam was exhausted. Sometimes, Senkpiel and Seanie had to run out and get more whiskey. Senkpiel had told the mother and son all about growing up in Grand Rapids, about his hopes for rising in the agency, and he had even confessed that lately he'd been thinking about going back to law school and leaving the agency. They were wonderfully encouraging.

He would often go down to "Ma Paton's," as he had learned to call Sheila. In cold weather they would sit in the house and sip doctored tea while Sheila revealed another sexy secret about the Hollywood stars. By now he had learned about Charlie Chaplin's huge penis, that Tallulah Bankhead preferred her own gender, as did Danny Kaye! As the days lengthened, however, and it began to warm up, much to Senkpiel's relief, they might go for a drive and end up at a tavern, perhaps one of the cheerfully noisy and messy ones, the Irish ones, like Dink & Myrt's. There they would find Seanie and any number of genial characters, drinking beer all day, playing a little pool or darts.

Senkpiel had completely changed his mind about Sheila, and about a lot of other things, too. Where once he had found her vulgar and appalling, that had quickly given way to a condescending admission that she had a raffish charm, and then to a grudging recognition that she was pretty shrewd, a tough lady; and lately, he had begun to find her strangely attractive. The woman was easily thirty years older than him and not in the best of shape, but by gosh, she knew how to get under a man's skin. He had strangely erotic thoughts about her, at odd times.

CHAPTER SEVENTEEN

I have just come upon a perfect word for what I do: word-pecker. I wish I'd heard it before. It saves a lot of embarrass-ment. I was never embarrassed when I was a detective. Not even when Dewey said, on that long ago morning in the Big Ship, "Lemme guess. Yer a dick." I was taken aback, but not embarrassed. Truth be known, I was rather gratified–to be known as a detective, even if I had to deny it. And anyway, it was all part of the game. I was prepared to lie. I wasn't embarrassed to say, in that context, "I'm a reporter, a writer, a school teacher, a soldier, an Indian chief." But when I was a writer, it made me uneasy to say so. I knew it was a lie, I guess. Odd, because the writer's game *is* lying.

My old mother used to say, Don't be vain. And the idea that one was a writer was vanity, because a writer was sup-posed to *be* somebody, and I knew it was presumptuous of me to claim it. But wordpecker is anything but presumptuous.

I wonder if this is what Kafka had in mind when he had Gregor Samsa wake up one morning to discover that he was a beetle. I wonder if Kafka woke up one morning to discover that he *was* something . . . something a little unnerving, maybe not quite true–a writer. I've been thinking about Kafka because of that famous line from another of his stories: Some-one must have traduced K, because one fine morning he was arrested. I know that isn't quite the way it goes, but it was sort

213

of like that for me. I wasn't arrested, but it started a train of events that led to this prison cell. The interesting thing about it was that I immediately felt relieved.

For some time I'd been having trouble writing, or at least, with being a writer. I think I could have gone on writing Damian Knight stories until one day they'd find me dead at the typewriter, just as I'd typed "I stepped over the body, careful not to get any blood on—" That is, I could do that if I could think of a reason to do that. Maybe as a discipline. But, I wasn't writing those stories. And the ones I wanted to write, I couldn't.

I wasn't arrested, but I got a call from my lawyer, a very nice guy named Bill Browning. I was pretty hung over. I said, "Who?"

Bill said, "Frank Little."

"Yeah, I knew him. What about him?"

"Who was he?"

A good question, I thought.

That's when I felt relieved. I told Bill the simple facts, that Little was an organizer for the I.W.W., that he'd been murdered—assassinated, was the usual word—in 1917. Hung off a railroad trestle in Butte, in 1917. He didn't ask if I'd had anything to do with it and I didn't tell him.

The reason I had a lawyer who would call me in the morning and ask me a question like that was because a congressional sub-committee had asked me to testify voluntarily about Communist influence in the motion picture industry. So far, I'd held them off. They hadn't subpoenaed me because they realized that I would be a reluctant witness and they didn't really have anything on me, or not enough. But now, I guess they thought they had something. They wanted me to come down to Washington, that very day, if possible, to discuss it with a senator.

214

Bill said this senator was "friendly." That meant that he wasn't necessarily interested in crucifying me in public, but if it looked juicy enough he'd find some nails.

It took thirty-four years for this day to dawn. I was not quite fifty-five, but I was about seventeen years older than Frank Little ever got to be.

The interview took place in the senator's office. He's not important, so I won't name him, but it went like this. There were four of us present, me and Bill, the senator and his assistant, or counsel, or whatever his role was. The senator was from one of those middle-border states, not quite southern, not quite northern. He was about my age. He'd read my books, he said, but from his conversation it sounded like he'd only seen the movies. He said he admired my writing, but he only talked about Ward Bond, who had played Damian Knight in "What A Way To Die."

"I loved that gal, what's her name, Sullivan, who played the moll," he said.

Actually, Miss Sullivan wasn't in that movie, but she was in "Cold To The Touch" (based on my novel, *Icy Hand of Death*). I didn't correct him. Anyway, nothing much was said about Frank. And nothing was said about Beverly LaFreniere, the woman I'd been hanging out with. But both of those names hovered in the air. Beverly was more at risk than me, since she was pretty outspoken in left-wing causes, had made a highly publicized trip to the Soviet Union right after the war and campaigned for war relief. Me, I was just one of those wishy-washy liberals. Any public-spirited program could get my support if they asked for it. But the point was, I wasn't working in Hollywood. Not anymore.

Why be coy? I was washed up. The word was, I was a lush who had drunk himself into a condition where he couldn't write anymore. Nobody had asked me to write a screenplay in years, although there was always interest in filming one of my novels, or remaking an old movie. The Damian Knight radio series was still running, but I never wrote any of them. Now television was the rage, and while I got occasional nibbles about a Damian Knight series, nobody from NBC or CBS ever suggested I write it. To tell the truth, that didn't bother me much. I never went to movies, watched television, or even listened to the radio, unless it was a ballgame. I had a little money from royalties and reprints, stuff like that. It was enough. I could have as much to drink as I wanted, more than I needed. I didn't eat much. I mostly read books. Dostoevsky and guys like that. I never read any of the new mystery guys I was supposed to have influenced, me and Hammett and Chandler. Hell, I didn't even read them, and they were pretty good, better than me. Beverly always hated it when I talked like that, but it was true. Anyway, I should have been happy.

I couldn't figure out what it was. I had something to do, but I wasn't anywhere near doing it. I couldn't see it. Then Bill Browning called. Things didn't exactly clear up, in the senator's office, but I had a feeling, a kind of electricity in the air. It made me strangely excited. At first, I thought maybe it was the weird set-up, the guys in the office, all standing around and waiting, waiting for me to say something. They were strange people. Not just the senator, but this weird guy Kahane, who was counsel for the committee, or something. He was really intense, nervous. He kept looking at me and licking his thin lips, like he wanted to eat me, or something. He'd ask a question, but Bill would stifle it.

Kahane asked about Butte—Had I ever been in Butte? But Bill would say, "Is this a hearing?" And they'd revert to something more general, like, "How do you feel about the hearings? Have you watched the hearings on television, or read about them in the papers?"

Of course, you couldn't avoid the subject. It was everywhere. And, of course, Beverly was very het up about it all. She had lectured me extensively on how this intruded on our civil rights, how it was prior censorship, and so on. I understood all that. And I understood that it was serious stuff. But I wasn't about to join any protest parades. I figured, if they wanted to subpoena me, I'd go and tell them and the public what I thought. And it looked like that was what would happen. After a few more questions—Did I ever know Frank Little? What did I think of the I.W.W.?—which Bill quashed, the senator said he wanted us back the next week. His staff would try to work out the schedule. In the meantime, he hoped I would think about the seriousness of the communist menace in the arts, especially the movies, and that I'd be ready to cooperate when they asked me to appear. As a final shot, Kahane said something about "indictment." But when Bill asked what that meant—indictment for what?—Kahane just smirked and said, "Ask your client."

On the train back to New York I asked Bill what he thought would happen and he said he thought they wanted me to testify, but it wasn't clear what it was all about. Were they after Beverly? Why didn't they ask about her? What about Frank Little? I told Bill more or less what had happened.

We'd made the train with only minutes to spare. I went directly to the club car and ordered a large gin. I downed it and got another before the train lurched and slid away from the station. Bill Browning sighed and ordered a martini. The train rolled through the Maryland countryside, I gazed out the window and remarked, casually, "Ah, the good old B&O. I like the B&O. Don't you?"

"It's all right," Browning said.

"All right? You ever take a ride on the Reading?"

"Only in 'Monopoly'," Browning replied.

"I had an uncle who was a conductor on the Reading," I said. "When I went out to Butte he let me ride for nothing. There were Pinkerton spies on the train, he said, who watched the conductors to make sure that they didn't pocket ticket money. But the union knew who they were, they issued posters of the spies. My uncle kept me safe. He didn't know I was with the Agency. He saved me enough to buy a new suit for the trip. It was green tweed, very prickly. You know how cartoonists draw tweed suits in the funny papers? 'Mutt and Jeff'? 'Moon Mullins'? They show little lines sticking out around the edges. You could scratch yourself raw on that suit."

"There's another card in 'Monopoly'," Browning said. "'Go Directly To Jail'."

"Yeah. 'Do Not Pass Go, Do Not Collect $200.' You think I'm going to jail?"

"I don't know what to think. Evidently, the Senator thinks he's got something on you. Has he?"

I frowned into my gin glass. "What do they want?"

"They want names," Browning said, "so they can go on with their dog-and-pony show."

"And if I give them names?"

"You might not have to testify. Not publicly, anyway. But this talk of an indictment has got me puzzled. What went on in Butte in 1917, Goody?"

"It's a hell of a long time ago, Bill. Do you remember what you were doing in 1917?"

"It doesn't seem so long ago to me, Goody, but I haven't lived an adventurous life. I know I was in law school at Princeton. I remember that much. I was stepping out with a girl named May."

"Oh, well, if we're talking about girls. . . . " I smiled. "There was a girl in Butte. The world is a hell of a lot different, now. We're older, sure, but I wonder if things ever changed so damned fast before? Or so completely?"

"Every generation thinks that," Browning said. "Maybe it's the effect of two World Wars. Or the Depression."

"The atom bomb," I suggested. "Radio?"

We ordered another round of drinks and stared out at the New Jersey countryside, both of us a little misty, remembering our youth.

"I was a fledgling Agency dick in those days," I said, finally. "I knew nothing about communism and politics. I wanted to join the Army and fight the Huns. I wanted to join the Air Corps. Airplanes! More like kites, really, just wood and cloth."

"It's radio," Bill said, not quite soberly. He was not used to drinking martinis in the afternoon. "Radio and the auto- mobile."

Beverly met us at Pennsylvania Station. I was pleased. She looked like a million bucks in a knee-length silk dress and a fox stole. We dropped Bill at his building, with a promise to call the next morning, and went on to a good dinner at Dahlberg's.

During dinner Beverly didn't bring up the hearing, but it couldn't be avoided. When we got back to her place she took me into the library, a room that she knew I liked. The maid had set the logs quietly burning in the fireplace. I stood with my back to the fireplace, enjoying the heat while she poured cognac into a balloon glass for herself, a whisky and soda for me. I watched her avidly. She was not a beautiful woman, but damned attractive. She was large-boned with a handsome face, tall and angular with a substantial bosom but slim hips —a combination I particularly liked. She had presence and intelligence.

219

"Now, Geed," she said brightly when we were settled into chairs, "what kind of shenanigans did you get up to in Butte?"

"Ugh! Don't talk to me about Butte. I'm sick of Butte. Let's talk about you and this damn rumor I keep hearing."

"I told you there was nothing to it," Beverly said.

I sipped whisky and stared at her. I shrugged. "Your life is your life."

"No it's not, Geed," she said sharply. "We've been through too much together for you to say that."

I nodded. "Still, we haven't always told all, have we?"

"Not everything," she admitted. "Are we supposed to tell everything? Is there something you want to know?"

"I don't know. Maybe I don't want to know everything. We never said anything about the Party, for one thing, and right now it looks like that was sensible. A lucky idea, anyway. You didn't see that little shit, Kahane. The so-called counsel." I simulated a shiver. "Gives me the creeps."

"I saw him on television. He seems repulsive. Tell me, are these people really interested in all that Party gossip?"

I thought about it for a moment. "No. I get your drift. They don't seem to have any real idea about the Party at all, about Marxism and all that, anyway. They don't care about the Party as an idea, or a movement. To Kahane and the Senator it's just a means of getting publicity. Funny, Kahane reminds me of certain Commies I've met. An 'apparatchik', as they say."

"Why were they so interested in Butte?"

"Butte," I sighed, and shook my head. I was tired. But then something flashed in my mind. I hunched forward, making a retching sound and blaring out "Beee-yooot!" I had to laugh at Beverly's shocked face.

But that laugh almost killed me. It degenerated into a brutal cough. Once started I couldn't stop. Beverly's shock turned to horror. She forced herself to remain seated, I could tell, while I coughed and coughed and coughed until finally I stopped, flopping back in the chair, gasping like a beached trout, exhausted.

"Jeeziss, I thought I was going to hell on that one. That's what I get for trying to joke about it."

"Too many cigarettes . . . " She attempted a flip laugh.

"Too many years. Anyway, I already cut out the cigarettes. And don't blame the booze." I shook my empty glass meaningfully.

She got up and refilled the glass. I sipped at the whiskey and relaxed, leaning my head back on the couch.

"What's the big joke?" she asked.

"Ah nothing," I said. "Just, Bee-yoot." I sat up. "A guy I knew out there used to pull that vomiting gag all the time. Called it 'bugling into the basin'."

"Frank Little?" Beverly said.

"No, no. Dewey." I shook my head slowly, marvelling. "Dewey Thacker. I'm surprised I even remember his name. Another lifetime. Not only do you forget a lot, even important things, but you probably had a completely different outlook at the time and what seemed all-important then doesn't even register now. A woman came up to me a few years back—at a party in Beverly Hills, it was. She says, 'Goody, remember me? Baltimore? We went to school together. We were crazy about each other.' Well, I remembered her, finally, after a lot of prompting, but not as my girlfriend—I never touched her— but I guess that's the way she remembered it."

Beverly ignored this little anecdotal dodge. "I get the impression that the Senator thinks they're onto something important," she said. "Something special. What was so special about Butte?"

"Aw, for chrissake, Bev. You know that's the impression he likes to give. He and that creep, Kahane. They don't know a damn thing. But, what the hell, everybody's got a few skeletons. I'd rather talk about something else. How's the play going?"

"Horrible. My characters won't get off their butts. They just sit there quacking. It's like a high school play."

"Action has to reveal character," I said. "You don't want some guy strolling over to the window, where you've got a piece of tarpaper tacked up, and saying 'Ah, Africa!'"

She laughed, then abruptly asked, "Who was the fellow in Butte? The one who did the vomiting gag?"

"Dewey? Just a miner I knew in Butte. Goofy kid from the Bronx, or 'Joisey'—I'm not sure. He used to say Butte was 'perzin,' meaning poison, see? A great kid. A shirt was a shoit, and a toilet was a terlet. We were all kids, then . . . "

"Geed?"

"Hunh?" It took a moment to focus. I hoisted the whiskey glass, but it was empty. "I guess I dozed off, eh?"

"It's late," Beverly said. "You've had a long day. Why don't you get some sleep?" She paused, then said, "You can stay here."

"Thanks." I stood up and stretched. I felt stiff. I went to the drinks counter and poured myself an inch of straight whiskey. I smacked my lips and replaced the top on the decanter. In the bedroom she laid out a pair of my pajamas. I put them on, exhausted. I thought of making some crack about being too tired—it had been a while since we'd made love—but I dropped it.

In the morning, I felt like hell and I hoped Bev wasn't still keen on hearing my recollections. The phone rang several times. It was mostly reporters, who had gotten alerted by someone, probably the senator's office, about my appearance there. About ten, Bill Browning called.

"Goody, we have to talk."

"I told you everything I know. What's the deal?"

"The senator wants to see you on Monday morning. We need to figure out what we're going to do."

I didn't respond. Finally, Bill said, "Well? What are we going to do?"

"You're the lawyer, Bill. What the hell can I do? Not go?"

"I can advise you on legal matters, Goody, but this is a career decision. Do you want to go on working in movies?" He went on to explain that many people were being black-listed, barred from working on films or in television, for not cooperating. Lately, all it seemed to take was suspicion.

"As bad as all that, eh? Well, what the hell, I haven't been working, anyway. Still, it isn't as if I'm in some kind of formal retirement. I wouldn't want to actually be told I can't work. Hell, maybe I should go back to being a dick."

Bill didn't laugh. "This is serious, Goody. I called a friend in Hollywood. He said he heard you were in trouble. The word is David has talked to Kahane."

"Selznick? I never worked with Selznick."

"Maybe it's someone else. But he says that Kahane is approachable, he'll deal."

"I thought we already knew that. It's names, right?"

"I'm betting they'd settle for a closed hearing and all you'd have to do is state that you are not a member of the Communist Party."

I thought about that for a long moment. I was in Beverly's dining room. She drank coffee across the table. "No names?" I said.

There was a slight pause, then Bill said, "Some witnesses have simply read a list of names . . . names that have already been, uh, mentioned."

"Are you kidding?"

"Well, no, Goody."

223

"What kind of jokers are these guys? What about Bev?"

"Bev?"

"Yeah. I've been hearing a lot of rumors that Beverly is going to be asked to testify. Does this let Beverly out?" I winked across the table at her. She shook her head and looked down into her coffee cup.

"I haven't heard anything about Beverly," Bill said.

"Bill . . . don't these guys strike you as kind of loony? How about if I read my own list, starting with Lenin and going on to Trotsky and Stalin?"

"Goody . . ."

"I'm not against reading lists, Bill. But even a closed hearing is a matter of record. Right? A few years from now, maybe no one will remember the names—except, of course, the guys who get named. But everybody will remember that I named people, even if it was Dagwood Bumstead and, oh, Ronny Reagan. I don't think I like that idea, Bill."

"Goody, how about if I call Kahane and say we're considering it? Okay?"

"I don't get it, Bill. Why not just go down there on Monday and play it as it lays?"

"All right, Goody. But call me."

I hung up and poured myself a large whiskey. There was something odd about this Hollywood talk. Why would anyone in Hollywood even care what happened to me? I looked across the table at Beverly. Now there was someone who they would be interested in, I thought. I drank the whiskey down and she looked into her cup.

I asked her, "How well do we know each other?"

She paused for a moment, then said, "We've known each other long enough, anyway. Why?"

"Would you be interested in writing a screenplay with me?"

She shrugged. "Why not? Do you have a project in mind?"

224

"No. I just wondered. Let's get the hell out of here. I can't take any more calls."

Beverly suggested a ball game. The Yankees were at home versus the Tigers, but I grimaced at the idea and she dropped it. Then she remembered a friend who had offered her the use of a cottage out on Long Island, somewhere beyond the Hamptons.

"Too far," I said, but she pointed out that while the drive was long, it was still early. It would be good to get away from the city. We could take a lot of terrific food from Laskewitz' delicatessen, walk the beach, spend the night, and drive back Sunday evening. This seemed attractive. We wouldn't have to see anyone.

It was fun picking out the food. I was no gourmand, not much of an eater at all, but I had a kind of curious interest in delicacies. We got mounds of prosciutto ham, a bucket of oysters, cream cheese, lox, loaves of rye bread, a nice wedge of Brie and a chunk of Port Salut, potato salad, cole slaw, three different patés which we sampled in the store, plus pickles, bottles of wine and whiskey and brandy. The deli packed all the perishables in Beverly's fancy new portable ice chest. I was short of cash, but Beverly was flush.

We stopped by my apartment so I could shower and change and pack a small bag, then we drove out over the Brooklyn Bridge. It was early fall and very fine. Beverly had a new Buick and she drove very authoritatively. There were a lot of cars on the road, but it got easier beyond Babylon. The Yankees-Tigers game was on the radio. The Yankees had a rookie named Mickey Mantle who had already hit two homeruns before I tuned in the game.

"Did you have a romance in Butte?" Beverly asked.

"Is this professional interest?" I responded.

"Just curious. You seem a little reluctant to talk about it, and it occurred to me that there might have been a romance. But I don't mean to pry."

I had to laugh. Obviously, she did mean to pry, but it seemed funny, after all these years. "Oh, there was a girl," I said. "It wasn't anything earth-shaking."

"What was her name?"

"Sheila," I said.

"Tell me about her." She looked straight ahead, seemingly concerned only with the road. We were somewhere around Shinnecock, with the Yankees well out in front. I twisted the radio dial until I found the Army-Cornell football game. That seemed appropriate for the brisk, autumn weather.

"I don't really recall the details," I said.

"Nothing? Oh, humor me, Geed. Tell me something amusing. And turn off that stupid game."

"Something amusing? Well, she was a pretty girl. We used to go up to a place called Columbia Gardens."

"What's that? A beer garden?"

"No, a big amusement park outside of Butte. You had to take a special trolley. One of the Copper Kings built the park. It had an artificial lake, a pavilion, a roller coaster."

"A roller coaster!" Beverly laughed. "I'm sorry. I had a vision of young Goodwin Ryder and this buxom Irish lassie—or is it colleen?—making love on a roller coaster."

I couldn't restrain a laugh. "Well she was Irish, as it turns out. You must be psychic."

"But not about the roller coaster!"

"Oh, no. It was up on the mountainside. You took a little trail, beyond the lake. There were some scrubby pines . . . I remember the pine aroma. It was warm in the sun. When we got there we didn't know how to proceed. We just sat there. Finally, out of desperation I started talking about the clouds.

I remember she said something about building cloud castles when she was a little girl, walking along the beach near Dublin, I guess. 'Along the strand,' she said. She used to imagine all sorts of things."

"We're coming to the strand ourselves," Beverly said, turning off the highway.

The cottage was small and tucked away behind the grassy dunes. There were other cottages around but remote and not easily visible. We put away the delicatessen things and walked out into the late afternoon sun, to the shore. We tramped a good distance, herding little flocks of sandpipers before us and pointing out to one another the virtues and defects of this or that large cottage. Beverly agreed that something more modest, like the cottage that her friend had provided, was a proper beach cottage. Beverly was pleased that I seemed more cheerful and reinvigorated. And I felt a lot better. For one thing, my hangover was gone, though possibly it was more than the fresh sea air that had done the trick. I'd downed a few sips from a flask I'd loaded up in the cottage. Still, we were cracking jokes and climbing sand hills one after the other without groaning.

As we neared the cottage we sat down in the sparse beach grass to watch a large freighter standing out to sea. There were still a few sailboats out. Immense rafts of white clouds drifted out from the mainland. We sat in silence for awhile, then Beverly said, "Were the clouds like this?"

"What clouds?"

"Your first date—with Sheila."

"Date!"

"All right, assignation, then. Or tryst."

I was amused. "Tryst is better."

"You were talking about clouds," Beverly prompted.

"They weren't clouds like these," I said. "They were flat, like discs."

When I didn't go on, Beverly said, "It's getting chilly. We should gather some driftwood for the fireplace."

"Good idea."

The cottage had an agreeable, musty sea tang, though the aroma of the fire soon replaced it. For once I was hungry and we ate ravenously. Afterwards, with the wine, we lounged around the fire, smoking and talking about nothing of consequence. I knew that Beverly wanted me to resume the recollection, but I resisted. Beverly became impatient.

"This girl . . ." she started.

"Woman."

"All right. Woman. Was she good?"

"Good? What the hell?"

"You know what I mean," Beverly said with a smirk.

"Aw, you don't want to hear about that."

"Of course I do. Tell me all about it."

"Everything?"

"Well, hell, Geed. What was it, some kind of sex epic?"

I almost laughed. "Not quite. You're close, though. Sheila was . . . well, she was very energetic."

Beverly laughed. "That's something. How did it start?"

"Oh, nothing really happened, not that first time, anyway. Almost, but we—well, I—just couldn't get things going. All that confused talk about clouds . . . until finally, things just happened naturally."

"Naturally," Beverly said. "I've always had a fantasy of making love in the open."

"I don't recommend it. You feel awfully exposed. It's like the whole town of Butte—not to say the people at the Gardens —can look up and see your naked ass."

"You were in love," Beverly said.

"Let's just say I had a crush. I thought I was in love."

"Hadn't you ever been in love before?"

"Not . . . not quite like this. Not with a grown woman."

"Were you a virgin?"

I sipped at the dregs of the wine and shrugged. "Yeah, I was." I stood up and stretched. The fire was nearly out and Beverly seemed to be asleep, curled up in a blanket at the foot of the musty old sofa. But when I threw a few more sticks of driftwood on the fire they caught readily and Beverly looked up. "Tired?" she said.

"Worn out. Let's go to bed."

"I wanted to hear the rest," she said sleepily.

I stood for a moment, hands in pockets and stretched my neck backwards, gazing at the ceiling. Shadows from the fire flickered in the dark corners. Finally, I said, "It wasn't much."

"Well, would you like some tea? Something to eat? There's paté . . . "

"Nah." I poured a little whiskey and drank it quickly. I lit a cigarette. Beverly waited, watching.

"There's not much to say. We had a fling and then one morning I went down to the station, early, and got a ticket to San Francisco."

"That's it?" Beverly sat up.

I hitched my shoulders. "I don't know . . . it was disappointing, in a way. Things hadn't worked out for me in Butte. Sheila was married, see. Anyway, it wasn't any of my concern anymore. I went out to the coast and kicked around for a few weeks, then joined the Army."

"And you got gassed."

I laughed. "That was just something the studio flacks put out when I started working for Paramount. How could I get gassed? I never saw any action . . . never even left the States. Nah, I got TB. The Army docs always maintained that I'd had it before I got in, but I'd passed the enlistment physical so that didn't wash. I spent some time in the hospital, then and later. I got a disability benefit. It wasn't much, but without it I guess I'd never have become a writer. I had lots of time, a little money. I couldn't do manual labor, not that I'd ever done any before. I wrote advertising copy, wrote some short stories for the pulps. I even did a few jobs for the Agency, once in awhile."

"You worked for the Agency after Butte?"

"Why not? Nobody ever said anything about it. Not a peep. The work I did was on the West Coast. I wrote those early stories . . . they did all right. I sold a couple of novels, then I did the movie stuff."

Beverly shook her head, with a laugh. "That's the fastest career I've ever heard of. I mean . . . I knew you were successful when I met you, but . . . I guess I just didn't understand how it all came about. I read the novels . . .. I don't know. . . . " She shook her head again. "You make it all sound so easy, but I guess you're just glossing over the hard times."

"Hard times are boring."

"Well, what was the Senator driving at, asking you about Frank Little?"

I shrugged. "Beats me. I guess he was trying to make a connection with the communist movement, maybe with the labor movement. We'll know Monday, I guess."

"And Frank Little? Did you know him?"

"Oh, I knew him."

"Well? What happened to him?"

I shrugged. I turned away toward the bedroom and began to unbutton my shirt. Without looking back, I said, "I never saw him after that."

"No? Well, what happened in Butte?" Beverly followed me into the bedroom. I sat on the edge of the bed and watched as she shrugged out of her sweater and let her skirt slide down.

"Oh, they had some union trouble. Frank was an organizer for the I.W.W. But they lost the election. Hell, they never won an election anywhere. In fact, a few days later there was some rioting. I heard that the governor called for federal troops. They had martial law, I guess. And no union, at least, not for a few years. The men just went back to work."

"What a shame." Beverly turned out the light and crawled into bed, naked. She snuggled up against me and repeated, "What ever happened to Frank?"

"Frank . . . " there was a long pause in the darkness, then I said, "well, I guess Frank just went on down the road. What do you know about Frank Little, anyway?"

"I never heard of him until Friday," Beverly said. "I guess he was a big guy in the labor movement."

"Not so big. Not like Haywood or Moyers. Or Eugene Debs. Who remembers those guys anymore? Frank . . . I haven't heard his name mentioned in twenty years. He was . . ." I hesitated.

"What?"

"Just one of them people." My laugh was a little shaky.

We lay in each other's arms under the musty blankets, warming ourselves against each other. After a long time, Beverly said, "What about Sheila?"

"What about her?"

"Well, what happened to her?"

"Oh, she left her husband eventually, came out to the coast. I saw her for awhile, then I lost track of her."

"Did she have kids?"

"Yeah, she had kids. I saw the oldest a couple of years ago. He had some job in the movies, something technical."

231

She was silent for a long time and just when I thought she was asleep, she said, "America."

Yeah, I thought. America.

CHAPTER EIGHTEEN

After awhile, Beverly began to breathe heavily. I stared up into the darkness. The wind licked at the flimsy cottage and I thought I could hear surf.

Well, that's the short version, I thought. It was all right. It got the job done. The long version had too many ragged edges. Not for publication.

Beverly was a fine woman. Not too young, not too old. She could still make me feel like sex, which was nice, and you didn't have to explain everything, which was even nicer. We had known each other for a long time. We'd even been in love for awhile, and still were in some less passionate manner. She was the only woman I'd ever felt completely comfortable with. We could talk. She never made me feel guilty about drinking or not writing, although she occasionally scolded me about both. But there was an understanding, there. She forgave me everything, even occasional affairs with other women, although there had been damned little of that in recent years.

One of the reasons we got along so well, I thought, was that we didn't talk much about ourselves. There was a lot we didn't know about one another. We talked about books and writing, about art, or politics. Grown-up conversation. Serious stuff, but nothing more personal than opinions.

I was surprised that I'd told her as much about Butte as I had, last night and today. But it wouldn't be fair to her to tell it all. It would be a burden on her, though I was sure she wouldn't complain. Anyway, what she didn't know couldn't hurt her.

It would be a nice thing to write someday, though. But you would have to write it the way something like that should be written. You wouldn't leave anything important out and you would tell the story as simply and as honestly as possible.

Was it possible to tell such a thing completely honestly? I didn't believe it. Even if you could remember all the details after thirty-odd years. That was what made fiction necessary. The factual truth, I'm convinced, is not possible, even if you could be absolutely assured that there would be no repercussions—an impossibility itself. But supposing that you could be sure? It still wouldn't be possible. The greatest of writers had agreed on that. Hell, even two eye witnesses of a simple auto accident could never completely agree on what they had seen. But fiction was a way of telling the truth, of saying how it had been, without worrying about the petty details.

Something happens, and you witness it. To your description of the event you bring all the emotional and intellectual baggage you have acquired throughout your life. It reminded me of the old joke about the elephant. After years of study the Jew writes *The Elephant and the Jewish Situation.* The Frenchman writes *The Sex Life of the Elephant.* The German writes *The Elephant, An Introduction,* in six volumes. Goodwin Ryder writes . . . what do I write?

The Elephant Dies Alone? Something like that.

Well, that was the problem, wasn't it? Somewhere along the line something had happened to my fiction. It had gotten too predictable, or something. They had seemed like good stories, lean and cruel . . . true, in the way of good fiction, but I couldn't write it anymore. It was pointless. I had written myself into a corner. Damian Knight had gotten too real. Or no, that wasn't it. The effect of Damian Knight had become real, had become onerous, because others took it more seriously than they should and so I thought I had to. But it was all too clear to me that Damian Knight was a miserable failure, a shallow, facile, glib creation, and it was painful to deal with it anymore.

The cottage creaked and grass brushed against a dry clapboard. I felt cold and wary. I wasn't sober, but I wasn't drunk, either. I was in some other state, beyond booze. A kind of super-sobriety. Everything seemed empty and hollow.

Empty. Where had everybody gone? It was eerie. A path suddenly opened out before me, out of this crowded corner. The corner that included myself, Damian Knight, the sensuous dames, the stupid thugs, the burly cops, the wise-cracking newsboy, the hackies. I didn't want to step out into this path, but for a fluttering second or two I understood that it might be possible. Just one step. All my familiar people sat at my table, thronged my corner, smiling knowingly, cheering me on. They had blocked my vision for such a long time that I had forgotten to look past them . . . I'd grown weary of trying to push them out of the way. And now, as if a cool breeze had parted the mist, there was the path, down a narrow corridor still crowded with shadows, shamuses and dames, but with at least room for passage if a guy would take one step.

If I could say to myself, as I hadn't been able to say to Joe Davis and the guy in the Packard . . . Okay, let's do it.

It was Frank, I saw. I'd meant to write about Frank, always, but I'd never been able to talk about him. I could never see a way to tell who Frank was and what he had done and. . . . Even now a lump came to my throat and my eyes stung.

Damian Knight shoots first and "solves" the mystery with a little internal speech over the corpse. It was a way of doing what I had not done. Stories are like that. They do it for us. They have their own logic and their own rules. The stories had been good stories, but they had taken me a long way from Frank. Those rules and that logic had no room for Frank.

What Frank, or Joe Davis, or I had done . . . that was done. It would always be done. That would go on the way it had happened, in that time that it had happened. What I needed was a way of making it happen again, now and in succeeding times. It would happen in its own way, but it would bear a certain truth. Its own truth, of course, but one that had as much to do with Frank as I could bear. And for the first time in a long time I had an idea how it would go.

It would start, as always, with Dewey.

An hour or so before dawn I scared Beverly awake from a deep sleep—I was gasping for breath and felt frozen rigid, utterly unable to move. I felt like I was falling, tumbling through freezing space. But at the same time, I was aware that I was still. I wondered if I was dead. I had no idea how I'd gotten here, but I was horribly afraid. I knew that there was no point, no point at all, in further existence. If only I could wake up. Or if not, if everything would just cease.

But then I heard Beverly crying. "Oh god! Are you having an attack?" She leaped out of bed and turned on the overhead light. I was lying with my arms tight against my sides and my fists clenched. My eyes were wide open, staring but unable to focus; my jaw was clenched in a painful grimace, my lips drawn in a ghastly grin.

Terrified, Beverly ran into the other room and quickly returned with the whiskey bottle and a glass. She poured some, spilling it, and held the glass against my teeth. It rattled. But finally some of it trickled into my throat and I choked, then coughed, spewing the whiskey into her face. I convulsed, doubled up then, and gagged.

She crouched beside me and held me in her arms while I rocked back and forth compulsively, groaning, for several long minutes. At last I was able to heave a great sob and wrench away from her, tangling in the musty blankets. I was overcome with remorse. I knelt on the bed, my head between my arms and wept bitterly. "Ohh, ohh, ohh," I cried, over and over again. It was all I could say.

She crept closer and put her arm about me, hugging me tightly and trying to console me, helplessly murmuring, "Dear, dear." But she didn't understand what was happening and anyway, I didn't know myself. I was simply, totally swept away by this awful wave of emotion. I felt as if I'd been drowning and now was thrown onto the shore. I wept uncontrollably for more than ten minutes, until finally I began to get control of myself and gradually become aware of the present. I still wept, but now I began to softly moan and mutter words that made no sense to me, over and over, until the tears subsided and I expelled an enormous sighing breath and fell silent. Slowly I found that I could extend my legs until at last I was able to lie full length, face down.

Beverly straightened the bed clothes and crawled in beside me. I was still trembling, from time to time, but now I clung to her, burying my face in her warm bosom.

"Oh thank you," I told her, over and over, alternating that with, "I'm sorry, I'm so sorry."

"Oh my darling, it's all right," she crooned, hugging me and patting my back. Oh how I thanked her for her kindness, her sweetness and forgiveness.

It took a full half hour before I regained real control. Then I sat up, mopping my face with the blanket, not looking at her. Beverly lay propped on an elbow, extending an arm to me, but I felt ashamed now and gently pushed it away.

"Where's the booze?" I asked, finally, with a shaky laugh. When she handed the glass to me, I drained it and lay back down, on my back, loving that warmth that spread down my throat and into my chest, my stomach.

"The light," I said.

She got up and put out the light, then rejoined me in the bed. I turned to her gratefully and embraced her. After awhile I felt able to roll onto my back and I expelled a huge sigh. A few minutes later, I was enough in command to say, in a cracked, rasping voice, "I lied to you. I'm sorry, Bev."

"You lied?" she said, speaking into the dark.

"About Frank."

"What about Frank?"

"I killed him," I said, simply.

"Oh my god," she breathed. "You killed Frank Little? That's what this is all about? The Sub-Committee and all?"

"No, no, no." I shook my head, irritated. "They don't know anything about any of this. They can't. Anyway, I didn't . . . that is, I didn't actually kill Frank, myself. But I didn't stop them."

I sat up and felt around in the darkness of the floor until I located the bottle. I uncapped it and took a long drink. Then I lay back. I could sense Beverly waiting.

"I told myself and told myself that there wasn't anything I could have done, and then . . . well, I just quit thinking about it and after awhile I forgot all about it. I guess I just got to thinking of it as if it were a story I'd written once, a long time ago, that didn't work out."

I began to tell the story, in a brisk manner, relating only the essential details, in as flat and emotionless a way as I could muster. I was afraid to get too involved in the telling; I couldn't venture back into that maelstrom. Beverly lay beside me, I'm sure as chilled to her heart as I was to my core, as the disembodied words drifted in the darkness above us like smoke in a card room. I knew she was weeping finally, although she concealed it well. In the dim light I saw tears running down her cheeks.

"It was a frame," I said. "Joe was going to lay it all on me, if it came to that. I ran away, Bev. It didn't matter: Frank was dead, of course. They hung him off the trestle with a sign on his undershirt—the Vigilante business, '3-7-77. First and last warning! Others take heed.'"

"Poor Frank," she said, softly.

"Yeah . . . poor Frank." I lay silently for a long moment, then said, "He was . . . " my tongue caught, "Frank was fine."

• • •

It was noon when I finally awoke. Beverly had gotten up earlier and gone out, I was vaguely aware. I'd slept the most profound sleep of my life, dreamless, sweet rest. She had built the fire, made coffee, and even gone out for the New York *Times*. The remains of the picnic had been cleared, but she'd carefully left the whiskey bottle on the table. She had even gone for a walk, she said, although there was a misty rain.

I got dressed and came out, feeling a little sheepish. Beverly sat in an old rocker by the fire. She'd been reading *Taps For Private Tussy,* a popular novel that someone had left in the bookcase flanking the mantel. I went over and gave her a peck. My beard was coarse, but she didn't complain.

"Is that coffee?" I asked. My voice sounded like coal tumbling down a chute.

"Well, I'm glad to see you're alive," she said. "I'll make fresh. There's no shower, I'm afraid. But I can boil some water if you want to shave, or bathe."

"That'd be great. Is that the *Times?* Jeez, Bev, you're a wonder." I sat down at the table in the little kitchen.

The *Times* reported that the novelist, Goodwin Ryder, was in trouble with the Congressional Sub-Committee, but more revelations seemed imminent. I put it down without saying anything and watched Beverly. I wanted to say something about the night, but she pretended unconcern. Finally, I said, "Uh, about last night, Bev. . . . "

"I was very worried about you," she said. "Do you feel all right? I was afraid you were having a heart attack."

This was disingenuous. An offer, perhaps: if I chose, we could pretend that I'd just had a physical problem. I made a face. "I'm all right. I feel fine, now. It wasn't anything physical, you know. At least, I don't think it was. Don't worry, I'll go see Doc Whatshisname. It was the other stuff."

"What about it?" she said, building up the fire in the little wood range. "I'm glad that you told me . . . told someone, at last."

"Oh, well . . . I'm glad you know. That someone knows. I just hope you don't think that I'm usually so, uh . . . " I tried to laugh, unconvincingly, " . . . so weepy."

She gave me her best wise-guy grin, and said, "There isn't anything usual about you, Geed. But I'm glad you told me about Frank. Next time, it'll be my turn for the waterworks."

When the water had boiled and I had shaved, I returned to the kitchen, saying, "God, I'm starving!"

While she set about making breakfast, I glanced at the paper again, concentrating on the sports section and drinking the fresh coffee.

I ate four eggs and we finished all the bacon. "I haven't been that hungry for breakfast in ages," I said, finishing up the last of the toast. I looked her in the face and said, "You're awful swell to put up with me, Bev."

"You're not so hard to put up with," she said. "I've seen . . . well, I'm not exactly a baby, you know."

We washed and dried the dishes and straightened up the house. At one point I found myself looking longingly at the whiskey bottle sitting on the table. Bev turned her face away. A drink would be very welcome, now, but I sensed one of those doors standing ajar—perhaps like the one that had offered itself in Butte. I made a little decision that made me feel good.

"Geed, do you know Dick Krehling?"

I looked up from the *Times* Book Section. "Krehling?" The name was familiar but I couldn't place it for a moment. "Oh . . . yeah . . . well, I don't *know* him. I know who he is. . . . How do you know Krehling?" I put the paper down and looked at her carefully. She seemed edgy.

"I know Dick Krehling quite well," she said. "I've known him for some time."

I thought about that. At last, I said, "I see."

"I called him this morning," Beverly said, "from the village. He's on his way out here."

I sighed and stood up. I found a pipe and loaded it, lit it. I went over to the dying fire and absently placed a small chunk of split wood on the coals. The wind gusted, splattering rain against the shingles. Finally, I said, "I wish you hadn't done that."

"I had to, Geed."

"No, I don't think so. But you did it. And now he's coming out." I shrugged. "Well, I guess we'll just wait."

I sat down and picked up the paper again. Beverly sat looking miserable, *Taps for Private Tussey* lying in her lap. She made an attempt to read, but after awhile, she got up and took the yellow slicker from the peg.

"I'm going out for a walk," she said.

I nodded. "Okay," I said, looking at her. "That's probably a good idea. I'll wait for Krehling." I smoked the pipe. It actually made me calmer. I looked back to the newspaper.

The wind was picking up. I could hear the waves crash and I thought it must not be very pleasant out there for Beverly, but it might make her feel better, somehow. The brisk, wet wind might be a relief after the tension of the warm cottage. After a while I heard a car bumping up the lane toward the house.

Krehling was a short, jaunty man with an ordinary but nearly handsome face. He was dark-haired, about forty years old and compact. His eyes were intense, but otherwise he betrayed no emotion. He explained why Beverly had never told me that she was a member of the Communist Party. He had perfect English, but even without an accent he didn't sound like a native speaker.

"There was no reason to," Krehling said. "We asked her not to and, although she disagreed, she accepted it."

"Like a good Communist," I observed, wryly.

Krehling didn't even smile, just half-shrugged, tilting his head toward his right shoulder. "It was enough that she was publicly associated with you," he said. "No doubt many people assumed she was leftish, but then, they would have read that into her plays and her journalism. But there is nothing more to say about that. What we must know is, will you testify?"

"Of course not."

"We think you should," Krehling said.

I just stared at the man, absorbing this amazing thought. My second thought was that I had anticipated this.

Krehling went on, "By now, those who are disposed to believe that you are a Communist are convinced, and those who refuse to believe it will not be swayed—indeed, encouraged—if you show yourself to be cooperative toward the committee."

"But what good will testifying do? Surely, you don't want me to name. . . . "

"No, no, you won't name anybody who hasn't already been named," Krehling said. "We will provide to you a list of names, and the Committee will not object."

"But that's absurd!"

"As you say. But they will have accomplished their purpose, which is to show that there are prominent Communists in America, in the arts, especially in the popular arts—which, after all, we do not mind that people should know."

I thought about that, then about the trials in Moscow, at which famous old Bolsheviks had stood and confessed their wrong-doings. After which, they were taken out and shot. Presumably, I would not be shot. I couldn't repress a smile.

"So, this is the American version of Stalin's trials," I said. "It makes it appear that Stalin is not mad, that we do the same?"

"You think so?" Krehling lifted his brows. "It has to do with Miss LaFraniere, I think. They want to subpoena her, but if you agree to testify, she won't be called."

I absorbed this, then glanced around the room nervously. The whiskey bottle stood on the table, not fifteen feet away. I decided, instead, to ream out my pipe and spend a few seconds loading it and lighting it.

I felt entitled to reflect on this alternative form of execution. So, Beverly was more important. She was a kind of sleeper. It was important not to expose her. To expose Goodwin Ryder was of no importance, evidently. Not that I was a Party member, but that was a distinction the committee would not make.

"I'll think about it," I said, finally.

Krehling almost looked exasperated. "Why don't you simply decide now?" he asked.

"It's not so easy to decide. The senator was making funny noises Friday."

"Funny noises? I don't know what you mean."

"You don't? Well, he was making threats. The main threat came from that little worm Kahane. Threats about . . . well, it wasn't clear."

"Oh, yes. We wondered about that. Something in your past. In Butte, Montana. August, 1917." Krehling actually smiled. "A year of some significance."

"For me, anyway."

Krehling frowned. "They told me you were not well grounded in theory."

"No," I said. "I'm not. Theory was never a strength with me. Practice . . . I'm better at practice."

"You talk about 'good Communists.' Are you not a 'good Communist'?"

"Neither good nor bad," I said. "I have had some trouble, over the years, being a good anything. I'm a bad joiner, maybe." I relit the pipe. "I thought about joining, to belong to something, but I had problems with it."

"You do not disagree with the cause?"

"I thought socialism was a good cause, but the Soviet version . . . well, there are problems."

"Yes. You want to interpret socialism yourself. You don't want to accept the discipline. It's very American, really."

This time, Krehling managed a grimace—dismay, regret, contempt: all of these.

"What will you do?"

I did not answer. Krehling left.

The whiskey bottle was the last thing to be packed, but I made no move toward it, and finally Beverly snatched it up and thrust it into the bag with the boxes of left-over potato salad and carelessly re-wrapped chunks of stiffened cheese. I picked up the basket and carried it out to the car. I said nothing when she locked it away in the trunk.

It rained all the way back to New York. We were reluctant to speak to one another, it seemed, and after awhile the silence became oppressive. I didn't want her to think that I was angry with her, although I was angry with her, but not so angry. We were almost to Manhattan when I said, "I think I may have had enough booze, at long last."

She was clearly delighted, but she said nothing. She peered out at the steady rain. "Do you hate me?" she asked.

"Only a little." I smiled at her as she glanced quickly at me, then turned her attention to the road. The rain continued to pour.

I sighed. "It's awfully late to be learning so much," I said. "I thought I had learned most of what I had to know, by now."

We were approaching the city. The rain still fell. "Did you and Sheila . . .?" Beverly let the question hang.

"We lived together as man and wife for a few months," I said, casually, "in San Francisco, until I ran out of money. Then I joined the Army. I wrote to her a few times, sent her a few bucks, then we quit writing. I never saw her after that. She was a good woman."

"Oh, Geed."

"It wasn't a great tragedy," I said, gruffly. "It was never very good for us. I had some good times, after we broke up, and they came at a good time for me—when I was still young enough to enjoy it but old enough to appreciate it. Poor Sheila, though, she never got any good times, not with me anyway. I didn't mean for it to happen that way, but that's how it works out, sometimes."

Beverly turned off the bridge and worked over toward Riverside. "What about the kids?" she asked.

I shrugged. "I don't know. I heard Sheila went back to Butte —for a while, anyway. Somebody said she and Sean were back together, but that may just be something I dreamed. I did see her oldest boy, Devin, at Paramount Studios, once, when I was writing scripts. He was doing something technical in the movies—a rigger, or maybe it was something else. I never talked to him. I didn't think he'd know who I was, though I might have been wrong. The kids were still pretty young when we broke up."

After a moment, I said, "Well, she was a fine woman. She did a lot for me. But it was a long time ago."

"'In another country,'" Beverly said, adding under her breath, "'and besides the wench is dead.'"

"Eh?"

"Nothing. Shall we go to my place?" Beverly asked.

"Nah. Just drop me off. I better call Bill and get together with him, about tomorrow."

She pulled up in front of my building. "Geed, I want to go down to Washington with you."

"No," I told her firmly. "Watch me on television." I laughed. "Now don't look like that. I'll be back. Bill's a good mouthpiece. We'll figure something out."

"I'll be here," she said.

"Good. That's . . . that's what I want."

We kissed briefly and I got out into the rain.

CHAPTER NINETEEN

On Monday morning, the hearing room doors were closed and locked. A sign read, "Hearings postponed until further notice."

Browning swore. "Why in hell couldn't they have notified us?" he exclaimed.

As if in reply, an aide appeared. He was a thin young man with a sharp nose and an obsequious air.

"Mr. Ryder? Mr. Browning? I'm from the Senator's office. We tried to get hold of you earlier, but. . . . "

"What's this all about?" Bill demanded.

The aide looked around nervously but there was no one within earshot. "Some new evidence has come up," he said. "The Senator wonders if you'd mind stepping around to his office?"

I looked at Browning, who shrugged. We followed the aide. In his office, the Senator was smiling and agreeable.

"I want to thank you boys for coming 'round here on such short notice," he said. He gestured at the leather couch. "Have a seat. Son, get these fellas some coffee," he paused, glancing at me, "unless you want something stronger."

"Forget the coffee," Browning said, "what's all this about?"

I sat down and looked around the plush office. Two other men were already seated. One of them was the Sub-Committee's Counsel, David Kahane. The other was a stocky fellow in his mid-fifties who smiled amiably at me. He held his hat in his hands, between his knees, slowly revolving it. I thought he looked familiar but couldn't place him.

The Senator sat down behind his large, clean desk. "Well, you see, Browning, your client hasn't been a very helpful witness. Now, as you must be aware, the American people have shown a good deal of interest in these hearings."

"This circus, you mean," Browning said, "thanks to your television cameras."

"They aren't my cameras," the Senator said, mildly. "But I can't say that I mind them. The thing of it is, it isn't very edifying for the American public when a witness like Mr. Ryder comes up here and all he's going to say is 'I refuse to answer,' and takes the Fifth."

"What would be more edifying?" I said, drily. "Denouncing people?"

"It would be nice if you would denounce Communism," the Senator said, "and help us to get on with our work of unveiling the massive infiltration of the U.S. government and the popular arts by Russian spies."

"I have nothing to do with the Soviet Union," I said. "As far as I'm concerned, Stalin is pretty much in the same line of work as you are, with his show trials."

The senator seemed delighted. "Well, there you go, then. Why don't you just say that, or something along those lines? I can't say that I'd appreciate the comparison with Joe Stalin, but if you could bring yourself to leave that out. . . . "

"Screw you," I said.

The Senator looked sorrowful. "I was afraid you'd say something like that," he said. "Which is why I've invited Mr. Thacker here this morning." He gestured at the man with the hat in his hands.

The man smiled and said, "Hello, Goody."

I was puzzled. I looked from the man to the Senator. "Who is this?"

"Dewey Thacker," the man said, rising. "Long time no see, eh, kid? We've both changed a bit, but I'd recognize you anywheres."

"I don't know this man," I said.

"Oh, come on, Goody," Thacker said. Suddenly, his face lit up and he broke into a strong Jersey accent: "Yiz mean yiz don't remembah Butte? Da jernt musta been perziner dan I t'ought."

"Good lord," I said. "Dewey? What are you doing here?"

Thacker shrugged. "Ask them, kid. My guess is it has something to do with Frank Little."

"That's right," the Senator said, smiling. "We've been looking into your activities, Mr. Ryder. All the way back to 1917. A very memorable date in world history, incidentally."

"As I recollect, there wasn't even such a thing as a Soviet government at the time," I said. "Kerensky was trying to form a provisional government."

"There were Communists, though," the Senator said. "But that's really beside the point. The point is, a man named Frank Little came to an untimely end in 1917, and you were involved, Ryder. Thacker, here, can testify to that."

"Dewey?" I turned to him, incredulous. "Why, what can he know?"

"I was there, kid," Thacker said, apologetically.

"But you were a miner, you. . . . "

Thacker shook his head slowly, a look of gentle, almost amused embarassment on his face. "You were awful green, kid. I guess you could say the Old Man made a mistake in you. But then, maybe not. I read your stories, though, later. I enjoyed them! They were really good. I liked the Agency stuff, especially. And I loved 'Damian Knight'! Terrific stuff."

Browning broke into this friendly exchange, addressing the Senator. "What's the deal here?"

"Why, the deal, counsellor, is that your client is in a heap of, uh, crap," the Senator said. "Now, I take it that you communicated our offer to Mr. Ryder?" When Browning nodded, the Senator said, "And he turned it down?" He turned to the Counsel and said, "You explain it, David."

The Sub-Committee Counsel stepped forward. "As you know, sir, there is no statute of limitations on murder. As a matter of fact, no one has ever been indicted for anything in the Frank Little case. But that doesn't mean that your client couldn't be indicted and we believe that with the assistance of Thacker, a pretty convincing case could be brought."

I stared at the Counsel unbelievingly.

"Yes, we're pretty confident," Kahane assured me. "But the question arises: Who would benefit? And the answer seems to be, that it wouldn't be the Committee, nor you, Mr. Ryder, though it might create a Communist martyr of sorts, out of Frank Little."

"Who has been justly forgotten," the Senator chimed in. "You see, fellas? It's not something that we really wanta do. But it's sort of our duty, isn't it? You see, Ryder," the Senator pointed out patiently, "you kinda pissed in your hat when you admitted that you knew Frank Little. At the hearing, you will be asked about that. Now a lot of people, including some reporters, I reckon, will want to know who Frank Little was. But that's not so important. I think we can deal with that. What is important is that you will be on record as testifying, and about Frank Little. Now, if I choose to pursue this question, and if you refuse to answer, you will be subject to a contempt of Congress charge, at the very least. There's no telling what a grand jury might make of it, frankly."

At that moment a buzzer sounded on the Senator's desk and he pressed a button on the desktop intercom. A secretary's voice spoke: "You have a vote in ten minutes, sir, on the Korean intervention bill."

"Thank you, dear," the Senator said. He stood up and tugged his suit coat down and straightened his tie. "Well, the nation's business calls, gentlemen. I know you'll excuse me. I think you can work all this out with Dave. Thank you for coming in." And he bustled out the door, beaming.

Kahane waited quietly. Finally, however, he said, "What's it to be, gentlemen?"

Before Browning could respond, I said, "Could I have some time to think about this?"

Kahane raised an eyebrow. "What kind of time are we talking about?"

"A couple of weeks."

Kahane frowned and looked down at his brilliantly polished shoes. He shook his head and looked up. "No, I don't think so. You've already attracted press attention. A hiatus of that duration would suggest that a deal was being made. No. No, it wouldn't do, I'm afraid."

"One week," I said.

Kahane puffed his cheeks and slowly blew them out. "One week? Let's see . . . today is Monday, it's shot . . . so, really, just another four days . . ." Suddenly, he looked sharply at me. "Why do you want this?"

"It's a big decision," I said. "A life decision. It's going to blow me as a writer. I need to think about it."

Kahane considered for a long time, gazing steadily at me. At last, he said, "This Korea thing is a big deal. It could provide a reasonable excuse to suspend the hearings for a day or two. I think we can allow you forty-eight hours."

251

Dewey Thacker caught up with us as we were leaving the building.

"Say, kid," he called out, "I hope you're not sore."

"Mr. Thacker," the attorney said, "my client can't speak to you. Not now, at least."

"Oh, that's all right, Bill," I said. I stepped aside with Dewey and looked at him closely. The man was heavier and tougher-looking, but his eyes were as clear and blue as ever and he still radiated good cheer. I felt pleased to see him, despite myself. I couldn't help smiling at that face. "Nah, I'm not sore, Dewey. It's good to see you again. I just wish to hell I'd seen you for what you were, back in Butte. But you're looking good. I'm glad."

Thacker smiled. "You weren't ever cut out to be a dick, kid. I don't guess you had the stomach for it. Not many guys do. Well, it's not much of a job, is it? But you and a few other writers, you did a grand thing for the profession. Especially you. You made us out to be heroes. It made things a lot better for us. I got to thank you for that. But you weren't stupid. You saw what detective work was really about, I guess. We were just doing our job. We knew what it was all about. I don't have too many regrets. Do you? I hope not."

"No, it's okay," I said. "It just didn't turn out like I thought it would. I'll tell you what, maybe we can get together some time and talk it over, after this is all settled."

"That'd be fine, Goody. I'd like that," Thacker said. He knitted his brow sympathetically and added, "You're in an awful jam, kid. I wonder if there ain't something I could do for you."

"Like what?" I said.

"Oh, I dunno. I allus thought you got a raw deal, but then you seemed to come out of it all right and I figured it was no harm done. But now. . . . The thing is, Goody, I ain't kidding when I say I feel like I owe you . . . we all do. I, uh, I know a few things. . . ." He stuffed his hands in his pockets and looked down at his feet for a second, then said, "I'm still in the same line of work, you know."

I turned this over in my mind for a few seconds. What could this oaf do for me? This oaf who had so successfully fooled me some thirty-five years ago. Why, even Joe Davis hadn't fooled me so completely.

"You talking about McParland?" I said, quietly.

Thacker grinned. "You can reach me at this number." His hand came out of his pocket with a card. He thrust it into the handkerchief pocket of my suit coat. "Say hello to the Missus for me."

With a cheery wave he turned and walked away.

CHAPTER TWENTY

There is something very restful about prison. Not all prisons, of course. But in many cases it comes as a distinct relief from the tensions and agonies of real life. For one thing, every man or woman who is going to prison, who is finally sentenced and on his or her way, has been tremendously beset by nerve-wracking turmoils; e.g., pursuit, capture, interrogation, confession, lies, denials, the trial, the verdict, the judgement, the sentence . . . and so on. But at last, you're on your way. Your troubles are over. Now you are the responsibility of the state. The state must feed you and clothe you and provide you with medical and dental care. Of course, for many, this is the moment of greatest fear. Will the state protect me? Will it be hell? And for many it will be hell, because the state cannot, after all, protect you from your new-found companions.

But, prison is a society in itself. Most people can get along in it, albeit rarely with the comfort and ease they might have enjoyed on the outside. Still, how many of these people actually experienced any real comfort and ease on the outside? Didn't I just say that they had been through a kind of hell getting into prison?

I certainly did and in my case prison was a positive relief. It was a relief from the kinds of pressures I've just enunciated, and, interestingly enough, it was a relief from my friends and those who cared about me. Most of all, it was a relief from myself. And it wasn't a bad prison, which was a great relief. No burly homosexual thugs, no vicious and sadistic guards, no hard labor (just make your bed and sweep out the barracks, rake the leaves in the fall, clean up the grounds in the spring, help plant some flowers), good and nutritious food in abundance (if not very imaginative), amiable companions (mostly tax cheats and bank embezzlers), a handy ping-pong table, a television in the day room, daily strolls around the grounds, a modest library, PX privileges. . . .

What the hell kind of prison is this, you ask? A very nice prison. Couldn't have imagined a better one, if I were being fair. That is, if it is at all reasonable to send people to prison in the first place, which I deny, then one couldn't do much better than this. Much better than this would deny the whole point of prison, at least as punishment.

This prison was in Kentucky, a federal facility (as they euphemistically call such things) for non-violent, non-dangerous, relatively short-term convicts. Hell, it was what most of us would call a country club for white collar criminals. A former army camp, probably a repple-depot, or a discharge depot, or something. Nice wooden barracks, housing a dozen men each in small, but not too small, private rooms with a common dayroom. At first they issued us GI fatigues, as a uniform, but almost immediately you learned that the camp officials (that's what we called them, we didn't ever use the word prison) did not object if you replaced these duds with jeans and an old sweater, tennis shoes, loafers, whatever (as long as it wasn't too outrageous—no zoot suits, no pinstripes, no smoking jackets, please.)

Later, when I'd gotten a good gander at the joint, I had to laugh at the way Beverly had carried on at the train station. It was awkward. The federal marshall refused to release me from the handcuffs for the farewell and several news photographers got some good shots of "famed detective novelist, Goodwin Ryder, in chains." Beverly's eyes swam in tears. I tried to comfort her. "I'll be back before you know I'm gone," I said. "It's not like going to war, where you don't know how long it's going to last, or if you'll ever get back. Eighteen months is nothing."

"Oh Geed," she sobbed, "you're so brave."

I laughed and got off one of my best lines, ever: "I've seen brave, kid. This ain't it." Well, it wasn't just a line. I was thinking of Frank.

Browning understood, to a degree. "It could have been worse," he said. I didn't completely buy that, either. I'd told him from the outset that the Senator and his nasty pals would not want to get into the Butte affair, when it came right down to it. They didn't give a damn about Frank Little, of course, but flogging me publicly wasn't good for their image and they had also (for reasons I've never learned) given up on pressuring Beverly. But although they didn't pursue the Little murder, that was the pressure point. I had to take the fall for a bail rap: I'd cheerfully signed on as a bail guarantor for some guys accused of being officers of the Communist Party of the United States of America. I got eighteen months for contempt of court because I wouldn't reveal the whereabouts of these rascals when they bolted.

Beverly was never even invited to court, which was the tacit deal. I don't know if she was aware, but Bev felt bad about it, for five minutes. I know she'd been scared to death. I think I'd have been scared, too, because what she'd have been doing was perjury. She knew where the birds were hiding, I'm pretty sure. But I never asked and she never said. I just assured her that it wouldn't help me if she volunteered any testimony. And it didn't. This, I guess, is why she called me brave. Nuts.

What was it like? It was boring. The guards were pretty decent fellows. One of them, a lardass named Tucker Cecil, was always telling me his troubles. He'd married a knockout, a hot little number named Doreen who was driving him crazy. She was fifteen years younger than he, just out of her teens, and she appreciated the fact that he often worked the night shift. I'd be sitting in my room reading and Tucker would come by and look in. We were supposed to have lights out at ten P.M., but it wasn't enforced except in the dayroom–the guys even lugged the damn TV into one of their rooms, to catch "Broadway Open House," or some such bullshit. Anyway, Tucker would come in and start whining about the faithless Doreen. He knew she was down at The Owl Club, probably dancing with that worthless Kelsey Pape. Why couldn't she be true, he'd ask me, over and over.

"Hell, Tuck," I would tell him, "who knows why a woman does what she does? A woman does exactly what she wants. It doesn't make a damn bit of difference if it's self-denial, slavery, whoring, or murder. They do what they want. You know that."

"But, my Gawd, Geed, she's so young and so purty. Why would she throw it away on a shiftless sonuvabitch like Kelsey Pape? He don't care no more for Dory than his next drink. Why would she throw herself at. . . . "

"Goddamn, Tuck, I told you."

"Should I beat her?"

And, of course, I'd have to plead with him not to. "It doesn't help, Tuck. It's bad for them." And thinking of Sheila, I added: "It's also dangerous. A woman will have the last word, Tuck. Don't cross her. Just be glad she stays with you."

The bastard even borrowed money from me. He always paid me back, but I really didn't have it to lend.

One fine day, not long after I checked in, I had a visitor. Dewey Thacker. I guess the officials let him in because he claimed to be investigating a case and I could possibly help him with it. He looked uncomfortable, even sad. I tried to cheer him up.

Dewey said, "You know, kid, you don't look so hot. Can I bring you anything?"

I assured him I was comfortable.

Dewey shrugged. "Well, I did a little checking after I read about this," he said. "Made a few phone calls. Everything's copacetic."

"Copacetic . . . ?"

"Mac's still alive. Long retired, of course."

"That's nice," I said. "Where does he live?"

"You really want to know?"

I shrugged. Thacker somehow seemed younger than me. A lifetime of bulldog work had not tired the man.

"Mac wasn't all that bad a guy," Dewey said. "He never screwed me. He did what he had to do."

"Dewey. . . . " I sighed. "Don't hand me this crap." I tried to keep the weariness out of my voice.

Thacker looked thoughtful. He said, "Mac and me went through a lot together. I can't say that I liked the man, personally. Not like I liked you, Goody."

I didn't respond.

"I mean it," Dewey said. "You and me didn't spend all that much time together, but I allus felt like I knew you, even if you didn't know me . . . obviously." He laughed. "I ain't kidding you, Goody. I used to read your books and think, 'Yeah, now this is more like it.' None of them other writers ever came close to telling what it was like. I mean, what you wrote wasn't really it either. . . . "

"Jesus, Dewey. What are you, now—a critic?"

259

"No, no. Don't take it wrong. But you know—you knew, to a certain point—what the work was all about. But you made it better in your books. I liked that Damian. I never knew anyone like Damian, of course—there never was any dick like Damian Knight, that's for sure. But you know what I mean. Just reading about him made me feel better about the work."

I sat back. I realized that I had to listen to this. It's always nice to have a visitor. Dewey wanted to talk about it and until he got it off his chest there was no point in pushing him. "So, you liked Damian. Damian is fiction, Dewey. He's not real. He's just a way of talking about something that maybe can't be talked about otherwise."

Dewey nodded rapidly, agreeing. "Yeah, yeah, I get you. But it's more than that, somehow." He frowned, struggling with his thoughts, gazing off. Finally, he said, "But it helps. It's like . . . a guy who is actually in the life can't really see what it is. You understand? But a guy who was, say, sort of in it, but not really, can maybe get a better handle on what it's like. Am I making any sense?"

"Sure. I understand."

"You do? Swell. 'Cause sometimes, I swear, I thought I was Damian Knight. I'd be dogging some guy and I'd say to myself, 'Okay, Damian is on to you, jerk. You've had it.' Just playing, see? There was a guy in L.A., once, I. . . . "

I cleared my throat impatiently.

Dewey broke off with a laugh. "I used to think, sometimes, that you must of gotten the idea for Damian from me. But then I'd see that it couldn't of been. I mean, you didn't know that I was. . . . " He laughed self-consciously.

"What ever happened to Davis?" I said.

"Joe? Joe Davis? Aww, Joe. . . . " Dewey shook his head. "He got shot. I think it was in '29, or something. In Panama, I think. Joe was a little rough, but he. . . . "

260

"But McParland lives on," I said. "What does he do?"

"He lives out in Montana. Ain't that something! He's retired. Gettin' pretty old, but in good health. The Agency calls on him once in awhile, just for information." Dewey looked serious. "If I tell you where he is, what are you going to do?"

"Do? What can I do?" I said, gesturing around me.

"I mean, when you get out?"

"I don't think that far ahead," I said.

Dewey frowned. He said, "You know what I'd do?"

"What?"

Dewey made a gun out of his hand and moved his thumb up and down. He made a silent "pop" with his lips.

I took a deep breath, then slumped back in my chair. I stared at the table between us for a long time, then said, "What's it like for him?"

"Mac? Oh, I don't know. I haven't seen him in a good long while, coupla years. His old lady died. Cancer. They had a kid. She's married. Mac's got a grandkid. Loves that kid. He lives near them. Sees 'em every day, I think. I had to stop by to get some dope from him, a coupla times, about some birds we used to know."

I looked up. "Did he ever mention me?"

Dewey shook his head.

"Frank? Did you ever talk about Frank?"

"Frank? Nah. We never was much for talking about stuff like that. Just a little chit-chat about the Agency—who was still around, that kind of stuff. Then I'd get the dope I needed, if he could remember anything, and I'd be on my way. He's got a nice little house, buys a new car ever coupla years. Plays a little golf. He paints."

"Paints? Paints what?"

Dewey chuckled. He gestured with an imaginary brush. "Water colors, I think—mostly landscapes. Can you imagine it? Mac?" He shook his head, almost fondly. "Mostly he talks about the grandkid. His name is . . . " Dewey frowned, then shook his head, ". . . mmm, I can't remember. Kenny? Something like that. Must be a teenager by now."

He fell silent at last and waited for me to respond, but I couldn't think of a thing to say. Finally, Dewey said, "Maybe I shouldn't have come. Maybe you want to just forget Mac."

I looked up quickly. "Oh, no. I'm glad you came. I'm through forgetting. I forgot too quickly . . . or thought I did. No . . . I can't forget anymore."

Dewey watched me for a long time before saying, "Like that, is it? Yeah, I can see it is. Well . . . what do you want?"

"What is he like? Does it mean anything to him?" I asked. "Does he seem to be sane? Can he be sane? Can he have done all that—" I waved my hand toward the room, but meaning the world, the universe, "—and not be affected?"

Dewey raised his hands helplessly, palms out. "I guess so. Why not? It was his work."

"His work? His work was to kill people? That's a kind of work? To infiltrate, to befriend and then to betray and finally to murder? That's not work, Dewey."

Dewey's face had closed up. But after a long moment his irrepressible good humor thawed his countenance and he said, "Aw, c'mon kid. He ain't you. He ain't me. You never had it in you to do them things. I didn't. Well," he admitted, "I was into it more than you, but even I . . . I mean, I couldn't of done what Mac did. Only he could. I don't say that it wasn't wrong. But Mac stabbed you in the back. He shouldn't of done that to a guy who was one of the guys. But," Dewey shrugged philosophically, "I guess he never figured you for one of the guys."

"He didn't?"

"You were never in it, kid. Well, maybe you had one toe in the water, but you never got in. Oh, you got in enough to see what it was, but you pulled back, I guess. No, I can see you got a bitch coming, but . . .." He shrugged helplessly.

"Mac was wrong," I said. "What he did was wrong. What, is he to simply lie down in clover, now, and the angels will sing him home?"

"I don't know what Mac knew," Dewey said. "Maybe no one knew, except maybe for the Old Man—and he's long gone. Now there was a guy."

I waved that thought away. "I don't want to hear about the Old Man. I don't want to know about him. It's enough to know about McParland."

"But you don't know nothing about Mac," Dewey pointed out, calmly and sensibly. "You don't even know what I know."

"No, you're right. But I could find out."

"How?" Dewey scoffed. "You could never find out shit. Not enough, anyhow."

I realized then that Dewey was right. But where did that leave me? Could it be true that McParland was somehow beyond retribution? That the Case of the Mysterious McParland was and would remain a true mystery? That it was impossible to ever get at the truth? It seemed too awful to contemplate.

But suddenly I saw that it was so. And more. That it did not, at long last, matter. What McParland was, he was. It had very little, by now, to do with me. My problem wasn't McParland, it was me. McParland, I understood, finally, was not my business.

It was hard. I knew it instinctively, but I couldn't so easily surrender to the idea. I sat and fought it in silence. The thought occurred to me that it was somebody's business. Or ought to be. If I surrendered my own claims on McParland I could not speak for others. Frank, for instance.

"What did you think of Frank?" I asked.

"Frank? Oh, you know. . . . Look, don't try to lay Frank on me, kid. I liked Frank. Helluva speaker. A fighter. I didn't have anything to do with that . . . or not much."

"Unh-hunh."

"I wasn't in on the party, kid. You were. But, I . . . ah, well, I observed."

"You observed?"

"From a distance. It was dark, you know."

"Yeah, I recall," I said. "There was another car there, at the trestle, that night. It was McParland, wasn't it?"

Dewey's face was blank. "Who knows?" he said, finally. "Anyway, it don't help you. And not Frank, neither. So . . . Frank? Well, Frank was one of them people. You know what I mean?"

I wondered if Dewey knew what that meant. Frank was one of them people, going down that road. It was a road Frank had chosen. Now it was time for me to choose a road.

"You said McParland stabbed me in the back," I said. "What do you mean by that? I'd like to be clear on that."

"Well, you know . . . he kind of pulled you into something that was over your head. And then when you panicked and took off, I guess he kind of . . . oh, I dunno . . . kind of over-reacted. He was pretty hot. Said he'd teach you a lesson for running out on us. He was gonna lay it on you, but you got away. I mean they were left to clean up the mess, get rid of the car and all . . ."

"Who drove the car?"

"The one you drove? I dunno. I guess Joe had to take it up in the mountains and dump it in a lake or something."

"So they didn't really need me to drive, did they?"

"Is that what Davis told you? No, I guess they didn't. But Mac was hot," Dewey insisted.

"He set me up from the start, Dewey. Tell me," I asked, leaned across the table and looking directly into those blue eyes, "where was McParland during all this?"

"Why he was with me," Dewey said. "We were in the other car, the Packard. Mac was afraid you seen us."

I nodded thoughtfully, then said, "And what kind of lesson was he going to teach me?"

Dewey thought about that for a minute, then shrugged. "I dunno," he said. "Anyway, you got away. I guess nothing came of it, eh? I heard you did occasional jobs for the Agency on the coast, later."

"It was a setup," I said. "I was supposed to be the patsy. If anything went wrong, if the cops got pushed into really investigating Frank's murder . . . or more likely, if Wheeler, the U.S. Attorney, ever got onto the case . . . there was only one guy who would be fingered . . . me."

Dewey was a man of considerable control. At most, one might say that he froze. But after a long moment he tipped his head forward an inch to indicate agreement.

"So, do you want it?" Dewey said.

"What?"

"The address. Mac's address."

"No," I said.

"No?"

I looked away. "Forget it."

"Forget it? But Goody. . . . "

"What?"

Dewey frowned. "But what would. . . . " He'd started to say: What would Damian Knight do? But Dewey knew what Damian would do. There was no question.

I left Dewey sitting there.

CHAPTER TWENTY-ONE

ACCOUNTING

In the spring of 1951, in Billings, Montana, a burly man got down off Northern Pacific's "Mainstreeter" and checked into the Northern Hotel. That afternoon he took a walk, an ordinary looking fellow in middle age, wearing a good blue serge business suit with a black-striped silver necktie and gray fedora, smoking a cigar and blithely swinging a leather satchel. It was sunny and mild and he took his time, a half-hour to reach a quiet residential street and a pleasant bungalow. He let himself in through the wrought iron gate in the yard fence and strolled casually up to the door. There was no answer to his ring. He stood on the porch for a few minutes, gazing calmly about. There was no sign of activity on this street, but he knew from the twitch of a curtain or two that someone had noticed his arrival. He didn't mind. Any onlooker would readily identify him as a salesman of a superior kind, perhaps insurance.

After a brief wait, he looked about as if puzzled, then shrugged and stepped off the porch. He walked to the end of the block and turned. As he passed the unpaved alley he paused. Down the way a set of garage doors were open and he could see the trunk of a car jutting out. He strolled down and peeked in. An odor of turpentine and varnish hung in the cool Montana air. In the garage, beyond a shiny black 1947 Packard sedan, he could see an elderly man working at a waist-high bench, sanding a wooden kitchen chair. A similar chair, already revarnished, stood nearby. The doors had been opened and the car pulled back for the benefit of better light and ventilation while refinishing the chairs.

The older man sensed the shadow in the doorway and looked up from his task, frowning. He was a bit stooped with age, but still tall and seemingly in good health. He wore gold-rimmed glasses. His silver hair was sparse. He wore an old pair of shapeless, stained khaki pants and an old cardigan sweater over a plaid shirt protected by a stained cloth work apron. When he saw who it was he almost smiled.

"Oh, it's you," he said. "What brings you to town?"

"Oh, same old stuff, sir. Information—this and that. Been working on the archives."

"Archives!" The old man snorted derisively. "You ought to burn them."

"Oh, no sir! We couldn't do that! What would the Old Man say? He always insisted we keep up the archives."

"Foolishness," the old man said, "and dangerous too."

"Yes," the younger man readily agreed, "they are dangerous. There's stuff in them—" for some reason he hoisted his satchel and shook it for emphasis, "—that could send powerful men to prison. But that's why we have to maintain them, of course: if *we* stay on top of it, we control it. Less danger."

The old man wasn't captivated by the topic. He shrugged and said, "Well, let's go in the house. I'll make some coffee . . . unless you'd prefer a beer."

"Coffee's fine, sir. Here, I'll pull the car in for you." The visitor moved toward the Packard, but the old man headed him off.

"I'll get it," he said. He drove the car inside. Then, while the other man waited, he pulled the two large garage doors closed and made sure the spring-loaded bolts were securely in place. With the doors shut it was rather dark inside; the lone lightbulb was weak and there was only one little dusty window, and the yard door, which was all but closed.

The younger man stood by the yard door and now he said, "Come to think of it, I won't have time for coffee. I've got to be getting on down the road."

"Well, what's your business then?" the old man said.

"Well sir, it's about Goodwin Ryder."

"Ryder! Why, Ryder was nothing," the old man said. "Just a temporary. He was never involved in much, and what he did get involved in he managed to bungle." This last was spoken with at least a hint of contempt, but no anger. "Anyway, I understood he was in prison. Good place for him."

"He is," the other man agreed, "but that's the problem. He didn't testify about the Agency, or about Frank Little, or about you, or the Company. What you might call a stand-up guy. Except now he's sitting and you know how it is . . . a feller sits in prison for awhile and maybe he starts feeling bad for himself. Maybe he starts talking. Or, in Goody's case, writing."

The old man didn't seem to take this notion seriously. "Pshaw. Let him write. Pulp detective stories, isn't it? Who would listen to a broken-down drunk like that? Anyway, what's this have to do with the archives?"

"Oh you underestimate him. There's lots of folks would read just about anything Goodwin Ryder might write," the visitor said. "Hell, I would. And maybe even his memoirs would be worth something. It wouldn't do to stir things up. And the feller won't be in the pen forever, you know. As for the archives, why there's a helluva lot in there about you. I been reading it up." He opened the satchel and took out a pair of yellow leather gloves which he tugged on.

The old man's eyes narrowed. He considered the burly visitor for several long seconds. "What are you on about?"

he asked, finally. He leaned, as if casually, against the work-bench. His long, liver-spotted hand rested on a claw hammer.

"The idea has come up that maybe Ryder would feel a little better if he had some kind of document that absolved him from the Frank Little business. And maybe a pension."

"A pension! For that buffoon?" The old man snorted. "This is about as stupid as you are. Whose idea was this? If the Old Man were still alive, he'd—"

"The Old Man's long gone," the visitor interrupted. "Prob'ly a good thing, too. That kind of business is over . . . or just about. Seems like there's always a few ragged ends to tidy up, though—no end to it, somehow. But it ain't the same business, these days, Mac. It's a corporate business, now. Mostly what they call security. Very lucrative, too, and not nearly so dangerous."

"Pshaw! Dangerous! These *managers,*" the old man uttered the word with genuine contempt, "would know nothing about danger. Too busy pushing paper, fussing over archives, tricking the men out in fancy uniforms. . . . "

"Well, they're gonna offer Ryder a pension, whatever you say. I'm not sure he'd accept it. The big thing, though, is the statement absolving him of complicity, as they put it. He'd get a copy, unsigned of course, but with the assurance that the signed copy was in the files. Just a little insurance policy, you might say."

The old man stared at him. "And you want me to write it."

"Sign it, anyway. It was your show," the other said. He opened the satchel and took out a sheaf of papers. "Here, take a look."

The old man refused to take the papers, or even look at them. He stared speculatively at his visitor, his head cocked slightly. The other fellow made another offering gesture, shaking the papers.

"Go ahead, look," he said. "It's all about you, of course. Not exactly Sunday School reading. You were the man behind a lot of things that won't hardly stand the light of day, Mac. About sixty-five years of them, if I read the archives right. Starting with nearly twenty miners hung on your testimony, back in eighteen-ninety–"

"Miners! They were bloody anarchists," the old man snarled. "They were out to bring down the country! Why, I was an immigrant, no more than a kid, myself–"

"Ryder was a kid, too, in his time," the visitor interrupted, his face grown hard. "That didn't stop you from using him."

The old man drew himself up. He seemed schoolmasterish. "Mind your tongue! And do not presume to threaten me."

"Why, it's not a threat, Mac. It's just accounts, a little bit of history. There's some awful good stuff here–planting evidence, bribing witnesses, officials, even staging a couple of killings that others got hung for."

The old man said, quite levelly, "Well, you son of a bitch."

"What d'you think, Mac? Would you rather sign this damn thing or spend your last few days in prison? The Agency has ways of fixing your little wagon, you know. You think we can't show that you were acting on your own? Without the knowledge or support of the Agency? That we had no idea what wild schemes you were cooking, for money under the table? And don't forget, the Old Man, who might have been in it with you, is dead. We can repudiate him, too."

The old man was livid. He took a trembling step toward his visitor. "You, you rascal! To think that my years of loyal service–"

"Aw, screw your loyal service, Mac. You've hung enough men. You've lined your damn pockets and tightened the noose around too many necks, and all the time telling yourself and anyone who'd listen that you did it for the Agency, or for the country, for Gawd's sake! I've heard your damn high-flown speeches to kids like Ryder—nothing but self-serving crap. Hell, you preached the same shit to me, you old bastard. Did you think you'd never have to pay? That you were gonna lie down in clover and the angels would sing you into heaven? Why, goddamn your soul!" The visitor laughed, almost hysterically.

But he regained his control and his voice turned to steel: "You'll damn well sign and be glad to sign, you old bastard. Or else your poor old skinny ass will be parked on a steel bench like Goody's. Now what do you say?" He shook the papers again.

"You stupid fool," the old man said. "You have no idea, no idea what a man like me can do to you. I'll not sign any such trash, and now you'd better get out of my sight and hope I don't have you hunted down like a dog and thrashed."

"Won't sign?" the other said, quite unfazed by the old man's threat. "I was afraid of that. Or, to be honest, I was kind of hoping. Well, let's forget about the prison business. Hey?"

He thrust the papers back in the satchel and drew out something else. It was a length of hemp rope, already fastened into a hangman's noose on one end. He tossed the satchel to one side and held up the rope. "This is my real offer."

The old man's eyes widened. He glanced nervously about and realized that the visitor stood between him and the door and there was no real escape. "You wouldn't dare!"

"I'm a bold man, Mac. You always said as much. Sign, or—" he shook the rope, much as he'd rattled the papers. "Last choice. What d'you say?"

"Who put you up to this?" the old man demanded. "Who is behind this?"

The burly man's face grew cold. "I might as well confess, Mac. It was my own idea. I thought about it on the train. I was just gonna plug you, but then I thought, 'Give him one last chance to save his sorry old ass.' So I gave you the chance. But you wouldn't have it."

When the flatness of this declaration had died away in the chill air of the garage, the old man grasped the finality of it. He launched forward with the hammer in his hand.

The younger man swung the heavy coil of rope, knocking the hammer out of the old man's hand and striking him on the shoulder, spinning him against the hood of the Packard. With remarkable poise, the assailant pinned the old man against the car and, casting the rope aside, quickly whipped out a pair of standard handcuffs. He easily twisted the old man's frail arms behind him and locked the cuffs on the wrists. With one powerful arm pinning the old man, the assailant snatched up the rope and looped the noose over the old man's head and around his scrawny neck.

In the struggle he had dislodged the old man's glasses, but he paid no mind. He leaned against the old man's back and pulled tightly on the knot of the noose until the kicking and struggling ceased. The old man had lost consciousness. The burly man stopped then to catch his breath. Still bracing his victim against the cold metal of the car with his hip, he surveyed the scene. There were no sounds, nobody called out, nobody walked by or looked in. It was just a quiet suburban afternoon.

With his foot he hooked a rung of the chair the old man had been working on and dragged it over to him. Then, working quickly, he tossed the free end of the rope up over a nearby crossmember of the garage rafters, caught it and yanked it tight. Now he stepped away from the limp man and hauled on the rope with both hands until the body was upright, seemingly on tiptoes. But the old fellow was surprisingly heavy and the rope resisted being dragged over the 2x6 rafter chord.

"Dammit!" the killer swore. He seized the old man's belt at the back and hefted him up with one hand, ignoring as best he could a sudden flurry of furious kicking of the high-top black shoes–either the victim had revived, or this was some kind of violent involuntary spasm. He hoisted with one hand and drew down tightly on the rope with the other. The old man was lifted into the air. The rope stretched, but then held the struggling and kicking figure off the concrete floor. The body rotated, facing him. The eyes bugged out, the tongue began to protrude. Muscles contracted and writhed.

The killer backed off then, grimly pulling on the rope. After a few minutes the dangling man went totally limp, his neck pinched smaller than one would have thought possible. It was clear that he was dead. The killer moved closer, hoisted the body higher, high enough that the feet could have been on the chair, then he himself stood on the chair and tied the rope end around an adjoining rafter chord. Then he tumbled the chair on its side, near the dangling feet.

He saw that he had stepped on the old man's glasses and broken them. That was too bad, but there was nothing for it. He found a broom and swept up the glass and dumped it, along with the bent frames, into his satchel. Putting away the broom he noticed a thick piece of blue carpenter's chalk on the work bench. He smiled and bent down to scrawl an obscure set of numbers on the floor, then he tossed the chalk back onto the work bench.

He stood, hands on his hips, inspecting the scene. There was plenty of free space for the hanging body, between the work bench and the parked car, enough room so that a man bent on suicide but perhaps panicking, would not have been able to scramble onto either the hood of the car or the bench to save himself. He brushed himself off, straightened his suit and tie, then picked up the satchel and composed himself, looking about the garage to be sure he hadn't overlooked anything.

When he was satisfied that everything appeared as it reasonably should, he took a deep breath, then bolted out of the yard door, satchel in hand, and raced for the house. He wished to give the impression that he was not quite in panic, but obviously in urgent haste. Once inside the old man's house, he found the telephone and dialled the operator.

"Operator," he said, urgently, "quick, give me the police. There's been a horrible accident."

• • •

One day Bev brought me a portable typewriter, on one of her monthly visits. (One good thing about lending money to Tuck was that it was possible to take Bev up to the room for a little, ah, privacy.) I guess I thought I was going to write a novel, or something. But except for letters . . . Well, I started a couple of short stories and I did a partial re-write of one of Bev's screenplays, although she later threw out every line of my revisions—but it did get her thinking more clearly. I don't know, I just couldn't get started. I thought about at least jotting down some of my impressions of Frank, but I didn't get very far.

About six months before I got out, I received an anonymous letter. I don't think our mail was censored, though I'm fairly certain that it was opened and read. The envelope was postmarked "Seattle, Wash." There was nothing in the envelope but a newspaper clipping. No letter, no note, no source and no date, just the clipping.

CORONER'S JURY RULES SUICIDE

Billings, Mont. A coroner's jury concluded yesterday that the death April 17, of John James McParland, 82, was self-inflicted. Mr. McParland, who had resided at 2213 S.Parkland Ave. for some eight years, apparently took his own life by hanging. The body was found in the garage behind the home. Mrs. James Malloy, 46, of this city, appeared unsatisfied with the coroner's verdict.

"My father was not ill, he was not depressed, he never contemplated suicide," Mrs. Malloy told the jury. To reporters she hinted darkly that "there is more to this than meets the eye." To the *Gazette* reporter she complained that the police had ignored a chalked message which she had seen on the concrete floor of the garage, near the site where the body of her father had been found. The message, she said, was "3-7-77." She claimed it had not been there before her father's death. Also, she noted that her father's glasses were missing. "If he was supposed to be working on furniture," she said, "where are his glasses? He wore his glasses all the time."

Detective Sergeant Kenneth Moreland, the investigating officer, testified that "there was absolutely no indication of foul play." Asked afterwards about the chalked message, he said he didn't recall seeing it. "What could it mean?" the officer asked. "He could have written it himself." As for the missing glasses, Moreland believed they would turn up, eventually. "I don't see that their absence is evidence of a crime," he said.

An autopsy confirmed that McParland had been in good health and that the body bore no indications of violence other than that associated with self-inflicted hanging. Dr. Cornelius Van de Wetering, a medical pathologist at Deaconess hospital, who had performed the autopsy, testified that there were some bruises on the wrists and forearms of the deceased, whose hands were manacled behind his back with a pair of regulation handcuffs which were shown to have long been in the deceased's pos-session. The pathologist said the bruises were consistent with a futile last minute struggle by the deceased to release himself from the handcuffs. A kitchen chair, one of a set from the deceased's kitchen, was found overturned nearby. The official cause of death was "strangulation with a ligature."

Some jurors showed concern that no "suicide note" had been found. But a psychologist, Dr. Erving Weissmann, who is a well-known forensic specialist and on retainer by the Police Depart-ment, testified that "The absence of a suicide note means nothing. Many people do not leave a note. That's just something from mystery novels." Dr. Weissmann, however, did hold out the possibility that Mr. McParland may not have "truly intended suicide, but he prepared for it quite thoroughly and, as it happened, he was unable to draw back from the fatal moment." He suggested a verdict of "death through misadventure" might be entertained, but the jury obviously rejected that notion.

Mr. McParland had been a special agent for the National Detective Agency for many years before his retirement, in 1946, when he purchased the home on Parkland Avenue, to be near his daughter and grandson.

Someone, the anonymous sender no doubt, had gotten hold of a rubber stamp and had stamped across the clipping, "PAID," in pale red ink.

• • •

I was kind of sick for awhile. Although I'd pretty much quit smoking–no cigarettes, no cigars, just an occasional pipe–I came down with pneumonia. I don't know what brought it on. I hadn't been exposed to the cold that winter. Maybe it was just living a more sedentary life than usual. But it laid me up for several weeks. After awhile, when I wasn't simply sleep-ing all the time, I began to read again. I reread a lot of Jane

Austen and then Flaubert. By the time spring hit Kentucky, I was feeling pretty good. The prison doctor was delighted.

One day I came back from my usual walk around the grounds and screwed a fresh sheet of paper into the little Smith-Corona. I typed:

"Bee-yoot!"